Praise
Evenfall

"In *Evenfall*, Liz Michalski weaves magic and fate, love and history, risk and desire into a novel that is rich with human frailty and emotion. This is one of those books you will not be able to put down until its last beautiful pages."

—Ann Hood, author of
The Red Thread

"*Evenfall* possesses the tranquil beauty implied in its title. The rural New England setting, combined with the characters' efforts to resolve past heartbreak, yields a story full of healing calm."

—Laura Brodie, author of
The Widow's Season

"Graceful, gentle . . . an orchestra of characters I won't soon forget, including the unexpected: a dog, a cat, a house, and the ghost of a man whose longing and affection for a woman keeps him tied to this earth."

—Diane Meier, author of
The Season of Second Chances

"A haunting, exquisitely written novel of steadfast love and enduring regret. Like the ghosts in the story, this novel will linger in your thoughts long after you finish it."

—Mary Alice Monroe, *New York Times*
bestselling author of *Last Light Over Carolina*

evenfall

LIZ MICHALSKI

BERKLEY BOOKS, NEW YORK

THE BERKLEY PUBLISHING GROUP
Published by the Penguin Group
Penguin Group (USA) Inc.
375 Hudson Street, New York, New York 10014, USA
Penguin Group (Canada), 90 Eglinton Avenue East, Suite 700, Toronto, Ontario M4P 2Y3, Canada
(a division of Pearson Penguin Canada Inc.)
Penguin Books Ltd., 80 Strand, London WC2R 0RL, England
Penguin Group Ireland, 25 St. Stephen's Green, Dublin 2, Ireland (a division of Penguin Books Ltd.)
Penguin Group (Australia), 250 Camberwell Road, Camberwell, Victoria 3124, Australia
(a division of Pearson Australia Group Pty. Ltd.)
Penguin Books India Pvt. Ltd., 11 Community Centre, Panchsheel Park, New Delhi—110 017, India
Penguin Group (NZ), 67 Apollo Drive, Rosedale, North Shore, 0632, New Zealand
(a division of Pearson New Zealand Ltd.)
Penguin Books (South Africa) (Pty.) Ltd., 24 Sturdee Avenue, Rosebank, Johannesburg 2196,
South Africa

Penguin Books Ltd., Registered Offices: 80 Strand, London WC2R 0RL, England

This is a work of fiction. Names, characters, places, and incidents either are the product of the author's imagination or are used fictitiously, and any resemblance to actual persons, living or dead, business establishments, events, or locales is entirely coincidental. The publisher does not have any control over and does not assume any responsibility for author or third-party websites or their content.

PRINTING HISTORY
Berkley trade paperback edition / February 2011

Library of Congress Cataloging-in-Publication Data

Michalski, Liz.
    Evenfall / Liz Michalski.—1st ed.
       p. cm.
    ISBN 978-0-425-23872-1
    1. Mothers and daughters—Fiction. I. Title.
    PS3613.I3447E84 2011
    813'.6—dc22   2010012575

PRINTED IN THE UNITED STATES OF AMERICA

10 9 8 7 6 5 4 3 2 1

For my family, the listeners and the storytellers both;
and for Bill, at last and always

Acknowledgments

First and foremost, to my agent, Mitchell Waters, who somehow manages to be the personification of kindness and professionalism both; and to my editor, Jackie Cantor, a delight and a dream to work with.

To Christine Greeley, who read every word twice, to Lisa Myerson, whose honesty can always be depended upon, and to Al Padilla, who read with a critical eye. To the inhabitants of Zoetrope, specifically, Ellen Meister, who introduced me to the best women's room on the web; Louis E. Catron, a good man and kindly scholar; Thea Atkinson, who opened her attic to me; and Terri Brown-Davidson and her office mates, who taught me the finer points of the business that is writing.

Greg Seay deserves a special shout-out. Greg, I confess, I've taken your name in vain more than once after you made me redo my lede for the umpteenth time, but you taught me more about writing and revising than any course could have, and I thank you on a regular basis.

To my family: Mom, for writing the notes that gave me access to the whole library; Dad, for never balking at buying

Nancy Drew books in bulk; and Maureen, my first listener. To Emma for letting me write, and Alex for making me stop. You make my life a Technicolor wonder every day.

To all the good dogs who inspired me—George, Calvin, Griffin, Phoenix, and Nina. May you catch the bunnies of your dreams. And to Harley, who is not allowed to catch any in this life.

Finally, and most important, to my fabulous husband, Bill, for his support and encouragement, for which you deserve your own page. Thank you for all that you do. I love you.

june

Frank

NINA sees the man first. It's a warm summer day, the kind where, when I was alive, you'd have found me down the creek. Fishing, I'd have said if anyone asked, though the only thing worth catching there was a long, cool breeze.

There's no such breeze in the attic today—not even the ghost of one. A dry heat radiates from the wooden beams above me, although the floor itself is cool, squeaking slightly under the movement of my rocking chair. The wide, solid boards, the angular shape of the room, the boxes and trunks that fill the dark corners, all put me in mind of a ship, as if I'm taking some kind of voyage up here instead of just passing time.

Beside me, Nina lifts her head, and her ears prick forward. "What is it, girl?" I ask. She looks at me mournfully. Nina wishes she could speak. Instead, she barks once and glances at the window.

A swatch of lace curtain blocks our view. In our forty years together, Clara tatted enough lace to cover every window in the house. If she'd lived, I would have had a lace-lined coffin. But of course Clara passed before me.

Nina barks again, impatient. Through the patterns in the lace I see something moving. "All right," I say. "Hold your horses." I think of the breeze down the creek, and the curtain flaps sideways and stays there.

The fellow's young. I see that right away. He parks his red truck on the side of the lawn and steps out wearing faded jeans, hiking boots, and a white T-shirt. He stands in the drive, shades his eyes, and gazes up at the house.

Even if I close my eyes, I can still see the place the way he does: the arbor to the right of the house, plump Concord grapes ripening in the sun; the fieldstone steps, laid by my grandfather and carved with his initials; the shady patio, where Clara used to bring me lemonade. And the house itself, rising out of the Connecticut ground at the edge of the woods, its white facade peeling a little but still proud after two hundred years. There's plenty that he doesn't see, too, and keeping it safe is what concerns me.

The boy—for that's what he truly is—passes a hand along his jaw. He stands still, taking in the house and the valley spread below. I look at Nina.

"Doesn't look like a thief," I say, and she whines in agreement.

"Still, best to make sure." Nina stands, shakes herself,

and trots toward the door, where she sits and looks back at me.

"I'm coming, I'm coming." These days, it's easier for me just to think of the place I'm going and find myself there, but Nina finds it disconcerting, and so, I suppose, do I. Instead I raise myself from the chair and follow along behind her, and the two of us make our way downstairs.

At the front door, she sits and barks once, a command of sorts. I stop and remember the feel of the wood, the coolness of the brass handle, and the door swings open. Not very much, but enough for Nina to wriggle through. She bounds down the steps, barking and growling, a black and tan bundle of uncontained fury.

The boy takes a step back. "Whoa. Easy, there." He puts one hand out, slowly, then stays very still. A good idea. Nina may be a mutt, but her broad head and mouthful of white teeth are pure shepherd. Her body's something else—maybe Rottie—but all told she's a solid one hundred pounds of pissed-off dog, and the boy's got the message. He doesn't seem afraid, though; just cautious. He keeps his voice low and calm. "You're telling me this is your place, huh? I hear you."

He waits until the dog settles a bit, then cups his hands around his mouth and hollers toward the door. "Hello? Anybody home?" No answer comes from the empty house.

"How'd you get out? You do that by yourself?" he asks the dog. She's still barking, random woofs of warning, but it's halfhearted now, and at his tone she tentatively wags her bushy tail. He extends his hand again, and this time she sniffs it.

"You're a smart one, aren't you?" he says, and rubs behind her ears. She groans in pleasure, thumps her tail on the ground, and leans into him so that when he shifts, she topples over, pink belly exposed and legs in the air.

The boy laughs. He bends over and scratches her stomach, making her writhe with delight.

"Some watchdog," I say from the door. Nina rolls a sheepish brown eye in my direction, but doesn't get up.

The boy stands, giving Nina a last scratch, and she scrambles to her feet behind him. He pushes the front door so that it's fully open and calls inside.

"Hello? Anybody there?"

He takes one step over the threshold, hesitates, and shivers. Perhaps he senses me, floating just where the door's shadow pools into midday darkness. Perhaps it is simply that he's been raised with better manners than to wander around a strange house when nobody's home. Whatever the reason, he turns and heads outside.

He's standing on the rise, looking toward the old north pasture, when I hear them coming through the woods. There's two of them, about the same size, but it's not until they're almost through to the clearing that I realize one of them is Gert.

Nina is standing by the boy's side, still a little excited from her efforts to chase him off. She hears them just after I do, and gives a low warning bark. The boy spins around just in time to see them step into the sunlight.

"Quiet, fool," I say to the dog, and she grumbles her way into silence. Gert's moving at a quick pace, faster than I've seen in some time. A few wisps of hair have escaped her braid, and they float about her face like strands of silver, as thin and fine in the morning air as spider webbing. As she strides toward us, her energy comes in waves. Touch her and she'd shoot sparks.

"Un-oh," I say to the boy. "You might want to leave now." But of course he doesn't hear me. Instead, he comes down off the rise, crossing the lawn to meet them. He's got a hand raised in greeting, but at the look on Gert's face, he lets it drop limply to his side. Nina, quite sensibly, is cowering behind his leg.

"Um, good morning?" the boy says. Gert's about to speak, but it's the other woman who answers first.

"Try something else," she says. "Like who are you, and what are you doing here?" She's dressed simply, in denim shorts and a man's white shirt tied at the waist, long brown hair pinned up in a knot. I should know her, I know, but she's so young, has so much energy, it's hard to keep her in focus. She strides up to within spitting distance of the boy, and for a second I think that's exactly what she's going to do. He's staring at her openmouthed, and in disgust she turns from him to Gert. Just before she speaks, the boy finds his voice.

"Andie? Andie Murphy?"

And like that, her molecules click into place for me, like the piece of a puzzle that makes the whole recognizable. It's my niece Andie, child of my heart, fully grown.

"Who the hell else would I be?" she's saying. "Do I know you?"

"You probably don't remember, but you used to babysit me sometimes. We used to catch frogs down the creek," he adds lamely. There's just the faintest flush of red around his collarbone.

"Oh my God," she says. "Little Cortie McCallister. All grown up!"

His flush deepens, but he manages a grin. "Over six feet. Taller than you, finally."

"Let's see, you're what, twenty-two now?"

"Um, no. Twenty-three."

"Great. Make me feel old."

She smiles, and for the first time I catch a glimpse of the little girl I knew, the one who spent summers running wild on this farm. She's got Murphy written all over her; Gert's strong jaw, softened by Clara's eyes and her daddy's—their brother's—wide, easy smile.

She turns to Gert. "Aunt Gert, you remember Cort, don't you?"

"I do indeed," she says, and at her tone Cort shifts uncomfortably. "But that doesn't explain what he's doing up here today."

It's an excellent question, and we all turn to look at him. "I, ah, I heard Evenfall might be for sale," he says. "I wanted to take a look before it got bought up, so I just took a ride out here. I'm sorry if I caused any trouble, Miss Gert."

"There's a modern device called the telephone," Gert informs him. "Old-fashioned as some people may think I am, I happen to have one. Next time, try using it."

"Yes, ma'am."

Andie crouches down and holds her hand out to the dog, who comes out from behind Cort, wagging her tail. "Cute pup you've got here—what's its name?"

"I dunno. I thought she was yours—I mean, Miss Gert's."

"Certainly not," Gert says. "You mean the mangy animal doesn't belong to you?"

"Nope. It looked like she came out of the house."

"That's impossible." Gert's clear gray eyes flick to the door, and I catch myself stepping back, although there's no way she can see me. "And I'd swear that door was locked tight when I left last time."

He shrugs. "Well, it's open today."

"It certainly is." She looks at him. "Andrea, excuse me. I think I'll check the house. And while I'm at it I might as well call the pound. I've seen this animal running loose before, and it's high time someone took responsibility for it."

"Sure, Aunt Gert."

I've been watching Gert so intently that I'm not prepared when she steps into the house. There's no time to move, no time to even think about moving. She steps firmly across the threshold and into me.

I feel her warmth first, just as she must feel the coolness of the air where I am. Her hands come up as if she's blind and bumped into a wall. They reach just to my shoulders, the way she used to hold them when we danced. With all my might I think of those days and whisper her name.

She sighs and stands still. Her long gray hair is pulled back in a loose braid and she grasps the end, a nervous habit I recognize from her youth.

I reach out to stroke her cheek, but before I can touch her, I hear Andie's voice.

"Everything okay, Aunt Gert?"

Gert drops her braid, startled, and the connection is gone. "Just waiting for my eyes to adjust," she calls, then strides off toward the kitchen and the phone.

For a second I debate going after her. But even if she can sense me, it doesn't mean she'll listen. It's not as if she ever has before. And besides, Andie's here, for the first time in I can't remember how long. My funeral doesn't count, of course. So I stay and watch.

She looks good. She's thinner than I remember, and there's a look in her eyes I don't like, as if she's seen plenty of what the world has to offer and is tired of most of it. But she's still a beauty, with that same wide-open face she had as a little girl. She could never hide when something was wrong, and she always gave me way too much credit for being able to read her mind. It was all right there, for anyone who cared to look.

"Sorry to hear about Frank," Cort's saying. He bends down to pet Nina, sprawled at his feet.

"Thanks. Frank and Clara really felt like my folks, you know?" She's quiet a moment, then turns and looks at the farm, waves a hand to take it all in. "This place hasn't changed much. It looks exactly like it did when I was a kid."

"You think?" He turns and looks with her. "It must seem like the ass end of nowhere to you. I heard you've been living overseas."

She laughs. "Henry still reading the mail down at the post office?"

He smiles back. "Just the return addresses. Anything else would be a federal offense. He told me the stamps were pretty, though. You were in Italy, right?"

"Yep. I finished my doctorate in art history this week, then hopped the first plane home to give Aunt Gert a hand. We were behind you on the road, coming in from the airport, when we saw you pull in here."

"My lucky day," he says.

They talk about Andie's flight, about the two-week camping trip the boy just took, and then the people they both know who are still in Hartman. All the while I'm seeing the place the way it must look to Andie. Ass end of nowhere, indeed. There are weeds sprouting through the gravel driveway and the lawn is almost knee high, sure, but it's nothing a few afternoons of hard work can't fix. Finally the boy circles back to the part that interests me.

"So you're really going to sell it?"

She nods. "You know how hot the market is right now. A couple of developers are already pretty eager. Aunt Gert thought you were another one poking around up here without permission. She's kind of had it—she was ready to call the police on you."

"She did seem pretty ticked," the boy says, and I snort. If Gert's worst threat is calling the police, she's mellowed considerably.

"She wants to get the house cleaned up and painted

11

before she calls an assessor in," Andie says. "I keep telling her, once it's sold, the house will probably be gone, but she doesn't want to hear it. You know how she is."

I'm still chewing over that one when the boy asks if the whole parcel is for sale.

"Aunt Gert will probably keep the cottage and an acre or two, but that's it. She can't handle more. That's why she's putting it on the market in the first place."

"Huh. What about you?"

"Me?" Andie says. "Right. There are still skid marks on the road, I left town so fast. I'm here to help out, nothing more. Then I'm out of here and back to civilization."

Her words remind me that Gert's still inside, trying to find somebody to collar my dog. *You*, I say to Nina. *You need to go hide*. She's sprawled in front of Andie, happily panting, and makes no move to get up. *Shoo*, I say. *Shoo. Quickly now*. I think of the pound, all concrete and chain link, and she reluctantly shakes herself to her feet. But still she doesn't run. Instead, she stands in front of the boy and gives two sharp, commanding barks. My niece jumps, but the boy doesn't flinch.

"Hey there, easy," he says. "What's the problem?"

She looks at me, and I could swear there's an apology there somewhere. Then she runs to his truck, stands there for a second, and runs back.

"I think she's telling you it's time to go," Andie says.

"I think she's saying she wants to come with me," he says. "How mad will your aunt be if I take off with the dog?"

Andie considers. "It's hard to say."

12

"Well, live dangerously. That's my motto," he says, squatting and looking Nina in the face. "Come on, girl. We'd best organize a breakout for you now, before Gert comes back with the law." He stands and stretches. "It was nice seeing you again. How long are you staying?"

"I'm not sure yet. Awhile—there's a lot to do."

"Well, if I can give you a hand at all, just holler. I'll be around." He starts toward the truck, Nina following. He opens the cab door and she leaps inside, moving over to make room for him and to claim the passenger window.

Cort turns the truck around, then brakes near Andie. He's grinning.

"Hey, tell Miss Gert I said good-bye—and thanks for not pressing charges." Before she can reply, the truck is rolling down the driveway, stirring up little clouds of sand-colored dust. Nina leans out the window and barks once. Andie and I watch them go.

Andie

ANDIE is leaning against a birch tree, idly stripping bark off its trunk, when Gert comes out of the house.

"Where did that boy go?" Gert says, shading her eyes and gazing around as if she expects him to pop out of the woods at any minute.

"Home, I guess. He took the dog with him."

"Then I spent the past twenty minutes on the phone for nothing. Although I suppose it will serve Roscoe right if he comes up here on a goose chase—cantankerous old fool."

Gert starts off toward the guest house, her sneakered feet slapping briskly on the path. Every now and then she pauses to swat at a mosquito. Andie trails along behind, fingering the branches and leaves that reach out to block her way.

When Andie was a child, sleeping over at Aunt Gert's

was an adventure. Clutching her overnight bag, she walked the trail between the two houses, pretending to be a fairy-tale character—Gretel, perhaps, or Little Red Riding Hood, or, on her more melodramatic days, any one of the endless sisterhood of cartoon princesses who had managed to lose their mothers at birth like her. By the time the front of the cottage came into view, partially screened by a stand of pine trees, she'd scared herself into thinking that every shadow, every twig that snapped underfoot, had ominous overtones. She'd have to stand on the front porch, shivering in the summer sun, until she got up the nerve to face whatever waited inside—witch or big bad wolf.

By now though, Andie has had too much personal acquaintance with wolves of the grown-up variety to be scared by the make-believe type. Instead, she sees the cottage for what it is—a faded, shabby structure—and her throat swells with sadness.

Gert plows up the steps, tugging open the screen door and letting it squeak shut behind her. Andie lingers on the porch, absently pulling off long curls of peeling paint until she realizes what she's doing and stops, appalled. She tamps down the piece she's been working with her thumb, but the curled edge won't lie flat. She kicks the corkscrews of paint that have already come off into the overgrown shrubbery around the porch railing, then goes inside before she can do more damage.

The afternoon sunlight is dim inside, filtered through the branches of the trees all around the cottage. The light casts shadows on the white walls, and as Andie's eyes adjust, she can see that not much has changed. The same blue sofa is positioned parallel to the door, dividing the living area from the kitchen. The cushions on the rocking chair in the corner are worn, but comfortably so. Postcards from Italy are tucked along the fireplace mantel, propped between pinecones and stones from the creek. A few more are stuck to the front of the kitchen's refrigerator with magnets.

Gert is standing over the white enamel sink, scrubbing potatoes for supper. Andie groans. Her aunt is a notoriously bad cook who believes food should be heated as long as possible, to kill germs. Andie has come to the rural southeastern end of Connecticut with hopeful visions of take-out pizzas and Chinese food, and armed with a secret stash of soy granola bars.

"Here, Aunt Gert. Let me do that." She moves to take over the chore, but Gert blocks her with the brisk efficiency of someone used to being in charge.

"Nonsense. Go unpack, if you feel the urge to do something."

Dutifully, Andie wanders into the guest bedroom, where she'd thrown her suitcase before rushing off to the big house with Gert. Her aunt has placed it neatly on the single bed, a towel underneath to prevent dirt from staining the white bedspread.

With a sigh, she unzips the bag, then takes a look around. There's a chest of drawers, wedged kitty-corner against the far wall. The closet—really an old-fashioned cupboard, with hooks set into the back—will hold perhaps a third of the clothes she's brought. The walls are bare, painted the same flat white as the rest of the cottage. Idly, Andie runs a finger along the top of the chest. No dust. Sitting on the bed, she recalls that, as exciting as her visits to Gert's were, as a child she was always glad to go back to the big house and Aunt Clara. After a meal of Gert's plain oatmeal, she'd fly along the path to the big house, in time for a second breakfast of pancakes with real maple syrup and butter. Her room there was wallpapered with a riot of yellow and pink roses, so realistic looking that as a child she swore one morning she could smell them.

She puts off unpacking. Instead, she takes her toiletry bag into the bathroom. There's a claw-foot tub with a hand-held shower attachment. An aluminum tray attached to the tub holds a neat assortment of items: Dial soap, a man's safety razor, a can of shaving cream, a small bottle of generic shampoo.

The rim of the tub is too narrow to hold any of Andie's things, so she opens the medicine cabinet. There's not much inside. A container of Bayer aspirin, a tube of toothpaste, some Ben-Gay, a bottle of roll-on deodorant. There's also a bottle of prescription medication. Feeling faintly guilty, she picks it up. The drug name—metoprolol—is unfamiliar. Gert hasn't mentioned being sick, but that's not surprising.

There's a knock at the bathroom door, and Andie jumps.

"Just a second," she calls. She turns the water on, then puts the vial back in the cabinet and shuts it. She splashes cold water on her face, dries it on the scratchy white towel laid out on the sink, and opens the door.

Her aunt is standing there, a dishrag over her shoulder.

"I was just looking for a place to put my things," Andie tells her. She holds up her transparent bag for emphasis.

"Lord, what fancy soap—I can smell it from here," Aunt Gert says.

When Andie doesn't answer, her aunt goes on. "I thought we'd have a meat loaf for dinner. I started it, but then I thought, living in a foreign country for so long, you might not eat meat anymore."

"Italy has meat, plenty of it," Andie reassures her. "And I do eat it, just not very often." Actually, for the last six months Andie has been a virtual vegetarian, but going down that conversational path with Gert, who firmly believes red meat is necessary for health, can only lead to trouble.

"Good," her aunt says. "The potatoes are in, and I'll finish the meat loaf. We'll eat at six." Andie glances at her watch. It's barely four p.m. now.

The two women squeeze past each other in the hall, Gert toward the kitchen, Andie toward her bedroom. She starts with her shoes, unzipping each pair from their compartment in her garment bag and lining them against the wall. When she takes out a pair of pale pink leather flats, she holds them up to the window, looking for scuff marks. The color reminds her of her favorite shoes when she was six, a pair of pink high-tops her father gave her when she was spending her first full summer at the farm. For two weeks, she wore them everywhere, and then they disappeared. She cried so hard Uncle Frank drove her into town to buy another pair. A week later the original ones turned up, unearthed from the depths of her closet at the big house.

The memory gives her an inspiration, and she hurries out to the kitchen, where Gert is beating an egg. Unbidden, Andie opens the old creaky hutch where the china is stored, and begins setting the table.

"Don't forget the place mats," her aunt reminds her, and Andie pulls out two faded squares of blue cotton, well-laundered, and matching napkins. She folds the napkins in half, smoothing out the creases, and carefully places them to the left of the plates, with a fork on top of each. Out of the corner of her eye, she catches her aunt's quick nod of approval. It gives her the courage to speak.

"Aunt Gert, I was thinking," she begins.

"No charge for that."

Andie plows on. "The cottage isn't really big enough for both of us, not if I'm going to stay awhile. There's no place for me to spread out my paints, and barely space enough for my clothes. We're stumbling over each other as it is, and I haven't even unpacked."

"Maybe you need fewer things."

Andie ignores this. "What I was thinking is, why not move into the big house? It has room enough for both of us. We're going to be spending lots of time there anyhow, sorting through stuff."

"No," says Gert. She turns away and rummages in the vegetable bin of the refrigerator.

"But why not?" Andie persists. "It makes sense."

Gert selects an onion, wipes it off with her apron, and carries it to the cutting board at the side of the sink, where she peels off the outer layer with a knife.

"Because this is my home, that's why." The skin removed, she chops the onion vigorously.

"You stayed at the big house when you were nursing Uncle Frank, didn't you?"

"I did not. It wouldn't have been seemly."

Her aunt's eyes are red from the onion, and the corners are beginning to tear by the time she dumps the minced pieces into the bowl. Gert is usually the most practical person Andie knows, so she can't understand her answer, but she lets it go. Part of it, anyway.

"Well, if you don't mind, I'm going to move over there. It will give both of us a little more room."

"You're of age. Do as you like."

The day is getting cooler, so Andie retreats to her bedroom to change. She pulls on a pair of jeans, packs up her shoes, and stretches out on the bed, careful to keep her feet off the white spread. She hates fighting with Gert, whose icy anger is worse than any hot-blooded rage. Even as a child, the two of them butted heads so hard Andie was often left reeling.

The problem, according to Uncle Frank, is that the oldest and youngest Murphy women are cut from the same cloth, both too proud and too stubborn to sugarcoat the truth, or at least their version of it. Andie never had that difficulty with Clara, who somehow had the knack of coaxing a stubborn nine-year-old to eat her vegetables and go to bed, all the while making it seem like it was Andie's own idea.

Andie sighs. More than once she's wished she had Clara's talent, particularly when it comes to men. If she's honest, she's not here just to help Gert out. She's put a whole continent between herself and Neal, a man she swears she loves but who drives her to dish-breaking fury and tears. Andie's not sure the distance is enough.

But love affairs gone wrong are hardly a dinner table topic in the Murphy household. Andie can't once remember her aunt talking about old boyfriends, although there must have been some. Even in her late seventies, Gert retains the high cheekbones and glamour girl legs of her youth. It strikes Andie suddenly how little she knows of her aunt's life.

She's still musing on this when Gert calls her to dinner. Her plate is filled with green beans, a potato, and a blackish slice of meat loaf. Store bought white bread sits on its own dish, next to a beaded glass of ice water.

Andie slides in to her seat, and Gert immediately bows her head.

"We thank thee Lord for this our daily bread and all other blessings. Amen."

"Amen," Andie echoes. Gert looks sharply at her but says nothing.

Dinner is a quiet affair. Gert has never encouraged conversation at the table, believing it hinders digestion. Besides, choking down the meat loaf takes most of Andie's concentration. She fervently misses Max, Frank's old black Lab who spent many meals curled at her feet, his pink mouth open and waiting.

When she's consumed as much as possible, she sits back. Gert looks at her niece's plate and snorts.

"You didn't eat much."

"I'm not that hungry. It's probably jet lag." She yawns, covers her mouth. Suddenly she really is bone-tired.

"All those Italian fashion models have anorexia, you know."

Andie stands to clear the table, but Gert waves her away and carries the plates to the sink herself.

"Are your things all packed?"

"I guess so." An image of her aunt sleeping alone, her breathing the only sound in the cottage, fills Andie's head, and abruptly she changes her mind. "Aunt Gert, I think . . ."

"Well, then, let's go before it gets dark," Gert says. She unties her apron from around her neck, tossing it over a chair.

"You're coming with me?"

"Not to stay—just to get you settled. You can't carry everything yourself, can you?"

Gert's leaving the dinner dishes unwashed is as close to an apology as she can give for her contrariness, and Andie accepts by not mentioning it. Instead, she goes down the hall to her room and fetches her suitcase and the wooden box that holds her paints and easel. When she returns, Gert is standing by the door, a canvas bag in her hand. Moths cling to the screen, their furry bellies exposed, and Gert flicks them off one by one before opening the door.

Together, they step out into the evening. It's not dark yet, and still warm enough that the air has a liquid quality. When Andie was little, she, Frank, and Clara would eat ice-cream sandwiches on the porch, watching the sun go down and waiting for the first lightning bugs to wink out their secret messages.

Watching her aunt's straight back move away from her in the twilight, Andie wonders how Gert spent those same evenings. It's not a question she expects to have answered, so she lets it go. Instead, she concentrates on the sound of pine needles crunching underfoot, releasing their faint scent of winter, and the feeling of night air on her skin. Above her, a mockingbird trills a long, impassioned plea for love, then falls silent.

The house looms at the end of the trail like a large white ghost in the twilight. The two women cut under the grape arbor, their feet crunching on gravel. At the door, Gert fumbles the key out of her pocket, pressing it into Andie's hand.

"You might as well keep this for now. I have an extra at the cottage."

"You're not coming in?"

Gert looks up at the house and shakes her head.

"Here. Some fresh sheets and food in case you get hungry. Tomorrow we can go shopping and get you established."

Andie takes the bag her aunt proffers. She reaches for her aunt and they hug awkwardly, Gert pulling away first.

"I'll see you in the morning. And, Andie . . ." She hesitates, gives a quick glance up at the house. "I'll leave the cottage open in case you change your mind."

"Thanks. See you tomorrow."

Andie unlocks the door, and when she turns around, Gert is already walking away, her white shirt growing dim in the falling light. At the woods' edge she turns, cups her hands around her mouth, and calls "Sleep tight. Don't let the bed bugs bite!"

It's the phrase Gert always used to tuck her into bed. Andie smiles and waves in response, but Gert has disappeared into the forest.

Andie steps inside, closing the heavy door behind her, and immediately her body relaxes. It's as if the house itself were embracing her in welcome. She walks through the lower level, listening to the drip of the kitchen faucet, the quiet hum of the refrigerator, the silence in the parlor.

The exhaustion she'd felt at Gert's house returns. She cuts her exploration short and climbs the stairs, fingers trailing along the banister. She stops at the back bedroom, the one she's always called hers, even though she'd only been able to claim it a few months out of the year. Inside Gert's bag are soft white bed linens, and when Andie unfolds them, the scent of lavender wafts through the room.

As soon as the bed is made, she strips off her jeans and crawls between the sheets, the cotton cool against her skin. In the instant before unconsciousness, she thinks she hears a voice saying her name. The voice, dry and soft, is oddly familiar. "Night, doodlebug," it whispers. Before she can respond, she's asleep.

WHEN Andie wakes, sunlight is streaming through the windows. She yawns, wiggling her toes at the end of the bed. It feels like the first day of summer vacation, when she'd slip into shorts and a T-shirt—heaven after a school year of plaid jumpers—and run outside, ignoring Clara's call to breakfast.

She couldn't wait to feel grass tickling her feet and legs, to splash in the cool water of the creek. Like a puppy confined for too long, she used that first morning to burn off energy, racing about the farm for the sheer joy of it.

Uncle Frank usually found her about the time she'd thrown herself down on the bank of the creek to rest. He'd settle beside her, all elbows and knees, resembling nothing so much as one of the long-legged water beetles that skimmed the creek's surface. He'd draw a foil-wrapped package out of his shirt pocket, and the two of them would munch in companionable silence on strawberry Pop-Tarts.

Thinking of food reminds Andie of her dream. She'd been sitting at the kitchen table with Gert. At the center of the table was a blue bowl, banded by a ring of silver. It was piled high with apples, and when Andie reached past Gert to take one, the bowl shattered. The falling blue pieces became the cool rushing waters of the creek. It swirled through the room, stranding a school of little silver fish at Gert's feet.

Andie frowns, stretches again. There's something she's forgetting, but the dream won't come back to her, so she lets it go, swinging her legs over the side of the bed. Sitting there, she's eyeball to eyeball with the pictures lining the dresser. She knows them by heart—they've sat there since she was a child—but today they're covered with a slight fur of dust.

She picks up the first frame and gently polishes it with the hem of her shirt. The photo inside is of her mother, fragile and lovely in her wedding dress. Growing up, Andie studied it so often she knew the tiniest details: the way her mother's veil twists slightly near its end, the way her eyes shine and her slender fingers are wrapped tight around the bouquet, the way the flowers are positioned to hide her stomach. Seeing the picture now, what Andie notices most is how young her mother was. A baby, really, a whole decade younger than Andie is now, forever frozen in time at the age of twenty-three.

When the frame is clean, she replaces it on the dresser, then picks up the next photo. In it, her father, looking as if he could use a cigarette and a drink, cradles Andie, who is pink and wrinkled and wrapped in a pale blue blanket. Andie remembers the blanket. It had a satin edging, and she carried it with her from New Hampshire to New York to Florida and back again, following her father, who was following the ponies in their endless cycle. The satin edge wore out, rubbed between her fingers until it was threadbare, but the blanket went with her to college, stuffed in the back of her underwear drawer.

The third photo is the most recent, although it's more than ten years old. Taken at her graduation from boarding school, it shows an eighteen-year-old Andie with big hair and dramatic eye makeup. Clara's hugging her on one side, Gert has an arm about her shoulder on the other, and Frank stands behind all three of them, his head just above Andie's. All four wear broad grins. Her father is to the left and slightly blurry, just beyond the camera's focus, though Andie can picture his expression perfectly well. She puts the photo down.

As she's rummaging in her suitcase, she hears a voice outside her window. Quickly she strips, pulls a clean white T-shirt over her head, yanks on the same jeans from yesterday, and looks outside. There's no one there.

An instant later, a power mower roars into being. It's coming from the front of the house, and Andie can't see it from her room. She hurries to the bathroom and brushes her teeth, then heads downstairs.

The scent of fresh-mown grass reaches her even before she's outside, a smell so sweet and rich it clogs her throat and makes her head ache. She has to wait a moment before she can open the door, and when she does the scent is stronger. It crowds about her like a ghost, bringing with it the memories of all the other days that started just like this, with an open door and the summer stretching before her.

It's those past summers she's seeing, not this one, so at first she doesn't recognize the figure pushing the mower. She thinks Aunt Gert must have hired a landscaping crew and forgotten to tell her, and is unreasonably annoyed as she looks at the boy stripped to the waist, grass flecking his shoulders.

But then the dog rises to its feet from the shadow cast by the house. It wags its tail, tentatively at first, then harder and harder as she strokes its head, until the air around her legs is fanned by a steady breeze.

Cort catches sight of her and cuts the power. The mower idles, fades into silence. He wipes his face on the T-shirt draped across his neck, and Andie is mortified to find that she uses this time to stare at the long, flat expanse of skin above his shorts. As he approaches her, she averts her eyes.

"Morning," he says, and there's no way she can look at him. She focuses instead on the dog, now leaning into her leg and panting madly, so that it looks as if it's grinning.

"Morning. Guess you decided to keep her."

"It's more like she decided to stay with me, I think. She's pretty smart, aren't you, girl?" He squats, rubbing the dog's head, and Andie is forced to examine him. His black hair is a little long, falling over his eyes and trailing down the back of his neck. His shoulders are wide, with just the hint of a sunburn. He glances up and his brown eyes meet hers.

Andie blushes. For crying out loud, he's just a kid, she tells herself fiercely. Get a hold of yourself.

"Did Aunt Gert ask you to mow?" she inquires, and her voice is cool even to her own ears.

"Nope. Looking around here yesterday, it just seemed like the thing to do." He shrugs and stands up, so that she has to tilt her head to keep eye contact. "Your uncle always kept this place perfect. The grass looked a little high yesterday, so I figured I'd come back and take my chances. With Gert and the law, I mean."

"Well, thanks. We'll pay you, of course."

"I probably should have called first, especially after yesterday."

"Probably," Andie agrees.

"I figured you'd be staying over at the cottage, though. Hope I didn't wake you."

"No."

"Well, I guess I'll finish up. It won't take long."

He turns around and is almost at the mower when some impulse she can't explain makes her call after him.

"Cort!"

He wheels around.

"Have you had coffee yet?"

"Nope."

"Well, if I can find some, you want a cup?"

"Sure, if you don't think it will stunt my growth."

Andie eyes his six-foot-plus frame and can't help but laugh. "Not much chance of that. Come in when you've finished."

Cort turns back to the mower, and an instant later the sound of his whistling is drowned out by the engine. Andie heads for the house, the dog following.

Once inside, the dog makes straight for the kitchen. It's as if she's been here before, but Andie can't imagine how. The dog sits in front of the kitchen cabinet and barks expectantly.

"I don't know what you're looking for, girl, but you've come to the wrong place," Andie tells her, wondering what she was thinking inviting Cort in. "The cupboard is bare."

But when she opens the door, she finds—next to some cans of green beans and creamed corn—coffee filters and a small glass container of coffee. Tucked behind them is an almost empty box of dog biscuits.

"Here you go." She hands the last one to the dog, who lips it daintily from her palm and carries it under the kitchen table to eat. Andie opens the jar of coffee and sniffs. It smells okay, so she sets about measuring the grains into the ancient coffeepot. There's nothing in the refrigerator, so they'll have to drink it black, which is fine by Andie.

She finds two mugs and rinses them before setting them out. She's wondering what she can possibly serve with the coffee when she feels the lightest touch against her leg. She jumps, but it's just the tip of the dog's bushy tail. She's finished her snack and is panting at Andie's feet.

"Sorry, girl, no more cookies." The dog seems to accept this, staying still while Andie slides her hand to the animal's collar. Made of faded purple nylon, it has a thin tag with the name "Nina" scratched in the metal.

"Nina? Is that you?" The dog thumps her tail happily, licks Andie's hand. "Well, Nina, nice to meet you." Uncle Frank always had a soft spot for animals, Andie knows, and it's just possible this one kept him company those last few months. She gives the dog a final pat, then straightens, and Nina scrambles to her feet.

Andie makes a quick survey of the rest of the cabinets. They're almost empty. She finds a half-eaten jar of peanut butter, a dried-out squeeze bottle of mustard, and a few crumbly tea bags. She's about to give up when she remembers the bag Gert packed for her last night. It's unlikely, but there might be something edible there.

Nina trails along behind her as she climbs the stairs. Quickly Andie makes the bed, snapping the crisp white sheets so they float in the air before gently settling back onto the mattress. Finished, she looks for the bag, but stops when she catches sight of the dog.

Nina's standing with her chin resting on Uncle Frank's old chair, her brown eyes mournful. The chair is rocking slightly under the pressure of her great shaggy head. The pose reminds Andie of the nights when Frank would read her to sleep. Before sneaking onto the bed, the old Lab Max used to stand the same way, head pillowed on her uncle's lap.

There's a lump in Andie's throat, and she's about to cough to clear it when she hears the front door open. Nina's ears cock forward, but she doesn't change her position.

"Hello?" Cort calls.

"Hey. Coffee's made; feel free to pour yourself a cup," Andie calls back. "I'll be right down." She rummages in the bag, pulling out a tinfoil-wrapped parcel. Inside is the meat loaf from last night.

"I have just the thing to cheer you up," she tells the dog. She grabs some soy bars from her stash and hurries downstairs. Cort is sitting at the kitchen table, two mugs of coffee steaming in front of him. He's put his shirt back on, Andie's happy to see. He stands when she walks in the room, but his first words are for the dog.

"Made yourself right at home, haven't you?" he says, but Nina ignores him. She's too intent upon what Andie's carrying. He laughs and sits back down.

"What happened to man's best friend?" he asks.

"She's been seduced by Aunt Gert's home cooking."

The dog sits, rapt, small ribbons of drool pooling in the corners of her mouth, while Andie unwraps the blackened lump and puts it on a plate. To her surprise, Nina doesn't wolf the food in one bite. She smells it carefully before taking a dainty mouthful.

"And for the two-legged creatures . . ." Andie hands Cort one of the soy bars. He brings the wrapper to his nose and sniffs it suspiciously, his expression so much like Nina's that Andie laughs.

"I'm not a nuts and berries kind of guy," he says. Nevertheless, he unwraps the bar and takes a dubious bite. He chews, washes it down with a swig of coffee, and looks glumly at the meat loaf Nina is rapidly polishing off.

"What do you eat on all those camping trips you take?" she asks.

"Mostly beef jerky. Sometimes venison." At first Andie thinks he's joking, but his face is serious. She'd been about to make some smart-ass comment, but catches herself just in time.

"A week of Aunt Gert's home cooking would turn you into a vegetarian," she says instead.

"I dunno, that meat loaf looked pretty good." By now Nina is done eating and is lapping the plate. When she finishes, she butts her head hopefully against Cort's arm.

"Trust me. This time, I came prepared—I've got a case of these things." Andie waves her empty wrapper for emphasis.

"You're welcome to them." He feeds the last of his bar to Nina, who takes it enthusiastically and carries it underneath the kitchen table. "Well, if you ever want a change from rabbit food, a new restaurant opened in Franklin, in one of the old mills. I'd be glad to take you if you want to check it out."

His eyes are on the dog and his tone is so casual that Andie isn't sure if he's just asked her out or not. By the time she decides that he has, Cort's already moved on.

"Where's Miss Gert?" he asks, looking around the kitchen as if he expects her to jump out at any second. As a child,

Andie remembers, Cort lived in terror of Gert, who always made him scrub his hands and behind his ears after their forays to the creek.

"She decided to stay at the cottage." Andie shakes her head. "I tried to talk her into coming here. It would be so much easier, but you know how she is."

Cort snorts, runs a hand along the back of his neck. "Still, it's got to be tough for her. Lots of memories in this place."

The two of them fall silent, listening as the old house breathes around them, the weight of the empty rooms upstairs forcing a kind of sigh from the ceiling and floor-boards. Even the kitchen where they sit seems curiously bare, the deep porcelain sink gleaming in the sunshine like bone.

Cort stands, stretches, and carries his cup to the side-board. "Well, I'd better be going. Thanks for the coffee."

"It's the least I could do. What do I owe you? For the lawn, I mean."

"Aw, forget about it."

"I can't do that."

"All right then, when we go out to dinner, you can pay." His smile catches Andie off-guard, and she feels her heart-beat pick up speed.

"Deal," she says, although a date with Cort is the last thing she's planning on. She's done with men for a bit after Neal; there's no need to complicate her life with a boy.

Cort whistles, and Nina goes to him, her brown body wagging with pleasure. But at the door the dog pauses. She looks around the kitchen and whimpers softly, and in the stillness the sound seems to echo back.

Cort looks down at the dog, then at Andie.

"It's a pretty big house, to be staying in all by yourself," he says.

"Mmm hmm." Andie takes her cup over to the sink and busies herself with rinsing it out. When she takes a step to reach Cort's cup, the floorboard groans, and she has to suppress a jump. She can feel Cort watching her.

"Tell you what," he says. "I'll take the dog with me during the day, keep her out of your aunt's hair, then drop her back off at night. Joint custody. What do you think?"

"I don't know." The dog's bulk is comforting. But Andie's never even been responsible for a goldfish, let alone a dog, so she hesitates. "What if her owners are looking for her?"

"I've called the pound, and no one's reported her missing. Even if they had, I'm not sure I'd turn her in." Andie knows what he means. There are burrs in Nina's coat, and her nails are long and twisted. When Andie runs her hands lightly over the dog's furry sides, she feels ribs.

"So what do you think?" he says again.

"It sounds like I just got myself half a dog."

"Okay then. We'll see you tonight."

Andie listens as the door shuts behind them. She hears Cort's footsteps crunch across the gravel, the slam of the truck door, and the slight rumble the engine gives before it turns over. When they've gone, the house is silent, but she finds she doesn't mind. She pours herself more coffee, gets a pen and piece of paper from Aunt Clara's old junk drawer, and starts making a list of the groceries she'll need to pick up in town. Milk, dog food. She hesitates, then adds beef jerky to the list.

Gert

GERT can tell right away it's not going to be a good day. For one thing, her back is aching before she even gets out of bed. Too much lifting yesterday, she thinks.

She lies in bed and listens to the early morning ruckus the birds are making. The quilt that covers her was once blue and red, made by her sister in another lifetime. The red has faded to a rusty brown, the color of a nail in water. Gert rests beneath its weight and gazes at the picture propped up on her dresser across the room. Painted by Andie her senior year, it's a tiny watercolor, no larger than a paperback book, depicting the woods surrounding the farm. Hidden in the branches is just the faintest suggestion of a doe and her fawn. Look quickly and you'll miss it. Gert can't see it from this distance, but she knows it's there.

When she can't stand being idle a moment longer, she slowly slides out from under the sheet and leverages herself to a sitting position, the way she's seen pregnant women do. There's a glass of water on her nightstand, and in the drawer a bottle of extra-strength Tylenol. She takes two before setting her feet onto the floor and shuffling toward the kitchen.

A yowling at the front door causes her to detour, and the metallic sound of a claw running down the screen quickens her pace. Buddy is waiting on the porch, nine pounds of sleek, muscular tabby.

"I'm coming, I'm coming," Gert scolds, opening the door just wide enough for him to slip inside. He brushes against her legs, butting his head against her ankles before stalking off to the kitchen, long tail twisting in the air.

Gert follows behind, admiring his sinuous grace, the way he doesn't seem to care if she's coming or not. She found him a year ago, a tiny, malnourished bundle of fur that fit in her palm. He was shivering on the banks of the deep, creek-fed swimming hole. Gert's never particularly cared for cats, but fifty years of nursing wouldn't let her turn away from a creature in need. Every now and then, when she passes the spot where she found him, she wonders how many of his siblings didn't make it to shore.

She opens a can of tuna fish, dumps it onto a plate reserved for Buddy, and painfully lowers it to the floor. The cat sits before it and licks his paw, as if to show that he really doesn't need her handouts to survive.

"Oh, go on," she says, nudging him with her foot. The cat yawns, stretches, and daintily takes a bite.

While he's eating, she makes herself a cup of tea before settling in a chair to watch him. Gert doesn't consider herself lonely—at least, no more so than she's ever been. But sometimes there's an aching that won't stop, particularly on fine spring evenings when the mockingbird sings outside her window. Most of the time she attributes the pain to old age, but a few nights a year she knows better. That's usually when Buddy shows up, taking a break from his nocturnal wanderings. She's learned to leave the screen in her window open so she doesn't have to bother getting out of bed to let him in. Instead, she waits for his plaintive meows with an eagerness she hasn't felt since she was a girl. Only when Buddy is curled up against her back, his small body radiating warmth, can she sleep.

The cat finishes his meal and leaps into her lap, rubbing his head against her hand until she gives in and pets him. She strokes his ears, the broad furrow between his eyes, until the cat is purring in pleasure, gently kneading her nightgown between his paws. They stay this way for perhaps five minutes, until Gert glances at the clock over the stove.

She stands, unceremoniously dumping Buddy from her lap. No matter how fast she hurries, she's going to be late, and that fact makes her irritable.

"Come on, come on," she urges the cat, guiding him to the door with her foot. Buddy mewls loudly in protest.

"Well, some of us have better things to do than sit around all day," she retorts, letting the screen swing shut with a snap. Through the wire she sees the cat shake himself before leaping onto the porch railing. He digs his claws once, twice, three times into the post, his golden eyes unblinking.

"Scat," Gert hisses, and he does, jumping off the porch and streaking into the woods.

Once the cat is gone, Gert washes his dish, using hot, soapy water and paper towels, and makes her bed. She takes a shower, throws on her summer uniform of khaki shorts and white shirt, and is heading down the path to the big house by ten a.m. She expects Andie to be inside, poking through closets and excavating rooms, so she is taken aback when she finds her niece sitting on the ancient porch swing, looking thoughtful.

"Morning," Andie calls, standing up at the sight of her. "Want some coffee?"

Gert's about to shake her head—she's never been a coffee drinker, prefers the subtlety of tea—but something about Andie is different. To buy time to figure it out, she agrees to a cup.

"You'll have to take it black."

"That's fine." As her niece disappears inside, Gert sits down on the swing. The wooden seat is hard on her bones, and she shifts, trying to get comfortable. Frank and Clara used to have cushions, she remembers. Blue and yellow floral cushions that Clara must have sewn. If Andie is going to stay for a while, perhaps they should look for them.

Her niece returns and hands her a mug of coffee. Gert takes it, bends her head to take a sip. It tastes every bit as bad as she expected.

She puts the cup on the floor next to her. The bitter coffee fumes have thrown another scent into sharp relief—the sweet smell of freshly mowed grass. Gert looks at the yard, then at Andie, cool and serene in her denim and cotton T-shirt. Her niece did not cut this lawn.

Andie catches her aunt's eye and blushes just the faintest bit. "Cort McCallister stopped by this morning to cut the grass. I thought you might have sent him."

Gert snorts. She remembers Cort as a wriggling, loud eleven-year-old, one of a cadre of boys who toilet-papered her cottage every year at Halloween.

"Well, it was nice of him," Andie says. "He wouldn't take any money, either."

Another image of Cort comes to mind unbidden. Gert once found him standing in the woods, watching as Andie drove off with a Saturday night date. The boy's hands were shoved deep in his pockets, and he looked so downcast Gert didn't have the heart to come upon him unawares. Instead she crept backward, careful not to make a sound, until she was out of sight. Then she marched forward, whistling and breaking branches underfoot to give plenty of warning. When she reached the spot where he had stood, the boy was gone.

"Hmmm," is all Gert says.

The two women sit quietly, the swing gently rocking, until Andie swallows the last of her coffee and stands up.

"I guess we should get going," she says, stretching. Her fingers can almost touch the porch ceiling. "What should we tackle first?"

Gert has been planning on cleaning out the attic or the basement, but when she tries to suggest those places she finds she can't. The thought of spending the day filling boxes and bags with the remnants of someone else's life weighs down upon her so she can scarcely breathe.

"How about a quick trip to town to get you set up?" she says instead, and is relieved beyond words when Andie doesn't argue, only nods.

Frank's car is parked behind the house, in a broken-down shed that once housed horses, and later, cows. A tan Chevy Nova, the car is at least twenty years old and hasn't been driven in ages. Gert's afraid it won't start, but Andie insisted on grabbing the keys when she went inside for her grocery list. To the surprise of both women, the engine turns over on the second try. The car sputters a bit at first, as if waking from a long nap, then runs smoothly.

Andie pats the wheel. "Good car," she says, as if it were a horse. Now they won't have to share Gert's ancient station wagon.

Gert insists they stop at the gas station first. She doesn't want Andie driving the car if it is unsafe, and lord knows the last time Frank took it in for a tune-up. The attendant, an older man who looks vaguely familiar, checks the oil, adds air to the tires, and fills the gas tank while her niece fidgets behind the wheel.

"I can do all this, you know," Andie says, but Gert ignores her. When the man is finished, he knows enough to come to Gert's side of the car. She adds five dollars to the total, and he tips his baseball cap respectfully.

"Thanks, Miss Murphy."

"You're welcome," Gert calls as Andie pulls out.

They stop at the hardware store next. The house has been

unoccupied for months, and the mice must be having a field day.

"I haven't seen any," Andie says.

"They're there. Trust me." Gert picks out six traps—the spring-loaded kind that break the mice's necks—and Andie winces.

"How about these?"

She holds up a box that bills itself as a humane trap—a catch-and-release program for mice. "Plus, you can reuse it," she says, reading the box's cover.

"And you do, catching the same mice over and over."

"Well, I'm going to try it."

"Be my guest." Gert shrugs as her niece tosses the trap into their cart.

They bicker even more at the grocery store. Andie wants to run in and just get the items on her list, while Gert maintains the only way to shop is to go aisle by aisle.

"Now, what about furniture polish? Is that on your list?" she asks, as Andie sighs impatiently behind her. Gert, reaching for the yellow can of Pledge, doesn't turn around. She knows she's being perverse, but can't seem to help herself. The only thing she's done today that she's proud of is turn a blind eye to the sack of dog food her niece snuck into the cart. If Andie wants to take on all the strays in the world, she's welcome to them.

By the time Andie has finished loading the brown paper sacks into the trunk of the Nova, it's past one p.m. and Gert's stomach is growling.

"I know what we need," Andie says, slamming the trunk shut. "Lunch."

She drives to the center of town and parks under one of the wrought-iron lamps. In front of the car is Lena's, a pizza place that has been around since Andie's parents were young. The smell of yeast and onions wafts out through the building's vents.

"I don't know . . ." Gert says. She rarely eats pizza, afraid the acid from the tomatoes will give her indigestion. Andie pays no attention. She marches inside, swinging a plastic bag filled with the milk and other perishables they bought. Gert can feel the coolness from the air-conditioning as she follows.

It's past the main lunch hour rush, and the restaurant is almost empty. A pair of teenage girls sit near the front, chewing on their straws and giggling. Andie picks a booth at the back and slides in, laying her purse on the table. When the waitress bustles over, she orders two Cokes and a small cheese pizza.

"So," she says, shutting her menu. Gert knows that tone, but whatever Andie has to say, she's ready. "Have you called the real estate agent?"

"No. There are things I need to set right first," Gert says. She knows her niece believes that she's stalling, that it's merely a matter of calling up a Realtor and handing over the key. She wishes it were that simple. The truth is, owning Evenfall makes her uneasy. She'd have preferred Frank to will the house directly to Andie and let her step out from the tangle the property has woven around her all her life. She understands, of course. He'd wanted to spare Andie the grief of dismantling the closest thing to a home the girl's ever known. All the same, it's a burden she'll be glad to set down.

Andie doesn't say anything, just waits, so Gert continues. "We really do need to clean out the house. I swear Clara kept the ketchup packets from every take-out meal she ever had, and I don't think Frank threw a thing out after she died."

"Uh-huh," Andie says.

"And I thought we might get the outside painted, too. We may as well show the house off to its best advantage before we get an appraisal." She owes Frank that, at least.

"I still think it's a waste of money. Whoever buys the property is just going to tear it down. It's sad, but it's all about the land these days."

"Perhaps, but it's my money, Andrea, and that's how I intend to spend it." She makes her tone final, and Andie sighs. But she's quiet for only a moment before she plows ahead.

"Well, have you at least thought about what you'll do when the house sells?"

"I'll do what I've always done—stay on in the cottage." Gert unfolds her paper napkin and places it across her lap. Strictly speaking, that's not quite accurate, of course. For some thirty years, ever since Andie's birth, the cottage has been the place Gert returned to for summers and holidays, like some migratory bird, with Andie herself as the homing point. It's only since Frank got sick that Gert's given up her apartment in upstate New York. There are still mornings when she wakes in the cottage and doubts her decision. Truthfully, she can't picture herself living on the edges of suburbia, watching mothers in tight jeans and designer T-shirts herd their children into the car for soccer practice and piano lessons. Maybe she'll be dead by then, she thinks, and oddly enough, feels comforted.

"It's just . . . you're so isolated here. You know, there are some nice retirement communities out there. We could just check them out and see what you think." Andie's opening up her own napkin as she says this, a task that seems to require so much concentration she can't look up to meet Gert's gaze.

Gert knows the type of place Andie means. One of those cookie-cutter developments, where there are five women to every man, and everyone is so busy there's no time to dwell on the fact that each day is a borrowed one. The type of place Clara would have gone, if she'd outlived Frank. An image of her sister happily playing bingo comes to mind, and Gert feels a momentary pang.

She takes a sip of the soda the waitress has just brought, and clears her throat. "No," she says finally. "The cottage is my home."

The waitress comes with their pizza. For a while they concentrate on the food, which drips with oil. Andie blots her slice with a napkin, and Gert follows suit, although she refuses to pick up the pizza the way her niece does. Instead, she uses the plastic fork and knife to cut it into bite-sized pieces.

It is better than she expected, and she eats two slices before pushing her grease-stained paper plate away. She'll pay for this tonight, she thinks, and hopes she still has a roll of Tums at home.

By the time Andie's finished eating, the restaurant is starting to fill up with the dinner crowd. The two teenage girls have been replaced by a young family. Andie stares at them, and Gert glances over to see what's caught her attention. A harried mother dangles an auburn-haired baby, maybe nine months old, on her arm. Two children, a boy and a girl, keep dropping their toys on the floor. The man they're with—Gert presumes the father—mostly looks out the window. "Knock it off!" he snaps once, and the children glance at each other, then at their mother, and keep still.

"Ready?" Andie asks, and Gert's drawn back into her own life. While she's been woolgathering, Andie's paid the check. Gert tries to make up for her lapse by pressing money into Andie's hand, but her niece won't hear of it.

They slide out of the booth and walk outside. The heat feels good after the artificial coolness of the restaurant, and Gert stands on the sidewalk, soaking it up. It's too late in the day to tackle the big house, and relief, followed by guilt, floods through her. Tomorrow, she decides. First thing.

The cottage has its own driveway, although it is seldom used, and this is where Andie drops her off. She offered to drive right to the door, but Gert insisted on walking this short way. After the pizza, it will do her good.

"Got everything?" Andie asks. Gert nods. She'd asked the checkout girl to pack her groceries separately, and now she picks up the small plastic bag that holds a loaf of bread, a box of macaroni, and oatmeal.

"I'll be over first thing in the morning, and we'll get started," Gert says.

"All right. See you then."

They're not the type that touch much, but as her niece drives off, Gert has an urge to run after her, stop the car, and enfold Andie in her arms. She shakes her head to clear it and starts up the driveway, then stops, listening. In the distance, she can hear her phone ringing. Well, it can't be Andie, and anyone else will just have to wait. She shifts the bag to her other hand and takes a step, then another, concentrating on putting one foot in front of the other, the way she's always done.

Frank

THERE are rules to being dead. Unwritten and hard to discover, but there all the same. Figuring them out is like waking in an unfamiliar room and stumbling toward the light switch: You bang your shins repeatedly until you find your way.

The first one I found out by accident, the very same day I died. A lucky thing I did, too, or that might have been the end of it. Of me. Although whether I was lucky that day or not remains to be seen.

Death is different from how you picture it, although I confess I never spent much thought after the War thinking about how I'd go, much less what would come after. Even at the end. I suppose I had other things to think about. But then suddenly it was the end, all panic and gasping for breath and knowing, knowing this was it, even though from the outside no one could tell I knew anything. Then silence. Like flailing on top of the waves before diving below, quiet and calm and still. At first there was nothing. A long stretch of nothingness, passing by. Then, gradually, light, green and watery, and at the end of the light, Gert. Gert with someone, being helped out the door of the big house. She paused on the top step, looked back inside, and I saw her face as plain as if I were standing in front of her. I've a lifetime of memories, but somehow the ones that have stuck with me all have Gert walking away.

"Don't go," I said, loud as I could. "Don't leave me here. Stay." I said other things, too, but it all meant the same. For a second, she looked as if she heard, but then the visiting nurse came up and touched her on the elbow, and Gert pulled the door shut. She hadn't heard me after all.

But the dog did. The dog did, and that's what saved me. I'd seen her the first time about six months earlier, a shivering, cringing bundle of fur, no bigger than a basketball. She was crouched outside the front steps, looking as if she'd been waiting there a long time for someone to come out. I used to sit out on the front step just to feel the warmth of the sun, to get out of the shadows of the house, and I remember that day was unseasonably warm for June. I sat there and the dog came over to me. I was pretty weak by then, not given much to moving around, but I went back inside and fished through the trash until I found the meat loaf Gert had brought over the night before for my dinner. The dog ate it as if she'd never had a meal before, and when she was done she just curled up at my feet and went to sleep.

We stayed that way a long time, the dog and me, until it seemed like there was nothing left to do but to bring her inside when she woke up. I was in no shape to care for anything by then, and I knew it was going to get worse, but somehow turning her over to the dog warden seemed like ratting out a friend. I bribed the home aide to pick up a few boxes of dog biscuits for me, and fixed her up a nice little bed in the shed. On cold nights, I brought her in the house with me. I'd have had her in every night, except that I was afraid I'd sleep right through the morning. Gert or the nurse was usually there by nine, and if either of them had seen her there'd have been hell to pay. Especially Gert. Those last few months she was awful to watch, so cool and efficient; it was as if we'd never met before I started dying on her. She'd gotten rid of all the houseplants Clara had collected over the years, just because they needed to be watered once a week. There was no way she'd take care of a dog.

So we muddled along, the dog and me, me sneaking her food whenever I could and her pretty much staying out of the way, until the last couple of weeks when I was too weak to get out of bed. Every now and then I'd see a flash outside the window, and I'd turn my head and it would be her. I'd named her Nina, after a pretty little French girl I'd met up in Boston. They shared the same long black lashes and a way of tilting their heads when you talked. I'd scratched the name on an old dog collar I'd found in the barn. I was going to tell the aide about her, see if we could figure something out, but then it all got really bad and I forgot about Nina altogether.

When Gert walked away that last time, it was as if she'd taken what was left of me with her. I was sliding back into the nothingness again, plunging down and down, when the dog barked. Not a loud sound. A conversational kind of woof, but it stopped me from sliding and let me focus again. She was sitting outside the screened porch, and somehow I was there, too.

I stayed there, not fighting for breath, exactly, but something like it, until the space around me fell into some kind of sense. Like I was concentrating myself into being one cell at a time. It was exhausting. The dog stayed with me all that afternoon, and all the night, too. She didn't move, just stayed where she was and watched me, her head resting on her paws.

I never believed in ghosts before, and I'm not sure if that's what you'd call me now, but I've had some time to think about the old stories. The ghosts who wail and mutter and bang things aren't trying to scare the living off; they're trying to reach out, to connect, maybe in the only way they can. Without some kind of a connection to this world, they can't survive.

There are other rules, too, other ways to exist, although none so important as the first. As time passed and I grew stronger, I took to exploring the house, room by room, in a way I'd never been able to see it before. The dark, cool molecules of wood; the smooth, slippery atoms of china. Always, I felt strongest in the attic. I learned to control my energy, to keep some in reserve—like a runner in a marathon—so that after the dog left I could continue to exist without her for a bit. It was easier there, as if the room itself were a power source.

One morning, after the dog had left me, I was in the attic. The dust fragments were drifting through the beams of sunlight coming from the eastern window. In and out, a slow dreamy dance to the floor. The movement captivated me, made me want to follow. If I concentrated hard enough, I thought I might be able to influence their path. I drifted with them, from one end of the attic to the next, and then I felt it—a white-hot burst of energy. A tiny whirlwind of dust motes traveled across the room and vanished over the rocking chair.

It was the ring. I'd left it there more than half a century ago, hidden under a loose board, and I hadn't touched it in all those years. At times I'd thought about it almost daily— its cool, silver shape; the spidery engraving that encircled the inside—and then weeks or months would go by and I'd forget until something jarred my memory, brought the bitter taste of disappointment to the back of my mouth. But in all that time I'd never touched it, and the ring stayed where it was.

The first time I'd seen it, I was about eleven. Even then, I was drawn to the attic—the dry, woody smell; the still air and the quiet. I'd come up during the beginnings of an afternoon storm. Storms always seemed louder here, the thunder closer. There was lightning just visible over the woods, and the sky was beginning to darken. From its spot at the top of the hill, Evenfall had seen its share of close calls, but this just made the storms more exciting.

I was waiting in that heavy, suspenseful time just before the rain started, and I had my marble bag. I was too old to really play anymore, but I still liked to hold them when I was alone, the cool glass globes pouring through my hands. But one slipped from between my fingers and rolled across the room, disappearing beneath a floorboard. I thought about letting it go, but it was a blue aggie, one of my favorites. The board was against the attic wall, and there was a hole, just large enough for a marble. I hooked my finger underneath the board and pulled up.

The marble was there, but so was something else. A faded square of cotton, folded and tied at the corner, too neatly done to have been placed there by accident. I picked it up, unfolded it, and caught the ring as it fell out. Cool and silver, polished to a bright sheen after all this time. It was a tiny thing, too small to slide over the knuckle of my little finger. I held it up in the darkening room. There was writing inside, and I had just enough high school French to make it out. *Je rêve que j'espère que j'aime.*

I jumped at the first crack of thunder. I could hear my mother calling me—she worried about my being in the dark of the attic by myself, afraid I'd light a candle that would burn down the house. I thought about taking the ring with me, but no hiding place I could think of was as secure as where it had been resting. I wrapped it back in the cotton—a handkerchief, I saw, embroidered with the letter W—and placed the bundle back under the floor. It stayed there until I was seventeen, when I took the ring out and kept it in my pocket every day for three months.

Love, rage, bitterness, betrayal—the power behind these emotions is enormous. We feel them in our hearts, in our bones, in the very atoms of our being. A metal object, cool and untainted by human hands, could remain the bearer of those emotions, could contain the energy within it for years. A portable power source, if you will. One made more potent by its history and its hiding place, by the storms and the seas through which it was carried.

Even when I was alive, there were times I thought I could hear the ocean from this attic, landlocked as it is. But now that I'm dead, there are spells, particularly during storms, when the waves seem to crash so loudly I fear the house will wash away.

This house was built by my grandfather, a sea captain whose last voyage took almost two years. During his absence my grandmother's hair turned white, though she wasn't more than thirty. When he finally returned, he swore it was his last trip. He'd had enough, he said. He wanted to sleep in his own bed, feel solid ground beneath his feet, and eat apples plucked fresh from the tree, not dried and hardened into leather.

But the house they lived in then was in New London, just a few streets away from the Long Island Sound. My grandfather awoke in the mornings with his eyes already searching for the ocean. The smell of the salt air was like the perfume of a lover, intoxicating him from across the room.

My grandfather was torn. To go to sea again meant the risk of losing all. Even if he navigated his way safely through the storms that surely lay ahead, there were no guarantees for what he would find when he returned home: He could read the perils there each evening in my grandmother's eyes as she brushed her long, white hair and gazed into the fire. Yet living so close to the sea was torment.

To escape, he moved his wife and young family as far inland as he could bear. To my grandmother, the new house must have seemed like a reprieve, a testament of her husband's love. She planted peonies and roses, grapes and apples, filled the house with cut flowers and fruit. She named the farm Evenfall, for the space between the day and the dark. She lived as a happy woman and no trace of her remains, unless you count the harvest the land yields every summer.

But my grandmother was wrong. This house was built not for her, but as a shrine to her rival. My grandfather hired many of the same men who built his ship to construct the house, and their careful reminders of the sea are everywhere, if you know where to look.

I know where to look, now. I rest my hand against the beam that runs the length of the attic and feel it vibrate, like a mast in a high wind. The floorboards creak and slant as if they were at sea. The round window at the peak of the roof is no more than a porthole, really, and in storms I've almost seen him sitting there, brought out of the darkness for a split second during flashes of lightning.

My grandmother took one sea voyage herself, the summer her eldest daughter turned sixteen. They traveled to Europe on one of my grandfather's ships, bringing with them the girl's two sisters but leaving the baby, a boy of two, at home. My grandfather also stayed behind. The women filled trunks with the latest fashions, wrote letters describing the salons and dinner parties they attended. They set sail for home on a calm August night, eager to return.

But a storm blew up three days out from land. It savaged the boat, turned it around, tossed it upon the shoals. The captain survived, as did a handful of crew members. My grandmother and her children did not. Her body was found more than a week later, in what state the captain did not say. He buried her remains quickly, saving only her ring, which he returned to my grandfather himself. I dream. I hope. I love.

IN summer the trees are full, but in fall they drop their leaves, and the valley and surrounding land crouches below the house like a cat before it springs. If someone searched very hard, they could just see, from that attic window, the things they hold most dear: the faintest glint of sunlight on water; the white, circling wings of gulls; the remote, unreachable face of the woman they love, telescoping away into darkness.

Andie

IT'S ninety degrees and Andie can feel the sweat dripping down her face as she lifts a stack of newspapers tied with twine. She and Gert are in the shed, a euphemistic name for the small building behind the house. In Andie's childhood it was used to store wood; today the shed is cluttered with old magazines, clay pots, and glass jars filled with screws and nails.

Andie drops the newspapers in the pile she's designated for recycling and wipes her hands on her shorts. She lifts her hair off her neck in hopes of a breeze. None comes, and with a sigh she turns to her aunt.

"Is there somebody we could call to come pick up this stuff?" For years, Andie knows, Gert has driven once a month to the town dump. But the flotsam and jetsam that's collected in the shed over the past forty years is beyond the capacity of one ancient vehicle.

Gert, who is eyeing a box of canning jars, is noncommittal. "I don't suppose you'll ever use these?"

Andie just looks at her.

"Fine," Gert says. "Maybe we can donate them for the church fair. Let's start a pile for that."

The shed has a damp, earthy smell. Inside, despite the heat, a coolness comes up from the dirt floor. Andie remembers playing hide-and-seek here, the thrill of waiting in the dimness to be discovered, the almost erotic excitement. And once, the summer before college, she and a date snuck into the shed to escape Clara's eagle eye and make out.

"Andie!"

She starts and looks at Gert.

"Where were you? I was saying that perhaps we could pay Cort McCallister to take some of these things away. That truck of his is big enough."

"Maybe."

Cort isn't on Andie's list of favorite topics this morning. She came home from the grocery store yesterday to find Nina curled by the front steps, reeking of manure. It took several scrubbings with Andie's salon shampoo—the only kind in the house—before the dog was clean enough to come inside. And since Nina vigorously protested, howling and attempting to run every time Andie lost her grip on the dog's collar, the bath took twice as long.

At the end of an hour, Andie was soaked, her shirt spotted with muddy paw prints. An indignant Nina bolted into the house the second Andie opened the door, taking cover under the kitchen table and refusing to come out even for the sticks of jerky Andie waved under her nose.

By nightfall they'd reached an uneasy truce. Nina curled on the foot of the bed, her brown eyes watching Andie's every move. This morning when Andie awoke, the dog was gone. And seeing how the door was locked, Cort McCallister has some explaining to do.

But Cort breaking into the house to free a dog Andie's not supposed to have in the first place isn't something she wants to discuss. Especially this morning, when her aunt is already more cantankerous than normal. Despite the heat, Gert insisted on starting with the shed today, even though they both knew it would be a good ten degrees cooler inside the house.

"No sense putting it off," she'd said, stepping off the front porch and disappearing around the back of the house, leaving Andie no choice but to follow.

It's like being fifteen again, Andie thinks, except now she's smart enough to keep her mouth shut. She takes a deep breath, moves the box of canning jars to the spot Gert has indicated, and starts sorting through the piles of old magazines.

They work in silence for a while, each careful not to bump the other in the small space. The floor of the shed is about a third clear when Andie glances at her aunt. Gert's face is pale despite the heat, and beads of sweat are rolling down her forehead.

"Let's take a break," Andie suggests, and for once Gert

doesn't argue. They make their way past the neatly stacked piles of junk and exit the shed, blinking in the bright sun.

At the house, Andie is halfway to the kitchen before she realizes that her aunt isn't behind her. She retraces her steps and is relieved to find Gert gently rocking on the porch swing.

"Aunt Gert?"

Gert looks up. Her cheeks look pinker, although her brow is still dotted with sweat.

"Just thought I'd ask if you wanted water or lemonade."

"Water, please," Gert says. A breeze brushes past Andie, lifting the stray tendrils of Gert's hair and smoothing them off her forehead. Gert leans back and closes her eyes.

In the kitchen, Andie washes her hands, then fills a glass from the tap, gulps it down, and refills it with lemonade from a carton in the fridge. She fills another glass with water, then dampens a paper towel and drapes it over her arm.

Outside, she hands Gert the glass of water and the paper towel. "I thought you might want to clean up. It was pretty dusty in there."

Gert wipes her hands before bringing the towel to her forehead and neck. The water seems to revive her, and she sits more erectly on the swing. She takes a deep breath before speaking.

"I had a phone call last night."

"Who from?" Andie asks, but really she's wondering if she should hire someone to help clean out the house. Maybe Cort knows someone, she thinks. Or she could place an ad on the church's bulletin board, although if Gert saw it she'd kill her. Andie's so busy scheming ways to help her aunt rest that she almost doesn't hear her next words.

"Richard. Your father," Gert adds, as if there could be any doubt in Andie's mind.

There's a silence. Gert sips her water and looks off into the distance. The breeze has picked up, and Andie watches it swirl bits of grass and leaves near her feet. When she finally speaks, she keeps her voice carefully neutral. At thirty-three, she's old enough to know she no longer needs a parent, but that can't undo the years she spent wishing for one.

"What did he want?"

"He'd like to come for a visit. He'll be passing through in a few weeks, and he asked if you would still be here."

"He did?" It seems impossible that Gert could be talking about her father, who hasn't visited the farm since Andie learned to drive. So far as she knows, he still lives in New Hampshire, in the same two-bedroom condo he bought when she was a child. "What did you say?"

"I told him yes, of course. No matter what his faults are, Andie, he's still your father. And my brother, I might add. That makes him family. And as such, he's always welcome here." Gert puts her glass down by the side of the swing. "Now, I think I've sufficiently recovered to tackle the rest of the shed. Shall we?"

And with that, she stands and marches away. There's nothing for Andie to do besides collect the empty glasses and trail behind.

She's still thinking about the phone call three hours later, though, after they've called it quits for the day. Under Gert's direction, the dirt floor of the shed has been swept, the magazines and newspapers neatly sorted, the rubbish bagged and set aside. A shelf below the shed's only window holds jars filled with nails and screws. And, armed with a hammer and ladder, Andie has even hung the rakes, brooms, and shovels that littered the floor. Her uncle, Andie thinks, wouldn't recognize the place.

"Well, I believe we're finished here." Gert brushes her hands together to rid them of dirt. There's a faint smudge under her left eye and a few stray bits of spiderweb in her braid, but no other signs of the afternoon's exertions, and no trace of her earlier fatigue. "Shall I pick you up for church in the morning?"

"I don't think so, Aunt Gert." By contrast, Andie's T-shirt is smeared with dust, her hair is unraveling from its ponytail, and she's so tired she can hardly stand. Her head is throbbing, both from the heat and from thoughts of Richard's visit, and she's in no mood to humor Gert any further.

"Sunday is the Lord's day, Andie."

"Yes, and on the seventh day even He rested. That's what I'm planning on doing tomorrow."

Gert's nostrils flare slightly, but whether in anger or amusement Andie can't tell. "Very well. Perhaps next week."

"Perhaps." And perhaps pigs will fly, Andie thinks but does not say.

She sees Gert off along the path that leads to the cottage, then heads around the corner of the house. All Andie wants to do is sink into a cool tub of water. She's concentrating so hard she can almost smell the bubble bath, which must be why she doesn't notice Cort until she's just about to trip over him.

"Hey, there." He stands up from his seat on the front steps and stretches. Nina, sprawled in the house's shadow, wags her tail but doesn't get up. From the wary look in her eyes, it's clear she hasn't quite forgotten her own experience with water last night.

"Hey, yourself." A trickle of sweat runs down the side of Andie's nose. She swipes it away with her thumb, and when she glances at her hand, she's mortified to see a smear of dirt.

"Nope—you missed." Cort shakes his head. Before Andie can protest, he carefully wipes her face with the bottom of his T-shirt. He's standing so near, Andie can feel the heat radiating from his body.

"There. Got it." He smiles, and suddenly all Andie can think about is how bad she must smell.

"Wow, I guess it's time for me to hit the tub. Thanks for dropping off Nina," she says, and tries to squeeze by him without actually getting any closer.

"Nah, don't go yet." He bends down and fishes a beer out from the tangle of grass beside the steps. "Here." He holds the bottle up invitingly. "I've got a couple of cold ones in the truck—I thought maybe we could drink them down by the creek."

"Well . . ." There are beads of moisture on the glass, and as Andie watches, one slides down the bottle, leaving a tiny, slick trail. Nothing, she thinks, could possibly taste as good as a cold beer right now. Smell be damned.

"Sure."

Cort's pickup is parked at the far side of the drive, close against the house. He reaches over the truck's tailgate and pulls up four beers. Andie glances in and sees that the cooler is filled with slushy water.

"Been waiting long?" she asks.

"Kinda." As they walk toward the woods, Cort holds the beer bottles two in each hand, his long fingers hooked around the glass necks. "To tell the truth, I saw the two of you working back there, but you both seemed a little tense. I didn't want to interfere with anything." He grins. "Plus, Miss Gert looked like she was in a mood to call the cops on me again."

"For stealing Nina this morning? Next time just knock, would you?"

His voice turns serious. "I've been meaning to talk with you about that. I know this isn't the big city or anything, but you should still lock the doors at night, just to be safe."

She starts to protest, but they've reached the woods and are walking single file along the trail that leads to the creek, so she can't see Cort's face. She lets the subject drop, for now.

The path is overgrown, and as they walk she's busy fending off the pricker bushes, saplings, and branches that reach out to snag her clothes. Ahead of her, Cort's back is tall and straight. He's had a haircut recently, she notices, and the skin at the base of his skull is pink.

"So what's bothering Gert?" he asks over his shoulder.

"Oh, I don't know. Seems like everything does these days." Andie considers telling Cort about her father, but it sounds silly to say she's upset because he's visiting. "I think maybe the whole idea of selling the house is starting to get to her."

"Makes sense." He seems about to say something else, but Andie catches sight of sunlight sparkling on water.

"The creek!"

The trail ends abruptly. There's a small clearing on the creek's bank, a place where the trees give way to a smooth shoulder of rocks, moss, and fern, and Andie pushes past Cort to reach it.

At its deepest point, this bend of the creek approaches three feet. As a child, Andie loved to paddle in its shallow water. The memory of mud squelching between her toes causes an involuntary shudder down her spine. She slips off her shoes and settles onto a rock warmed by the small patch of late afternoon sun that has managed to filter its way through the branches above.

Cort nestles two of the bottles into the side of the bank and sits beside her, their feet dangling companionably into the cool green water below. He palms the top off a bottle, hands it to her, then does the same to his own.

The beer is colder than the creek water, and the first, icy swallow satisfies something deeper than thirst as it rushes down Andie's throat.

"This is just what I needed," she says, leaning back and closing her eyes. She can feel Cort shifting beside her, searching for a comfortable position.

"Did you miss it much when you were away?"

At first, Andie thinks he's talking about the beer. When she realizes he means the creek, she opens her eyes and considers.

"I don't think I thought much about it—I just kind of assumed it would always be here." She props herself up with an elbow and looks at him. "How about you?"

"I went to school out West for a couple of years. I loved it there, too, but I think I just have New England in my bones. I can live other places and be happy, but no place else feels like home, you know?" He glances sideways at her. "Especially here. I try not to take it for granted."

Andie leans back again and shuts her eyes. There was a time when to live at Evenfall—to be claimed by Frank and Clara—was all she wanted. To be claimed by anyone, really. Even Richard. She remembers the mornings before she'd leave for boarding school. Always, she'd spend those early hours walking the meadows and the woods. She'd carved her initials in the bark of more than one tree, desperate to leave some sign that she'd existed here, that she'd belonged. But she's an adult now, she reminds herself. She's built her own life, one far from here. There's no point in going over the past. Instead, she concentrates on feeling the shadows of the leaves move across her face, the puffs of breeze against her skin. She can hear the water, and if she listens carefully she can just make out Cort's slow, quiet breathing. It's peaceful, and she feels herself getting sleepy. She's on the verge of dozing off when she hears Cort's voice.

"So what was Italy like?" he asks. "Tell me about it."

"What do you want to know?" She doesn't open her eyes, just lets herself drift with the sound of the water.

"You were a student, right? So you took art classes?"

"Not exactly," Andie says. "My concentration was on

architecture, which means I focused on buildings. One building, really, for my thesis."

"But you were always drawing and stuff—I thought you wanted to be an artist."

Andie gives up on resting. She'd forgotten how inquisitive Cort was as a child. Apparently, he hasn't outgrown the trait. She sits up and drains the rest of her beer.

"I thought so, too. But my college advisor pointed out that art majors are a dime a dozen, and if I wanted to support myself, my paintings weren't going to do it." She recalls, with a shiver of distaste, the dismissive wave of her advisor's hand over her midyear portfolio. "So I switched to art history, with a focus on architecture, and then I liked it so much I kept going. I just finished my PhD. That's why I was in Italy."

"Congratulations," Cort says. He's in the middle of opening another beer, and he raises it in a toast. Andie nudges him with her foot, and he twists off the cap and hands her the bottle.

"Thanks." She takes a long pull of the beer. "Now if I could only get a job."

"Sounds like we have something in common." He clinks his bottle against hers. "So, tell me about this building. What's it like?"

"Amazing. It's a palace—a fort, really—built in the fifteenth century. It belonged to one family for almost three hundred years, and they just kept adding to it. I studied how it was built, who lived there, and how they used the space."

If she closes her eyes, Andie can see the palazzo, centuries-old dust motes drifting through its dark, cool halls. She's sketched its exterior so many times she can feel its shape beneath her fingertips: the slim Doric columns; the vaulted entrance; the grand courtyard. Births and deaths, marriages and affairs, have all taken place between its massive walls. Yet only the stone remains.

"Huh." Cort's quiet for a moment, considering. "So you basically wrote your thesis on what home meant to this one family."

It's an oversimplification, but close enough to the truth that she opens her eyes and nods. "Pretty much. But it took me two years and three hundred pages," she says.

He flicks a beer cap at her knee. It bounces off, coming to rest in the moss, and Andie picks it up, runs her finger along its sharp edges.

"So what did you do in your time off?" he says. "You did have time off, right?"

"Not much," she says, still thinking of the cool, silent space of the palazzo, the way the outside looked in the pre-dawn air. "I hung out with friends, mostly. Shopped some, ate a lot. It's kind of a different pace there." *Sensual* is the word she thinks of, like the memory of a fat, ripe tomato in her hand. Because she's with Cort she amends it. "It's slower, more of the moment. You can't find that here."

"Depends on where you look." He reaches up and breaks off a long, slender switch from a volunteer sapling, then idly brushes its tip through the creek. "So, you do all this by yourself, or are you with somebody over there? Some eye-talian stallion?"

The thought of anyone mistaking Neal, with his reddish blond hair and ruddy skin, for a native Italian makes Andie laugh out loud.

"What's so funny?"

"Nothing. It's just, I remember you used to do this when I babysat. Ask me a million questions."

"Yeah, and you never answered any of them then, either."

"That's because it's none of your business." She takes another swallow of the beer. "Now your turn. What are you doing these days?"

"Not much." He traces the end of the switch along the instep of her foot. "Mostly helping dad on the farm while I figure out what to do with my life."

"How's that going?"

"What, helping dad, or figuring out what to do?" The switch is tickling her calf now, and Andie swats it away. "It's okay. I got a degree in agricultural engineering—did I mention that? Not a PhD or anything, but pretty good for a country boy."

"Congratulations," Andie says.

"Yeah, well, it doesn't seem to be doing me much good. What I'd really like to do is have my own place, but that takes money. So I'll probably wind up working for the aggie extension or something, at least for a few years." He lays back, lacing his fingers behind his head. The leafy canopy overhead shifts and sways, casting shadows on the water below. It's quiet for so long that Andie starts to think Cort has, impossibly, drifted off to sleep. She's on the verge of dozing again herself when he speaks.

"Was this place ever a working farm when you were here?"

"Evenfall? It depends on what you consider working." She struggles awake. "Uncle Frank worked it, sure. But he probably never made much money. He was a security guard over at the GE plant most of the time I was growing up."

"But my dad says it was always good land. I wonder why they stopped."

Andie shrugs. "Who knows? Between Clara's sewing and the job at GE, they did all right. Maybe he just didn't want to farm."

"Maybe," Cort says. He sounds unconvinced.

"You know, it's kind of weird to think of him growing up here," Andie says. "He was always so quiet that Clara and Gert ran the show. I forget that this was his home first."

"Yep," Cort says. "Those strong-willed Murphy women will run you right over if they get the chance."

Andie rolls to her side and pretends to frown. "Who says that? Aunt Clara was as meek as they come."

"Maybe so," he concedes. "But you take after Gert."

She pummels him until he sits up, laughing, and grabs her wrists. "You do," he says. "Except she probably hits harder. Her hands are a lot bigger—yours are delicate little things."

It's true. Andie's always been secretly proud of her hands. "Another Murphy through and through, God help me," Frank would say, shaking his head and looking at her. "Except for the hands—those came from your mother."

Now she holds them up to the light. Her fingers are long and slender, but strong, with smooth oval nails. Cort places his right palm against hers, dwarfing it.

"You've got that Murphy jaw, though," he says. He brings his hand up slowly and cups her face, tracing his thumb along her jaw. "And the eyes."

Andie's urge to push Cort away is lessened by just how good his touch feels, like water on a plant that's been neglected for weeks. She makes no move to stop him from leaning closer. She can feel the heat of his skin, the soft cotton of his shirt against her arm. Her face is growing flushed, and her breath is coming faster. She closes her eyes. There's a touch of warmth against her lips, and then an ungodly crashing noise.

Andie's eyes pop open and she jerks away from Cort. A second later Nina comes tearing through the undergrowth. The dog dashes into the creek, paddles straight out, then turns and swims back. She claws her way up onto the bank and races in crazy circles around them, stopping just long enough to shake and spray them with water. Finally, she collapses panting at Cort's feet and rolls over, legs waving in the air.

"Jesus." Andie takes a deep breath. Her heart is pounding, and droplets of creek water dot her shirt and her hair. "That damn dog."

"She's something else." He glances up at the sky. "Shit. It's getting late—I need to head back and help dad feed."

He stands and extends his hand, but Andie ignores it. She's embarrassed enough by their almost-kiss that she prefers to scramble to her feet on her own. Cort doesn't seem to mind. He picks up the four empty beer bottles, holds back a sapling at the beginning of the trail, and lets her go ahead of him. All the way home she can hear him whistling behind her as she tells herself how crazy this is. He's not a minor, exactly, but with ten years separating them, he might as well be.

By the time they reach the clearing, she's decided their almost-kiss was a temporary lapse in judgment brought on by the beer, the heat, and possibly the fact that she's miles away and on a different continent from the last man in her life. She's calm enough to face Cort when he strides up beside her, and ready to let him down gently.

"Frank never kept cows, did he?"

"Cows?" She covers her confusion by pretending to rack her memory. "Nope, I don't think so. He did have one old milk cow when I was a kid, but that's it."

"I bet this field would be great pastureland. Look at the stone walls." He points, and behind the scrub trees that surround the clearing Andie can just make out the faint outlines of rock. "Somebody must have used it for that."

"I know Uncle Frank's father kept animals. I've seen pictures."

He stops and looks around the field. "You ought to clear those wild roses. They can take over a pasture so quick that before you know it there's no room for anything else."

"I kind of like them," Andie says. She doesn't stop walking. "And besides, in a few months it won't matter."

They don't speak again until they reach the house. Nina, who took her own path home from the creek, has reappeared, and Cort bends down to scratch behind her ears. Immediately, she flops over on her side, pink tongue hanging out.

Andie, standing on the front steps, can't help herself. "Do you always have that effect on females?"

"Only the four-legged ones." He straightens up and walks over to her, leaning against the door frame. "Prove me wrong—have dinner with me Friday night."

"Thanks, Cort, but I don't think so." Andie turns to go inside, but he puts a hand out to block her.

"Why not? You have to eat. And dinner with me can't be worse than Gert's cooking, can it?" He runs his fingers through his hair until it stands up in little spikes. He looks so woeful Andie can't help but laugh.

"You used to make that face whenever it was time to go to bed," she says, and immediately wishes she hadn't.

Cort, to his credit, doesn't go for the easy line, just arches an eyebrow. "You always let me stay up later, so it must have worked."

Andie doesn't tell him she simply didn't want to stay up alone. She remembers sitting with Cort on his parents' brown, scratchy sofa, watching late-night reruns of *The Rockford Files* and eating popcorn from the aluminum mixing bowl between them. No matter how hard he tried, Cort could never stay awake past eleven. He'd stop asking questions, his breathing would slow, and the next time she looked over, he'd be sleeping, his head propped up against the sofa's high back. His favorite pajamas had green and blue trucks on them, and by age eight he'd worn them so often the cuffs were starting to unravel. His wrist bones showed above the threads, impossibly thin and fragile for a boy.

"You were just good company," Andie says.

"I still am."

When she hesitates, he touches her lightly on the shoulder. "Look, Andie, I promise to respect your status as former babysitter, okay? It's just dinner—no strings." His face clouds. "Unless you're seeing someone. Is that it?"

"No." The answer pops out before Andie has a chance to think. "No, I'm not seeing anyone."

"All right." He grins. "Is eight okay? I could pick you up then."

Against her better judgment, Andie nods. Cort's grin gets wider, and he backs away, as if afraid she'll change her mind. "Eight it is. See you then."

"Right," Andie says, but Cort has rounded the corner of the house. He's forgotten the empty beer bottles, and Andie bends to pick them up. She's still holding them in her hands when the truck drives past. Cort honks the horn, and she raises a bottle in mock salute. The brown glass catches the sun and glints like a light on dark water.

Gert

THE dress that clings to Gert's calves is damp with creek water and heavy with the promise of coming rain. Of the three dresses she owns, this one—blue cotton sprigged with white flowers—is her favorite. Her mother hemmed it with tiny, precise stitches, her face tired under the glow of the kerosene lamp.

She walks along the creek bank, the muscles in her thighs bunching and releasing smoothly. When she glances down, there are no age spots on her hands, and the braid that trails past her shoulders is thick and lustrous. She knows she has been walking a long time, but she is not tired.

The air here is thick, a cross between water and glass, the type of air in which words or thoughts can hang, suspended, hidden, yet almost visible.

"I thought you might not come," he says, stepping out from behind the oak tree that grows just where the bank curves away. His face is smooth and unlined. He's thin, but with the leanness of a boy, not the wasting that came later with age. His eyes are unchanged; the same blue, open-hearted gaze that makes her catch her breath each time he looks at her. At first, she wondered how no one else noticed the intensity of that gaze. In time, she realized that he looks at everyone in the same penetrating way. This is part of his charm. His eyes are slanted at the corners, like a cat's.

"It took a while to get away. I've been home such a lit-tle time, they're still happy to see me," she says. She does not apologize. There is no apology sufficient for what she is about to do. Even if there was, it would not belong to Frank.

He doesn't answer, just takes her arm, and so they wan-der together, dizzy with touch. After a month of stealing glances, of letting their knees bump under the table and their shoulders brush as they walk along, Gert expected their first stolen time together would be purely for the ease of their bodies. So she's surprised when he begins telling her about the book he's reading, a leather-bound edition of Melville he found in an attic trunk. He talks about high school and his plans to enlist this summer when he graduates; he asks her what she'll do when she finishes nursing school. At first, she thinks he's nervous, but when he asks after her father, the old man she's left rotting in the shack she calls home, she understands. He's being kind, giving her a chance to change her mind before they do any real damage.

But Gert has walked the four miles to the creek knowing

where each step leads. If she were going to turn back, she would have done so before this. She stops walking, takes her arm away, and sees sadness and resignation in his face, but no relief. That's when she kisses him. Just as their lips touch, he dissolves into mist, the drops cool and wet upon her face.

Gert wakes from the dream as hungry for that kiss as she's been for any meal in her life. The loss follows her around all morning like a pesky fly, making her irritable and short-tempered. She's late to the house again, and when she arrives Andie's already started clearing out one of the spare bedrooms. The walls are papered with pink and yellow roses that climb from baseboard to ceiling, smothering the room in a riot of color. The air is hot and still, though Andie has wedged the window open with the old water-stained dictionary kept handy for that purpose.

Gert stands in the doorway. There's a pink glow to her niece's cheeks that, were she in a more charitable mood, Gert might credit to heat and exertion, as opposed to the red pickup truck she saw bumping down the driveway late yesterday afternoon. She knows her niece left Italy under unhappy circumstances, although she never talks about it. In Gert's opinion, any man who is too busy to come to the funeral of his almost-fiancé's father—and never mind what she told Andrea about Richard, Frank raised the girl as if she were his own—is a man whose priorities need to be reordered, and quickly. On another day she might take that into account. Today, however, Gert is inclined to think the worst of everyone, including herself.

"Good morning!" Andie says. "I thought I'd get an early

start, and this room is small enough that we can finish it up today. It will make us feel like we've accomplished something."

Like the other three bedrooms on this floor, the room is stuffed with everything from an extra chair to stacks of musty magazines. Gert fans herself with a sewing pattern book, one of a dozen Andie has stacked on the narrow single bed. From the colored sketches of clothes on its cover, Gert guesses the book to be from the 1960s. She sighs, not for the first time, at her sister's inability to let go of anything.

"I suppose this is as good a place as any to get started," she allows. "Do you have a plan, or are you just pulling things out of the closet willy-nilly?"

"That pile is for recycling—I've got some bags in the corner for trash and Goodwill," says Andie.

"And just how did you plan on deciding where each item will go?" Gert asks.

"I was hoping you could help me with that," Andie says cheerfully. "Maybe we could start by going through the dresses over there."

The closet smells like dust and stale perfume and is jammed with old clothes, most of them Clara's. Gert and Andie move in and out of the narrow opening, taking dresses off hangers, careful not to touch.

"What do you think about this one? Trash?" asks Andie, wrinkling her nose. She holds up a sleeveless lime green dress patterned with pink terriers. There's a tiny splotch of barbecue sauce near the neck.

Gert remembers the dress. The stain came from a church picnic the summer before Clara was diagnosed. She'd joked the dress was so ugly it would be chic by Hartman standards, and that the stain would blend right in. By the next summer, the dress no longer fit right. She'd lost too much weight, and the left side hung empty. Even when Gert brought home special padded bras, Clara wouldn't wear them. She claimed they made her scar itch.

This house should have been cleaned out years ago, Gert thinks. She should have done it when Frank got sick. If she'd started even a month ago, she could have done it without her niece around to witness Gert's unraveling over the debris of a life gone by.

"I'm sure someone could use that, Andie," she says. "It's expensive material. Save it for Goodwill."

"But it's stained. See?"

"Fine. If you know what to do with it, why bother to ask me?" Soon, Gert knows, her niece will quietly pack her bags, call the town's only taxi service, and drive away. Gert doesn't blame her. If she could leave herself, she would.

But today Andie doesn't go anywhere, just glances at her sideways and places the dress on the Goodwill pile. They empty the rest of the closet in silence, not talking beyond the occasional "Excuse me" as their shoulders bump. Andie doesn't ask Gert's opinion outright again. Instead, she handles each dress just long enough for Gert to comment if she chooses to. She doesn't.

Andie's worked her way to the back of the closet and is pulling out shoes, the ugly, thick-heeled ones made for older women who spend too much time on their feet. Each time she emerges, she tosses a pair into the discard pile.

"Hey, what's this?" Andie asks. Gert turns to look, expecting another pair of shoes, but the box her niece holds is too large. Andie carries it to the bed and lifts the top off gently.

"Photos, Aunt Gert. Look."

Gert would rather not. There's nothing here she wants to see. But she can't keep rebuffing Andie. Gert's never been the aunt known for holding on to things, but today she makes an effort.

"I see," she says, glancing at the top layer. The photos are in color, and are mostly of Andie: dressed in a yellow graduation gown, Clara, Frank and Gert clustered around her on the college green; holding a white rose onstage at her high school commencement program; sitting on the porch stairs as a gap-toothed seven-year-old, Clara's arm around her and a glass of lemonade by her side. If you didn't know better, if you excavated this box a hundred years from now, you'd think the girl in the photos had had four parents, instead of one.

But Andie sees something different. She scoops the top layer of photos out and places them on the bed, heedless of where they fall. The colored shots give way to black-and-white photographs, and Andie picks one out and holds it like a prize.

"You know, I've never understood why there weren't more photos of the three of you," she says. "Aunt Clara must have been saving these for a scrapbook or something."

"We simply didn't take that many photos back then, Andie. We were too busy living our lives to document them," Gert says. "And film and cameras and the like, all were expensive."

There's a faint thrumming, a whispery sound, coming from the corners of the room. Gert looks around but sees nothing, decides she's imagining the noise. She turns back to the closet, hoping that her brisk example will spur Andie back to work and away from the photos. But Andie's having none of it.

"Whose car is this? Where are you all going?"

"I have no idea, Andie. That was all a very long time ago." Her eyes skim the photo and move on, back to the closet, as if there's nothing more fascinating than the clothes hanging there. And really, nothing is. Gert's lived the life in the photographs already. This is all that is left.

The air in the room is thick with heat and the thrumming is getting louder. She glances at her niece to see if she's noticed, but Andie is oblivious.

Gert rubs her temples. There is something about this house that sets her on edge and has since the day she first entered it, the dirt-poor daughter of a drunken farmer. She'd known who Frank was, of course. Everyone in town knew the Wildermuth boys. Abe was four years ahead of her at school, Frank two years behind. He'd had the most beautiful eyes, even as a child. Not that it mattered. In Hartman there were only two classrooms, so small everyone knew one another, so compact it was easy to see who had food at lunch each day and who went without. There may have been plenty of times when Gert went hungry, but she still had pride. She'd felt Frank's eyes on her, but she never looked his way. Except once. The first day of school, she'd felt the strength of his gaze, and when she brushed up against him on her way into class, it was as if she'd taken her first breath of air, like she was awake and alert for the first time. She found she was trembling. But she'd have been damned before giving anyone the slightest reason to say a Murphy was setting her cap for a wealthy beau. She made it to her seat without stopping that day, and through the rest of high school without exchanging more than a handful of words with either of the brothers.

She'd have made it the rest of her life without seeing Hartman or the Wildermuth brothers again, too, if she hadn't gotten the call to come home during her last year of nursing school. Years of hard drinking and harder living had finally caught up with her father in the form of a stroke.

She recognized the irony. As a child, after all, she'd prayed for his death. Now, as she wiped the drool from his face and changed his soiled sheets, she saw how the answer had come, just not early enough to save her. After her mother's tearful call to the school, the director of nursing herself had put Gert on the train home. She was a good student, the woman had told her, but family had to come first. She'd try and hold Gert's spot, but there were so many worthy girls and so few scholarships she could make no guarantees.

She hated everyone that summer. Her father, for taking so long to die. Her mother and Clara, for being oblivious to what life offered. Herself, for knowing. And the minister on Sundays, for his endless sermons, a purgatory of sorts: They kept her from the hell of home, but offered no glimpse of a deeper salvation.

Until after service, standing on the steps outside, she

noticed a slim figure in pressed cotton trousers and a clean shirt. It was his eyes that caught her attention and wouldn't let her go. Like cat's eyes, Gert thought, watching Clara brush invisible lint off his shirt.

She found she could talk to him now. She was a nurse, after all, or almost a nurse, not just a farmer's daughter. They'd talked about Hartman and how little it had changed, about Boston and her classes. When he touched her bare arm to draw her attention, she shivered. Her sister, Gert saw, had the good sense not to ask him home, but he offered to take them for a drive after dinner in a way that made Gert think it wasn't the first time. When Richard, still in short pants, clamored at his elbow, he good-naturedly included the boy in the invitation, too.

"Frank Wildermuth?" Gert had whispered when he'd left. "How long have you been seeing him?"

"A few months," her sister said, removing her gloves as they walked along the dusty side of the road to their home. "Not long. He's nice. But his mother . . ." She made a face.

"His family owns half of Hartman, Clara. You know what people will think."

"He can't help what his family has, no more than we can help what ours doesn't have. Besides, who cares what people think?"

Gert thought of Mrs. Wildermuth, a thin woman with hands that constantly fluttered about her face, like small birds struggling to be free. She'd hovered by the side of the car the whole time Frank had been talking, making no move to join the group on the stairs. The only thing that would scandalize the neighbors more than news that one Murphy girl was dating a Wildermuth would be whispers that two were. And yet she found herself unable to stay away.

At school Gert has nothing but scorn for patients who follow the cool glass vials of morphine with their eyes like a lover, who twitch restlessly beneath the sheets while the needle is being drawn. No one has ever clung to Gert during rounds, begging for more even when the charts forbid it. By twenty, she'd developed an immunity to wanting anything too much and contempt for those who did. Which is why the feelings that flood her every time Frank's name is mentioned take her by surprise. She flushes, then grows pale in fear that someone will see. When they meet for the first time alone at the creek, after a month of denying what is happening, she's amazed by how easily she's able to lie about where she's been to Clara and her mother. A part of her doesn't care if they find out, that's how badly she wants to be with him. For the first time, she finds herself thinking of those patients with something approaching sympathy.

When his mother drives to New London to visit friends for the day, Frank invites her to the house. He's made tea and serves it around the back, where no one will see them. He's left the kitchen window open, and when a slow song comes on the radio, he bows and takes her in his arms. He's taller by a good bit. In her flat walking shoes, her hands just reach his shoulders.

After they've eaten, he takes her inside and walks her through, room by room. The house is filled with silk throws, dark heavy furniture, even Oriental rugs, and Frank points to each object and tells her where it's from: the tea set his grandfather brought back from China, the sampler his grandmother stitched with silk thread. It's not that he's house proud, more that each item reveals a bit about his family and himself, and he wants to have no secrets from her.

At home, Gert's mother braids her own rugs and cuts pictures from women's journals to decorate their walls. Gert might not be used to luxury, but she doesn't mind it. It's not till the attic that she starts to feel uneasy. They look through the round window, Frank showing her the lands spread below and the ribbon of road like a gift, as if all she had to do was say yes to accept. When he puts his arms around her waist and nuzzles her neck, she feels the first prickles of warning, as if they are being watched. She glances around, but no one is there.

"Shhh," Frank murmurs, as if he senses her unease. He turns her to face him, cupping her head against his shoulder as if she were a child. His shirt smells faintly of lavender and of cotton, warmed by his body heat. "Shhh. It will work out."

Work out for whom? she'd wanted to say, but didn't. No matter what happened, someone would lose. In the end, it seemed that everyone did. Except maybe Clara.

Gert's staring at the closet, counting up the losses, when Andie's voice breaks into her reverie.

"Aunt Gert?"

It's with effort that Gert drags her mind back into this room, into this body that is no longer twenty. She blinks, as if she's just walked out of the forest and into the sun.

"Aunt Gert?" Andie asks again, worry edging her voice.

"What is it, Andie?"

"We're just about done here, I think. If you want, I can finish up myself. Or we can take a break for lunch."

When Gert was Andie's age, she imagined old age as a calm, desiccated state, a desert of the emotions, and longed for that peace. At almost eighty, she still does, and wonders when it will come.

"No, thank you, Andie. Let's finish the job, and then we'll rest." She pulls a particularly ugly print dress out of the closet, drops it in the trash pile, and brushes her hands briskly together. Even if she can't completely banish her emotions, Gert's learned how to keep them under control.

There's a noise behind her, a long slow sigh, and at first Gert doesn't realize it is Andie—she thinks it is somehow connected to the whispery sound that's still echoing in her ears. There must be rats in the attic, she decides, and makes a mental note to remove Andie's Havahart traps and call an exterminator when she gets home.

But then she sees the photo in her niece's hands. The picture is black and white, but Gert knows the dress she wears is blue cotton, sprigged with tiny white flowers. Although you can't see it from the camera's angle, the dress is stained in the back, a combination of green moss and dirt, from where Gert's body pressed into the warm creek bank. He'd spread a handkerchief on the ground for them to rest on, an old-fashioned one with an elaborately scripted W, but it was too small to be of much use. On her face is a look of joy so real, so fragile, Gert can't bear to look, let alone remember. She turns away.

"You look so happy," Andie says, wonderingly.

The whispery sound is getting louder, filling Gert's ears.

"Who is that in the woods with you?"

Gert glances quickly at the photo where her niece is pointing. There's a shadow, the faintest suggestion of a figure, to the right and behind Gert. The shape is tall and slender. It could be the movement of the trees in the wind. It could be a spot on the film. It could be anything.

Gert sits on the bed. The noise is a rushing now, like the sound of a stream running. There's something wrong with my heart, she thinks, and struggles to remember if she took her pills this morning. Atrial fibrillation, according to the young physician who took over last year for Dr. Cushing. "It means your heartbeat is irregular," he explained, speaking slowly as if Gert were ninety-two and senile instead of someone who had been caring for people since before his parents were in diapers.

She rubs her temples, eyes closed. No matter what the doctor says, no matter what medication she takes, it won't help. The truth is, her heart has been frozen for years. Now when for some reason it has started to beat, it can't quite remember the rhythm. Instead, it's bumping along as fast as it can, leaving Gert no choice but to pay attention.

The memory of that afternoon has been with her for over half a century, a touchstone that reminds her joy once existed. Sitting in the rose-smothered room, surrounded by her dead sister's belongings, it occurs to Gert to wonder, not for the first time, how she ever let it slip away.

Frank

FROM the attic window I watch Gert walk away. Andie's following, worried, I suppose, but Gert pays her no heed, just doggedly continues on in the direction of the cottage. I press my fingertips against the windowpane and feel the molecules slide and shift beneath my weight, smooth as ice. I want to shatter the glass, let it fall like knife-sharp rain. I want to run down the stairs and block her path, grip her by the shoulders until she's finally forced to see me. I want to take her in my arms and weep.

But what power I have is featherlight, the merest echo of desire. I can whisper my yearnings through the walls of this house. I can alter the way an image appears. But I can't make Gert stay.

This isn't the first time she's left me. It's not even the most painful. The first day of fall term, when I was twelve, her hair rippled down her back like creek water, light brown shot through with strands of gold. I opened my mouth to say hello, but she brushed past me without a glance, leaving me gaping in her wake.

There weren't many in my youth who wouldn't pause to say hello to a Wildermuth. Abe and I both had our pick of seatmates at school, the girls vying to settle next to us when they opened their lunch pails. They'd pull out cookies and candy bars, home-baked breads and bottles of pop, as if we were as easy to attract as the flies that buzzed around the classroom. All the while, Gert would be sitting up front, her face buried behind some book. Princess, the other fellows called her behind her back, but they'd have come running if she'd looked their way; we all would have. But she never did.

To us she was as cool and remote as the moon. She glided through her days in Hartman as if she were biding her time, as if she knew better things were coming. Ask how she was and she'd hold your eyes with that steady gaze and thank you, all the while making you twist inside.

Clara was just the opposite. She came to class one day about a year after Gert had left for Boston. Clara was easy to look at back then, all softness and curves, with a halo of curls that framed her face and set off the blue of her eyes. Sliding into her seat, her hip caught the edge of her book bag, knocking it to the floor. Girls were always doing that, but this time it looked real, so I picked it up. I had a notion to ask her how her sister was, but when she reached to take the satchel from me, I saw the bruise, the size of a handprint, on her wrist.

She saw where I was looking and flushed, shaking her sleeve down to cover her arm. "I was helping my pa out around the farm last night and banged it, is all," she said. "You know how it is."

I did know. Jack Murphy had once worked for my father, who fired him not so much for sleeping on the job as for being a mean, loudmouth drunk. I carried her books home that day, or as close to her house as anyone ever got. That's how it started.

She was younger than me by almost three years. A baby, really. She knew what it was like to be left behind, so we had that in common. By then Abe had been gone for more than a year, and with my father passed, it was just me and Mother at home. Abe wasn't a big letter writer—we probably got one a month from him—and when he did write it was mostly about what he needed, like laces for his boots, more socks, things like that. My mother spent her days haunting the mailbox, and then like as not when she did get a letter she was disappointed. Either way, Abe was all I heard about, and it drove me crazy.

Clara was in the same boat. Gert didn't write much either, she told me, and when she did it was all about her classes and how hard they were, or how money was tight and she couldn't see herself coming home for the holidays. Clara didn't blame her, but their mother was upset. What with the old man, Clara and her mother were pretty close.

We'd fallen into a routine by then. I'd walk her home

most days, stopping about a quarter mile from the house. We'd talk about class or homework or the weather, little nothings that kept us from silence. Sometimes I'd slip in a few questions about Gert, thinking I was so slick, but Clara never wanted to talk much about her. On weekends, if there was nothing better to do, I'd swing by and take her for a ride into town, or along some of the less bumpy country roads in the fall to see the leaves change, and Clara would cut bittersweet to sell. It grows wild around here, and city folks still pay good money for its bright red berries. But it's a parasite, really. Cut it back and it twines around a tree twice as fast, holding on so tight that it chokes the life out of it.

For her sixteenth birthday I got her a Rollei I'd found in a pawnshop in New London. It was used but in good condition, with a couple of scratches on the camera itself that made the price right. When she saw it she squealed and threw her arms around my neck. Her lips were inches from mine, and her eyes so big and blue there was nothing for it but to kiss her. Gert had faded for me by then. I thought what I'd felt was nothing more than a schoolboy's idle crush, until she came back home.

If Abe had been home, or if my father had been alive, things would have turned out differently. That's what I tell myself, anyhow. I'd have had something to do, somebody else to talk to. I wasn't looking for romance so much as filling time. But I guess Clara didn't see it that way. I don't blame her, although I can't say I haven't tried.

I breathe on the glass of the attic window and watch her name appear in thick cursive script: *Gert*. The day I died, my grief filled the air like a gray cloud. I'd thought death would be the quiet shutting of a door, but it's more as if someone torched my house to the ground. All the chances, the days to come—there's nothing left beyond a few smoldering embers. Touch them and you'll burn your hands.

Andie

IT'S not as if she's nervous, Andie tells herself. It's just that dinner with Cort is a bad idea all around. She's picked up the phone a dozen times since last Saturday to cancel, but something always stops her. And now it's too late.

To distract herself from the disaster the evening is sure to be, she's focusing on what to wear. For the past forty-five minutes, she's been digging madly through her closet, tossing aside paint-stained shirts and ripped shorts in hopes of finding something suitable. Part of the problem is that she has no idea where they're going. If her date was Neal, her choice would be simple: the sexiest item she owned, preferably designer, the better to keep his attention at the intimate party or hot new restaurant he'd most recently discovered. But in Hartman, there's only the pizza joint and Johnny's

Bar and Grill, the kind of dive where the parking lot is still filled with pickup trucks at two in the morning and if you drive by after last call, you're liable to see somebody peeing in the bushes. Neither offer a great first date setting.

"But it isn't a date," Andie says aloud. She rests her hand on a black dress that has spaghetti straps and an open back. It's the nicest thing she's brought, and just for a second she thinks about wearing it. Then she pictures the expression on Cort's face and reluctantly leaves it on the hanger.

Instead, she settles on a dressed-up version of her regular jeans and T-shirt. She pulls on a straight denim skirt that falls just below her knees, wiggles into a black tank top, and drapes a black cotton sweater over her shoulders.

The phone rings and Andie has half a mind to ignore it. At Evenfall, there's only one phone jack, and it's in the kitchen. There have been a half dozen calls this week, and every time Andie has scrambled to answer it, only to find no one there. Her cell phone is useless in the States, and she hasn't bothered to pick up another one, since there's no one here for her to call, at least until she starts sending out her CV. But then it occurs to her that the caller could be Cort, so she races down the stairs in her bare feet. The phone is on its eighth ring when, breathless, she lifts the receiver, only to hear the line go dead.

"Hello?" she says anyway. "Hello?"

There's no answer, just the faint buzzing of the line.

"Asshole," Andie says to no one in particular, then hangs up. She glances at the kitchen clock as she walks out the door, automatically calculating the time in Italy. Almost midnight. If she were there, she and Neal would be going to bed, sleepy after a bottle or two of red wine. Loneliness floods her in a wave, making it hard to breathe. She leans her forehead against the cool hallway wall, then pulls back, startled. There's a faint humming noise. She leans in again and listens. Nothing. There must be a hive somewhere, she thinks, pushing thoughts of Neal away as she climbs the stairs.

The bedroom's ancient mirror hangs over the bureau, and when Andie gazes into it her reflection is wavy, as if she's peering through water. She frowns, and her image scowls back, an angry mer-twin. She rifles through the top drawer of the bureau until she finds the earrings she bought last year in Rome, tiny pearls set inside circles of silver. Smooth and cool in her palm, the earrings are almost weightless. She puts them on and looks again, twisting her hair up with one hand into an easy knot. Better.

Shoes are the only thing left to decide, and that should be easy. Her mules are right in front of the closet. She's reaching for them when she catches sight of a pair of black spiky heels, thrown near the back with her hiking boots. The toes of the shoes are open, and the straps wrap around her calves almost to the knees.

Neal called them her "fuck-me shoes," since whenever she wore them that's what they ended up doing, hurrying home from whatever club or party they'd been to, stopping only to press against each other in the dark, twisting alleys that led to her flat. She tries not to think about the last time she wore them, the cool night air, his hands under the thin fabric of her shirt . . . She puts the shoes down, then picks them up again. She's still hesitating when she hears Cort's truck bumping down the driveway.

By the time she's laced them up and made it down the stairs, he's cut the engine. The kitchen window is open, and from her place in the hall she can hear the car door slam, then the soft pad of footsteps on the walk. He's whistling softly, something that could be Bruce Springsteen, she's not sure. She feels silly suddenly, like a teenager waiting for her boyfriend, her pulse thumping in her ears as if she's been running.

Even though she's expecting it, his knock on the door makes her jump, and a strand of hair falls across her face. She brushes it away irritably. She's just about had it with herself and the whole idea of going out tonight. But it's a little late to cancel, so she reaches for the doorknob.

There's an awkward pause when they're face-to-face through the partially open door. It lasts about five seconds, the amount of time it takes Nina to squirm through the door, pushing it the rest of the way open with her body. She wriggles behind Andie's knees, whining, and almost knocks her over.

Cort reaches out a hand to brace her. "Guess she missed you."

"Looks that way," Andie says. "Though I can't imagine why."

Nina twists her way between them all the way to the truck, so that Andie stumbles and Cort grabs her arm. He's wearing khakis and a pressed white shirt, and when her nose bumps his shoulder he smells of heat and fabric softener. His hand on her bare arm is very clean, and Andie's glad she dressed up a little.

At the pickup, he shoos Nina away from the passenger door. She stops wagging her tail and puts her head down, but her ears prick up when Cort reaches behind the seat and pulls out a newspaper-wrapped package. Opening it carefully, he drops its contents to the ground. It's a long white marrow bone.

"Ugh." Andie wrinkles her nose as Nina swiftly picks it up and retreats to the side of the house, tail wagging once again. "I don't even want to know where you got that."

"No, you probably don't," he agrees. He balls the newspaper up and throws it into the back of the truck. Andie, who has been wondering how to navigate the distance between the ground and the pickup's seat in her skirt, takes this opportunity to swing herself up using the grab strap above the door frame. When Cort turns around, she's sitting in the front, knees primly together.

He eyes her for a second, and she gives him a demure smile.

"Nice shoes," he says, then shuts the passenger door.

ANDIE wasn't expecting the ride to be so quiet. After the initial small talk about where to eat, Cort seems content to let her gaze out the window. He's whistling softly again, eyes on the road, as she watches the scenery slide by.

Cort's silence is so unlike what she'd come to expect

from Neal, with his aptitude for easy conversation, that she doesn't know whether to be amused or insulted. But it's a comfortable quiet, she decides, one that takes the pressure off and lets her simply enjoy the ride.

The landscape between Hartman and Franklin is familiar yet strange, like the aging face of a friend after a long absence. The road that runs between the two towns is still dotted with dairy farms and vegetable stands, but now there are also banks, coffee shops, and gas stations. Andie even spots a mini strip mall, complete with a Laundromat and a Dairy Queen.

In Franklin, the huge brick mill stands forlorn, the broken windows of its outer office gaping like teeth. A huge plastic banner across the building's side proclaims "Quality Space For Rent!" but graffiti takes up almost as much space as the lettering.

Cort noses the truck between the two pillars that mark the entrance to the mill's courtyard, and the seats jounce a bit on the uneven surface.

"Um, what's this?" Andie asks, peering out the window.

"This," says Cort, bringing the truck to a stop, "is where we're having dinner."

There's a huge stack of firewood outside one of the mill doors. Weedy shrubs dot the foundation, and a crumpled scrap of paper drifts across the courtyard. But the lot is filled with cars and she can see lights on inside the building, so she shrugs and lets Cort open her door.

"It doesn't look like much on the outside," he says, as if she hadn't noticed. He offers his arm to guide her down, and after a glance at the cobblestones beneath her feet, Andie takes it. Her hiking boots wouldn't have been out of place here.

She's unprepared for the din that leaps out when Cort opens the restaurant door. There's a small entryway, just large enough for two couples to stand in, with heavy green velvet curtains at the end. She pushes past them and they give way to a room with soaring ceilings. Aside from the wooden beams overhead, the entire space is exposed brick.

To her left, a long wooden bar is just visible through the crowd milling around it. On the other side of the room, a huge adobe oven spits fire. A teenager not much younger than Cort wipes his forehead with the back of his hand, picks up a long wooden pole, and slides a pizza round into the flames.

Cort shoulders his way through the crowd to the hostess stand. After a few seconds of animated conversation with the skinny blonde behind it, he beckons Andie to follow him.

The blonde, wearing tight black pants and a white shirt knotted at the waist, leads them toward the back of the room. Here, away from the press of the bar, it's quieter. A few tall ficus plants along the back wall glow with necklaces of tiny white lights.

The hostess drops their menus on a small round table, revealing a small slice of her perfectly flat stomach in the process, and departs with a toss of her hair. Screened by a ficus tree on one side and an outcropping of brick on the other, the table is an oasis from the hubbub surrounding them.

Cort pulls out her chair, and Andie slides into it. He sits across the table from her and studies her face.

"Not what you were expecting?" he asks.

"It's definitely different. To tell the truth, I thought we'd wind up at Johnny's."

"Nah. That's for second dates."

Andie studies the menu to avoid a reply, and finds herself surprised again. It's short—just one page, without a fried item in sight. There's a list of pizzas, and a handful of entrees with ingredients like capers, creme fraiche, and olives. She's debating what to order when a short, plump man with a shaved head and the start of a goatee appears at their table and drapes an arm around Cort's shoulders.

"Hey, buddy!" says the man, dressed in the black and white pants and white smock of a chef. "How's it going?"

"Hey." Cort gives the man an affectionate whack on the back. "Andie, I'd like you to meet my friend Chris. He likes to pretend he's the cook at this dive."

"Nice to meet you, Andie. Pay no attention to our friend, here—he's unskilled in the ways of the world, doesn't realize you should never insult the man preparing your food. Make sure the waitress tells me which meal is for you when she brings the order back."

"I'll do that," she says.

"C'mon, Chris, if I wind up with food poisoning, there goes your one-star rating."

"Watch yourself, funny guy," Chris says. "Andie, enjoy yourself, despite the company, and I'll try to pop out here later and provide a little intelligent companionship for you as a change of pace."

He claps Cort on the back once more and strides away.

"How do you know him?" Andie asks. Her napkin is slipping out of her lap, and she stops its descent by catching it on the toe of her shoe.

"Chris? We met last fall through some hunting buddies."

"I didn't know you hunted."

"Yep. Been going out with my dad since I was a kid," he says. She's about to reply when the waitress arrives. The woman sports the same black pants and white shirt of the hostess, but the pants aren't stretched as tightly and the shirt is securely tucked into the waistband. She sets two glasses of sparkling wine and a small plate on the table.

"Compliments of the chef," she says. "I'll be back in a minute to take your order."

"Thanks, Mary," Cort says, and the waitress nods and hustles away.

"Do you know everybody here?"

"Just Chris and Mary. And Janet, the, ah, hostess."

The way he lingers over the name makes Andie suspect he's a little more familiar with Janet than with the others. Surprisingly, she finds it's a train of thought she'd prefer not to follow. Instead, she examines the small white plate's offering. There are two squares of toasted bread. On top of each sits a tiny asparagus spear with slender ribbons of prosciutto draped across it. Andie hesitates a moment when she sees the ham—she's not used to eating meat—but figures she's already had Gert's meat loaf and might as well. She picks up one toast and bites into it. A thin ribbon of rich, lemony sauce is beneath the spear. She finishes the appetizer in three bites. It takes Cort just two.

"Pretty good, huh?" he says.

Andie nods. "Amazing."

"Surprised?"

"To find a place like this in Franklin? You're kidding, right?" she says. "We couldn't even get McDonald's to come here when I was growing up."

"Chris has only been open a few months, but he's been pretty good for the area. He's bought a lot from us. And the asparagus comes from Old Lady Miller's farm, just up the street."

Mary bustles over to clear away their plates and tell them about the specials. "There's a goat cheese, onion, and red pepper flatbread. There's also a trout prepared campfire style that I highly recommend," she says, speaking to Andie.

"Any recommendations for me?" Cort asks.

"Yes. Be glad that it's me waiting on you, and not Janet. Now, what can I get you?"

"I'll have the pizza," Andie decides.

"The trout," Cort mumbles. The tips of his ears are bright red.

It's very quiet at their table after Mary leaves.

"So you and Janet, ahh?" Andie asks, amused.

Cort mutters something unintelligible.

"Sorry, I didn't catch that."

"Yeah, we went to high school together. She moved back around the same time I did and we've been out once or twice. It's no big deal. I didn't know she was working here, though." He glances toward the hostess stand, and Andie follows his gaze just in time to see Janet smile and give a little wave. Mary's cackle is audible from a table away.

Cort puts his head in his hands. "Maybe this wasn't such a good idea. I just thought . . . Chris's food is really good . . ."

It's clear a diversion is necessary. "So, you and Chris are hunting buddies?" Andie asks. "I had no idea you were so bloodthirsty."

Cort looks like he's wishing someone would put him out of his misery, but he rallies and sits up. "Ever been hunting? It's quiet, peaceful out in the woods. If you do it right the deer doesn't know what hit him. That's not a bad way to go."

"I guess," Andie says. She thinks of the deer that she's seen in the woods surrounding Evenfall, all big eyes and delicate, fashion-model bones. She saw a fawn watching her one morning, just after her first year at boarding school; its white spots blended so carefully into the sun-dappled leaves that, recalling it later, she wasn't sure if she'd really seen it or if her eyes, weary from a year of studying, had tricked her. It's of this deer that she's thinking when she asks Cort, "But why should he have to go at all?"

"I guess, in an ideal world, he wouldn't. But we've all got to eat, and all we can do is make the best choices we can. I'll tell you one thing—I'd rather come back as a deer than a cow."

"I don't know," Andie says. "I've seen your farm. The cows look pretty fat and happy to me."

"For now, yeah," Cort says. "But we're an abnormality in the dairy business. Dad just put in automatic milkers about eight years ago, and we're one of the last in this area to keep our cows on pasture. And pretty soon, if we don't start making money, we're gonna be out of business."

A busboy sets a plate of salad in front of each of them. Cort's looking at it, but Andie can tell he's not seeing it. His face is too bleak to be thinking about greens.

"Come on," she says. "It can't be that bad."

Cort stabs at a piece of lettuce with his fork. "Yeah, well, my mom's gone back to driving a school bus to pay for health insurance. My dad's selling some land to pay the taxes this year but . . . ." He shrugs. "It's probably pointless. In a couple of years it'll all be houses."

"I'm sorry," she says, and she is. For years, the McCallister farm has been her touchstone, the first sign of Hartman she's glimpsed coming off the highway. In summer the pastures were green and lush, unrolling before her like the weeks of vacation to come. In fall, when her father came to collect her, she'd twist around in her seat for one last look. The memory of the farm's trees, tinged the faintest shade of gold, had to sustain her the rest of the year, like a deep breath of air before entering the suffocating atmosphere of boarding school. Andie's always felt rootless, but she can see how having a legacy like Cort's and then losing it might be worse.

"Dad's not the only one," Cort says. "Every day, the state's losing small farms. The little guy just can't compete anymore."

"Couldn't your dad grow something else? Something that makes more money?"

"I'm open to suggestions, but the only profitable crop in Connecticut these days is houses," he says. "Cows just can't compete with $100,000 an acre."

Andie knows he's right. Everywhere she turns, there's a new subdivision. Driving in town last week, she took a wrong turn and became completely disoriented. Down the lane where she and Clara used to gather blackberries, a network of houses had sprung up like mushrooms after a rain.

"A whole way of life is disappearing," Cort says. "There's been farmers like us here since forever, and in a couple more years we'll all be gone."

"That can't be true."

Cort shakes his head. "You remember my brother Joe, don't you?"

Andie has to think a moment before she can nod.

"Joe's the oldest of all of us. He went off to school when I was a kid and never really came back. He's got an MBA, he married a city girl, and he lives a life with no manual labor required."

"My kind of life," Andie says, but Cort ignores her. "Summers, though, he likes to bring his kids home to the farm and let them run wild. Last week, his youngest was out in the yard playing near the chicken coop, and all of a sudden he starts screaming "Grammy, Grammy!" at the top of his lungs. My mother rushes over, figuring he's hurt himself. She grabs him to see what's wrong, and he says 'Grammy, do you know where an egg comes from? From a chicken's butt!' The kid wouldn't eat eggs the rest of the week."

Andie laughs, but she knows what he means. There's a disconcerting sterility to the supermarkets here. When she picks up a red pepper, its waxy surface gleams but has no scent. Cheese is wrapped so tightly she can't tell if it is crumbly or not, and the dairy case is too cold in which to linger.

"It's not like that everywhere, you know," she tells him. "In Italy, it's a completely different experience."

"Tell me."

Andie thinks for a moment. "I made this recipe once that had shrimp and garlic in it. When I bought the shrimp, they still had their heads attached, and I almost couldn't bear to unwrap them when I got home. Their little bug eyes looked so reproachful. The garlic was so pungent I could smell it through the paper bag. Carrying it home on the bus, I was so embarrassed. I was sure everybody was trying to figure out what the smell was."

"I'll bet you got a good seat, though," he says.

"It was one of the first dishes I cooked for company there. I kept thinking it was going to be a disaster, but it wasn't. The ingredients didn't look perfect, like they would have if I'd bought them here, but they tasted so much better."

She'd served a Pinot Grigio, she remembers, and Neal had brought flowers, a handful of daisies he said he'd picked alongside the road. After, they'd gone out for gelato. Across the street she'd noticed a bucket of the same daisies in the fiorista's window. Coincidence, she told herself back then. Now she knows better.

Cort says something, but Andie doesn't hear it. She's about to ask him to repeat himself when Mary swoops over, removes the salad plates, and serves their meals. The goat cheese on Andie's pizza sits in round white dollops across the crust, slightly browned on the edges. The red peppers are sliced thinly, and the whole pie smells faintly of garlic, onion, and yeast.

The food serves as a natural break in conversation, and it's quiet for a bit. Andie picks up a slice of pizza and bites into the tip, eschewing a knife and fork. It is, she decides, worth every single calorie. The cheese and red peppers are slightly sweet, offset by the tang of garlic and the smokiness of the crust. She devours half of her piece before she looks over at Cort.

He's just as intent on his meal, but he takes a second between bites to smile at her.

"Good?" he asks.

Andie nods, her mouth too full to answer. They eat in silence for the next few minutes. When she comes up for air, Cort's watching her.

"What?" she says. "Do I have goat cheese on my face?"

He shakes his head. "Nope," he says.

"Then what?"

"Admit it," he says. "I'm enthralling you with all my talk about land management and chickens."

"I'm fascinated," she agrees. "No wonder poor Janet fell for you."

"Yeah, well, it's a burden, being irresistible. Although you seem to be holding up just fine. Maybe I need to change my approach."

"Maybe," Andie says, surprising herself. Her left hand is resting on the table, and Cort reaches across to take it in his right. His palm is rough with calluses, and very warm. "How's this?" he says.

Andie's saved from a response by the arrival of Chris. She

pulls her hand away and places it in her lap as the chef drags over a chair and straddles it, resting his chin on the back.

"How was your meal?" he asks.

"Delicious," Andie tells him.

"Thanks. I have to say, I'm flattered Cort chose to bring a date here. We give him such a hard time, it must be serious."

"It's not really a date," Andie says without looking at Cort. "I used to babysit him sometimes."

"No way. Little Cortie had a baby sitter? I'll bet he was a real pain in the ass."

"He was," Andie agrees. "I was always dragging him out of trees and sticking bandages on him. Once he even broke his arm." She remembers the heart-stopping moment when he fell, the sick feeling in her stomach. His face when he landed on the ground was white as bone, but he never cried, just blinked back the tears so they pearled in the dark of his lashes, shiny as a spider's web.

"My babysitter was a seventy-year-old church lady with black hairs growing out of her chin. If I'd have climbed a tree, she'd have broken my arm for me," Chris says.

Cort looks pointedly in the direction of Chris's stomach, which plumps out the front of the chef's smock. "I have a hard time picturing that," he says.

"Yeah, well, some of us change between the ages of three and thirty, little buddy," Chris says. "It's called maturing, a concept you're obviously unfamiliar with."

"Really? I thought it was called getting old and fat," Cort says.

Andie raises an eyebrow. "So thirty is old and fat, is it?"

"Not on you," Cort says hastily. "Definitely not on you."

Chris laughs and stands up. "It's almost worth sticking around to hear how you get out of that one, but I've got to get back to work. Andie, it was a pleasure to meet you, and I hope to see you in here again soon."

"You will," Andie assures him.

"Cort, we still on for Thursday?" Chris says.

Cort nods. "I'll drive if you bring breakfast."

"Deal. See you then."

"What's Thursday?" Andie asks after Chris is gone.

Cort shifts in his seat. "We're kind of working on a project together," he says. "What do you think about dessert?"

Andie's sure she can't fit anything else, but after Mary clears the table, she brings over two plates. In the center of each is a small tart, no bigger than a half dollar. A tiny strawberry adorns the center of each one.

While Cort's ordering coffee, Andie takes a bite. The tart is so lemony it makes her mouth pucker, but there's a sweetness there too in the thin and brittle crust.

"You must have made a good impression," Cort says.

"Why do you say that?" Andie's saved the strawberry for last. She lets it sit on her tongue, the flavor unfolding like the essence of a warm summer day.

"Those are Chris's prize berries. Right now, he's growing them in a little greenhouse until it warms up, and he hoards them."

"You got one, too," Andie points out. Cort has eaten his tart in two bites.

"Really? They're so small I'm not sure I noticed," he says,

but Andie knows he's joking. Cort, she's starting to realize, notices everything.

When the check comes, they both reach for it, but Cort is quicker.

"This is supposed to be on me," Andie says. She tries to peek at the bill, to see what she owes, but he deftly keeps it out of her reach.

"We'll just have to do it again so you can settle your debt," he says. "I know how you Murphy women hate to owe anybody."

"I'll take you to Johnny's, then. That's not payment—that's punishment."

"Depends on the company," Cort says, standing. "Ready to go?"

The room is starting to clear out. Most of the tables are empty, and the crowd at the bar has thinned. On their way out, Andie spots Mary and Janet near the hostess station.

"Bye, Cort," Janet calls brightly. "See you soon!"

Cort mumbles a good-bye. Mary laughs and waves good-bye, including Andie in the gesture, but Janet's gaze is pretty cold.

Glad I'm not up against that, Andie thinks, amused, but puts a little extra wiggle in her walk anyhow as she slides past Cort and out the door. She can always blame it on the shoes.

THE silence on the ride home is different from the silence during the trip to the restaurant. It's heavier, laden with expectation. Andie's planning her exit from the truck almost as soon as they leave the parking lot, and Cort's first words don't help.

"So who's the guy?"

"What guy?"

"The guy you're cooking meals with shrimp and garlic for. The Italian guy. The one you don't want to talk about."

"What makes you think there's a guy?"

He sighs. "Andie, I've been . . ." The sentence trails off. There's a hush before he starts again, carefully. "I've known you since I was six years old. There's always been some guy. Why should now be any different?"

Andie doesn't speak for a second. "He's not Italian," she says finally. "He's American, and I'm pretty sure it's over."

"Is he why you left?"

"Partly. I needed to come home anyhow, to help Aunt Gert. When Frank died, I was in the middle of my thesis, so coming back for the funeral was about all I could manage." She shrugs, forgetting he can't see her in the dark. "She wasn't in a big hurry to get things settled, and said the summer would be fine. I think I was hoping the extra time . . . But it didn't work, and Neal and I broke up right before I came home."

"How come?"

She wonders which answer to give. She thinks about Neal, about the way the corners of his eyes crinkle when he smiles, his slightly spicy scent, his smooth, manicured hands. There's a vitality to him, a kind of humming energy, that draws people in. In the three years she was with him, she never knew him to sit still. His energy was enthralling at first, until she saw it for what it was. By always planning for the future, he could avoid being fully there, with Andie, in the present. She'd known that even before she'd discovered the affair. She thinks of his apartment, filled with sleek, sharp-edged objects, and then the palazzo of her studies, the dust slowly drifting through its halls.

"Remember when you were talking about living out West, how it never really felt like home?" she says finally, as they're bumping down her driveway. "Well, Neal never really felt like home to me."

"Where is your home, Andie?" Cort asks, but that's a question she can't answer. She only knows it's not here.

When the truck pulls up in front of the door, Nina rises from her place next to the steps, wagging her tail. Cort kills the engine and shuts off the headlights, so that the dog becomes a dark shadow, illuminated only by the moon.

He comes around to her side of the cab, but Andie is already on the ground, precariously balanced on her stiletto heels. He offers his arm, and she takes it gratefully.

"They're pretty, but not really made for the country," he says, nodding toward her shoes.

"Neither am I."

"Oh, I don't know about that. You seem to be holding your own okay."

At the door, Andie turns to him. He smells like warm grass, like rain. "Since you were six?" she asks softly.

"Yeah," he says. When she kisses him in the moonlight, his face is white as bone.

july

Andie

BEING with Cort is by far the craziest thing Andie's ever done. It's crazier than the time she "borrowed" her biology teacher's red Honda on a Friday night to visit her boyfriend at a neighboring prep school; crazier than when she and her best friend Samantha skipped classes and hitchhiked to New York sophmore year to see the Rolling Stones, geriatric but still hot in their Steel Wheels/Urban Jungle tour, and wound up alone in a trashed hotel room with two passed-out road-ies and some second-rate actor Andie still sees sometimes on late-night television. It's even crazier than moving to Italy alone, with no money and only her classes and cramped liv-ing quarters paid for.

Andie knows this. She knows Cort's too young, too wide-eyed around her. She knows she's on the rebound, that what she needs is space and quiet, time to think, not the complications of an affair. But she can't seem to stop. She refuses to think about how this will, inevitably, end, and concentrates instead on the slow, delicious pleasure of kissing Cort, the taste of sweat-slicked skin and the feel of his muscles beneath her hands. Her days have already fallen into a rhythm around him. She wakes early and begins work so as to have the rest of the morning free. She pretends it will always be summer, that there will always be a canopy of green leaves casting shadows on the walls of this room, that this time will never end.

He's in her bed now. It's late afternoon and the sheets are twined around their legs. She runs a nail across his shoulder, leaving an angry red line, and he catches her hand and brings it to his lips. From the waist up he is the color of sand, the color of the iced coffee he brings her each morning. His thighs and ass are glaringly white, as if someone had highlighted these parts to capture her attention.

He releases her hand and traces his finger across her collarbone, moving so slowly Andie shivers. She'd like to keep him here for the rest of the day, but in a few moments he'll start to look for his clothes, kissing her as he pulls them on. He'll tug her down the stairs with him and they'll kiss beside the front door until her lips are swollen. When he steps outside, he'll hold her hand until the last possible second. When he walks down the path to his truck, she'll turn the radio up, run the water, anything so she doesn't hear him leave.

Sex with Cort is refreshingly uncomplicated. He's not afraid to show how much he wants her, and he wants her pretty much all the time. There's no pretense, and Andie can't help but respond. She feels as vulnerable as if she's sixteen and in love for the first time, like a cut with a scab peeled off, all open and aching just when she thought she was healed.

He stretches and rolls over, putting his feet on the floor. She gazes at the long length of his back and can't help but touch it, running her finger up and down his spine.

"Hey, cut that out. Some of us have to go back to work," he says, and twists to kiss her before standing up.

She raises an eyebrow. "Going back would imply you'd actually been, and I thought you were out gallivanting with your buddy Chris this morning," she says.

"Good point. I almost forgot, he sent you these," he says, retrieving a slightly crushed brown bag from the floor along with his jeans. He drops the bag next to Andie. "He seems to think you need fattening up."

Andie peers inside. There are two small muffins, studded with tiny pieces of strawberries. The smell of sugar and corn reminds her that she hasn't had breakfast, and all at once she's ravenous. She pops a piece of muffin in her mouth. It's delicious, so much so that as soon as she finishes eating the first she polishes off the second one.

Cort laughs. "So can I tell him you liked them?" His pants are on, but he's on his hands and knees, searching for his shirt beneath the bed.

"I think it's in the hall," Andie says, and rises to help him look. "Just what were you guys up to today? Spreading fear and terror in the forest?"

"Nah, it's not hunting season yet. The deer are safe from us." He pauses, plainly distracted by the sight of her bare breasts. She tosses him his shirt, which she found puddled in a heap just outside the bedroom door, and it almost hits him in the face before he grabs it.

He pulls his head through the neck opening, and Andie quickly tugs on her own shirt, sans bra. She's buttoning it up as Cort comes over and slides his hands up her stomach, cupping her breasts and backing her up against the wall.

They kiss, standing up, until her labia are swollen and chafed from the friction of Cort's jeans and the hard mound of his erection. She pulls at his waistband, fumbling with the button, and he lets go of her long enough to undo his pants. She tugs his jeans and then his boxers over the round muscles of his ass, pushing them down so they puddle around his ankles.

She's reaching for him when he presses her back against the wall. He leaves a soft, slow trail of kisses along her neck, then tongues her nipple through the thin cotton of her shirt. Andie moans. She wants him inside her, but he moves his head lower, pushing aside her shirt and blowing gently on her belly, her pubic mound, and finally her clitoris. She arches herself toward him, and he cups his hands under her, holding her still. He brushes against her with just his lips, then the tip of his tongue, pressure so light Andie can barely feel it. She squirms and digs her fingers into his hair, urging him closer, but he gently holds her away. He waits until she's almost frantic before settling into a steady, firm rhythm, and Andie leans into him so hard she almost knocks him over.

She comes in a matter of seconds, gripping his shoulders to hold herself steady.

After the last spasm she's limp, a sponge wrung dry, but Cort stands and picks her up. He helps her position her legs around his waist, and enters her with a single slow drive, rocking her back against the wall. She squirms in his grasp, trying to take him deeper.

"Jesus," he gasps, burying his face in her neck. He bends and thrusts, bends and thrusts, clutching her so tightly when he comes, Andie's certain he leaves bruises. There's a slick of sweat pooling on their chests, and when Andie arches back to look at him, her skin comes away with a small sucking sound.

Cort staggers backward and collapses on the bed, still holding Andie to him. "Jesus," he says again. "I've had fantasies about you since I was twelve, and I swear none of them were like this."

"Luckily I can't say the same," Andie says drily, wriggling down the length of him and to her feet. She stands and begins searching once again for their clothing, now scattered about the room.

They dress, moving slowly in the summer heat and aftermath of physical effort, stopping to kiss, to touch. Cort tugs her close, stooping to rest his chin on her head.

"So what's going on this afternoon for you?" he asks, gently rubbing her earlobe. Andie leans into his touch. She can't help herself.

"Oh, I don't know. I guess I'll check on Aunt Gert."

"She okay?"

Since her dizzy spell in the bedroom two weeks ago, Aunt Gert has been scarce, coming to the big house only rarely, and never inside. Andie checks on her most afternoons and joins her for dinner when Cort can't get away. Gert is always polite but vague about how she's been spending her days, and seems to have no pressing need to resume cleaning out the house. Today, up early and restless without Cort's presence, Andie spotted her aunt wandering through the far pasture, looking ghostly in the early morning mist. The scene, cool greens and grays, stayed with her even after the mist had burned off, so that she had to get it down on canvas. To get a better vantage point, she's moved her easel up to the attic, where the round window frames the view of the meadow. The attic is cool in the early morning air, not hot as she expected, and the light is perfect, soft and golden. It's the first time in months she's been inspired to paint, and she finds she wants to keep the image of her aunt to herself, a secret even from Cort. She doesn't tell him about her aunt's wanderings.

"I think she's fine. Maybe just a little tired from the heat," she says instead. They walk downstairs and outside, arms wrapped about each other's waists. Nina's dozing in the shade of Cort's truck, which is filled with rolls of fencing wire, posts, and what looks like feed buckets.

"How about you? Looks like your dad has an afternoon of slave labor planned," Andie says, nodding toward the truck.

"Um, no, not really. It's for a project for Chris," he says.

Andie raises an eyebrow. "What, he's building a corral to keep customers in?"

"No, not exactly."

Andie waits, and after a pause he continues, looking sheepish. "Look, I haven't been exactly straight with you," he says, and the words are like ice to Andie's heart. She's learned the hard way that no good can come of a sentence that starts like that, especially when it comes from a man in her life. *I didn't want to tell you . . . I've been meaning to let you know . . . I haven't been exactly straight with you.* Dimly, she can hear Cort talking, but she's too busy imagining the worst to listen. There's another woman somewhere, and she's been a fool. Again. Although how another woman ties in to the supplies in Cort's truck, she can't imagine. Maybe the woman has children—children!—and there's an animal that needs a pen, a dog or a pony that Cort bought for them.

"Hey, are you all right?" Cort's rubbing her shoulders, and she takes a step away from him, crosses her arms in front of her chest to soften the blow.

"Just tell me," she says.

"You look angry already," he says, and when she doesn't reply, he sighs. "Look, I didn't say anything before because I didn't want you to get the wrong idea."

"Wrong idea about what?" she asks. As if there's a right way to look at it.

"About why I asked you out that day."

It's clear that she's missed something. "Tell me again," she says, and he does. He and Chris want to create a country inn with a five-star restaurant, the kind of place where guests can harvest carrots in the afternoon and be served them that evening at dinner.

The relief that washes through her must show on her face, because Cort leans over and gives her a kiss. "It's a good idea, right?" he says, and Andie's so happy she nods, although she's not convinced. But she'll listen as long as Cort wants to talk about designer vegetables for the garden and organic sheets on the bed, his plans for a gift shop with homemade jams and breads, although the idea strikes her as essentially flawed. She's heard of tourists paying money to sleep at lighthouses, polishing the brass and cleaning floors in exchange for reduced rates. But there's a difference between falling asleep to the sound of the ocean and waking up in the morning to the prospect of spreading fertilizer, or worse. There's a reality to farming that just doesn't lend itself to glossy vacation brochures.

"What happens when roasted chicken is on the menu?" she asks.

"It won't be the total whole farm experience," he admits. "But they could help bring in the eggs, milk the animals, churn butter, the works. We're talking about having some pick-your-own fields, like berries, and some beehives. Maybe even some grapes for wine."

"Sounds interesting," she says. "I'm not sure why I couldn't be trusted with the news, though."

"It's why I was looking around here, that first day. I didn't want you to think . . . When you said you'd go to dinner with me, I mean, it didn't have anything to do with this." He waves an arm around to take in the house and land beyond, and she finally grasps his point.

"If you have designs on Evenfall, you're seducing the

wrong woman," Andie says. "Everything here belongs to Aunt Gert."

"Yeah, well, I like Gert and all, but she's safe from me." He pulls her close. "So you're not mad?"

"No," Andie says. "Not even a little bit." She kisses him, just because she can, because he's honest and belongs to no one but her. They kiss for a long while, and when they come up for air she opens her eyes and sees the posts and buckets in the back of the truck again.

"So does this mean you've found a place?" She nods at the truck.

"You mean one that we can afford in this market? Not yet, but Chris found some goats at a price he swears we can't pass up. He wants to do goat milk and cheese, and somebody in Vermont is selling off their herd." He rubs the back of his neck. "My dad's going to have a fit when I bring them home. He hates goats—he's always said that they're for farmers too poor to buy a cow. He wouldn't say that if he knew what I paid for them."

"How many are you going to buy?"

"Two, for now. That's about all I can afford."

He looks so despondent, Andie can't help herself. "Maybe you could keep them here, till you find a place."

"Really?"

She thinks for a moment. It's the kind of harebrained scheme her uncle would have loved, and in her head she can almost hear him egging her on. The farm is big enough that Gert might not even notice, if Cort puts the paddock far away enough from the house. It's not as if she's planning on keeping the goats a secret from her aunt forever. She'll tell Gert—eventually. But saying yes means she'll see Cort again this evening. And most likely, he'll be shirtless. It's this last image that sways her.

"Sure," she says. "But just till you find a place, or till the end of summer. After that, they have to go."

"No problem," he promises. "Just let me run home and give dad a hand feeding and I'll be right back to build the pen. And if I finish up early enough, I'll even take you out to Johnny's for pizza."

"Right," she says, although she already has other plans in mind for their evening. The phone is ringing again, but Andie pays no attention to it. Summer is short, she thinks, watching Cort drive away. She might as well make the most of it.

Gert

IT'S been years since Gert's walked the meadow, but for the past two weeks, she hasn't been able to stop. There's plenty she should be doing instead. There are bills for Frank's estate that need to be paid, insurance questions that ought to be looked into, a meeting with the assessor to be arranged. But each morning, she comes out just after dawn, when the sun is up enough to light her steps but before the heat of the day begins. This morning the tall grass moves in the wind like the glossy coat of an animal. Mist floats above the ground, a wispy reminder of the departing night's cool air.

Ahead, she can just make out the tip of Buddy's black tail, twitching determinedly as he makes his way through the field. The cat keeps a few steps in front like an advance scout. He'll lead anywhere, stopping only when he comes to the deep end of the creek. There he crouches, hissing, as if at memories of his own.

For Gert, the meadow's open space is surprisingly peaceful. Her cottage has come to feel too small, a skin she's outgrown, and she no longer finds solace in its order. In the big house, there's a pressure, a weight that makes it hard to breathe. Only out here, in the rustle of the grass and the feel of the breeze, is there room for memories.

The milestones of her life have always been present, shaping her path like the bumps and hills that contour this land. But lately other memories, events she hasn't thought of in years, are coming back with a clarity that's frightening. This morning, for example, she awoke with the face of a boy she'd treated more than fifty years ago in her mind, his image as clear as though he were standing before her.

For hours she's been trying to recall his name, but it hides in the dark recesses just out of reach. The boy was southern, she remembers that. His words had a honeyed drawl she'd found soothing after a lifetime of clipped New England syllables. His face was dark with stubble, and when she took his boots off he'd groaned in relief. He'd asked her how such a pretty girl had wound up in such poor company. His ward mates shook their heads, told him not to waste his time.

"That one's got ice water for blood," the man in the next bed said, pretending to shiver.

She took the southerner's pulse, and he placed his own hot fingers gently against her wrist. "Naw, she's just spent too many years north with you Yankees is all," he said, and smiled up at her. "A few days down south would warm her up just fine."

Instead of the steady, reassuring beat she wanted, his pulse fluttered. She pulled down the blankets to look at his wound.

"What do you southerners do for fun?" she asked. The bullet had grazed his groin, the wound still covered by a field dressing; the bandage was clotted with blood and speckled with dirt and grass.

"Oh, we know how to show visitors a good time," he said, white-faced as she carefully pulled the bandage away. Bits of dirt and shreds of fabric from his trousers were buried deep in the soft tissue, and a bubble of blood rose in the corner. She swabbed it gently and the boy bit his lip to keep from crying out.

"Is that right?" she prompted. She stopped her work long enough to give his hand a light squeeze, low, by the side of the bed, where his buddies wouldn't see.

He smiled weakly, grateful for the distraction. "Oh, yes, ma'am. Come Saturdays, we get some of the finest bands around playing at the church hall. You can dance all night if you've a mind to."

"It's been a while since I've danced," Gert said, scribbling a note on the boy's chart.

"You come down to Georgia, then, anytime. Summer's best, though. There's an old stone quarry we use to cool off in after a high time. The water feels so good, you wouldn't believe it." He closed his eyes and Gert moved on to the next bed.

She'd been with the Army for a year, in Italy for a month, paying off her tuition debt to Uncle Sam with bad dreams and sleepless nights. Not even working in Boston's emergency room prepared her. Her first week, she cut off the mask of her long hair, scissored away the strands that dying boys grasped at, that tangled in blood no matter how many pins she used to put it up. The short bob left her little to hide behind, but it didn't matter. She'd stripped away everything that wasn't useful: emotions, longing, hope.

The physical hardship wasn't the problem. In Hartman, growing up, she'd spent the first years of her life in a house without running water, crouching in the one-holed outhouse and pouring in lime to keep the stink down. Bathing out of her helmet, using the leftover liquid to sponge a stranger's blood out of her uniform was no worse. At least someone else hauled the water, she told the girls who complained, and they looked at her curiously. Behind her back she knew they called her "the Boston Brahmin," mocked her reserve, wondered how a woman they believed meant for a life of oysters and little black dresses wound up eating chipped beef on toast and wearing olive drab.

Gert let them wonder. A year before, she might have been amused by their assumptions. Two years ago, terrified they'd find her out. But now when she looked in the piece of polished tin that served as mirror in her tent, the face that stared back had ice-sharp cheekbones and a gaze cool as death. Whether the other nurses thought she was aloof because of background or breeding didn't matter, so long as they left her alone.

Kenneth, that was the boy's name. It comes to her as suddenly as a blow, but her memory stalls before she recalls his fate. Dead, most likely, but from that wound or another, she doesn't know.

She's crossed the widest part of the meadow, and pauses for breath at the top of a knoll that marks the halfway point. A birch stump, the tree struck by lightning years ago, offers a resting spot. From here she can see the Wildermuth family cemetery, bone white stones rising from within a rough fieldstone wall. Volunteer saplings sprout along the wall's edges and the grass is high.

The cemetery holds—or rather, doesn't hold—its own secrets. Two bodies have escaped its grasp, although not death itself. Frank's grave is marked with a granite headstone that bears both his and Clara's names. But Clara isn't there. She rests in the church's cemetery, next to a weeping cherry tree. After years of living on the farm, she told Frank she wanted to be buried like civilized people, in a proper town cemetery.

The other secret lies beneath a simple white stone, gone gray with time and furred with moss. It's where Abe Wildermuth, Frank's older brother, should be. But Abe is missing as well, killed at twenty-two when the boat ferrying him to Italy came under attack. There's nothing beneath his headstone but cool dark earth.

Gert can no longer recall Abe's face, but she remembers his hands from school. Broad, strong hands, the hands of a farmer. Not like Frank's, with his long, slender fingers and narrow wrists. Although after his brother died they became callused enough.

Rested, she descends to the graveyard. She skirts the edges, considers going in but decides against it. She'll spend more than enough time there, after all, although if she has her way she'll be cremated. Might as well save the cost of the coffin, and it's not likely many people will feel a need to visit when she's dead. It's ironic, really: the two people most responsible for her flight from Hartman and this farm are irrevocably lost to it. Yet she'll be here for all eternity.

She thinks of the day she left, of the way the air smelled of pine and earth, even though it was high summer. There was a coolness to the air, although perhaps that's her imagination playing tricks after so many years. She sees the walk to Frank's house clearly: the way the scrub roses lined the road, scenting the air with clove; the gravel that stuck in her shoe as she turned into the Wildermuth's lane; the way the house itself reared out of the early morning mist, as sudden and shocking as a gravestone.

She'd paused to get her breath at the top of the driveway, resting her hand on her belly. Wonder and dismay competed as she realized how clearly the signs were visible. She'd been a fool not to have seen them before, with all her training. She pushed the worry from her mind, concentrated on filling her lungs with air. Standing there, panting a little, she was struck by how quiet the house seemed, the blankness of the windows. It was early yet, and she was counting on being able to catch Frank alone, before his mother saw them. She needed that time to convince him that they had to leave now. If they left earlier than they'd planned, if they didn't wait for the end of summer, everything could still be all right.

What she hadn't considered was that Frank might have news of his own. The door to the house was open, so she'd stuck her head inside and whispered his name. He was sitting at the kitchen table, and she'd known even before she saw the black-bordered telegram between his fingers that something was wrong. It was in the way he stood when he saw her, as if it were an effort, as if at almost eighteen he were an old, old man. The blue eyes she loved were hooded, and when she heard the smothered wails of his mother from up the stairs, there was no need for him to speak. Abe was dead.

Looking back through the years, Gert has the gift of prescience. She can see the moment that doomed them, pinpoint the exact second that sent them in separate directions. Watching as the scene plays out, she'd like to tell the girl she was that it will be all right, that she will survive this, that it will make her stronger. But in her heart, she'd be lying.

The girl takes a step forward into the kitchen, then stops. If she touches him now, she will never leave. They will spend their lives together on this farm, weighted down by work and by years, by the stares and whispers of the townspeople, by the reproaches of their families. If she touches him now, he will come with her, leaving behind ruin and wreck, the loss of the farm, the death of his mother, who has already given one son to war and will not survive the absence of the other.

She cannot stay, and he cannot come with her: it is as simple as that. They look at each other in the still morning air, and she makes her decision. The boy moves to speak, but she holds up her hand. When she has taken a last look, stored up in her mind the blue of his eyes and the long lean length of him, she simply turns and walks away. Out the open door and down the driveway without once looking back, although she can feel him watching long after she must have disappeared from view. All the way to the train station, with just enough money in her purse to purchase a ticket. She'd borrow the money for the rest later. It was early yet; she still had time. She knew a friend of a friend who was an intern and would help her out, for a price. And she was lucky, in a way; she was almost a nurse, so she had connections, access to a safe place and sterile instruments that other girls would not. And in wartime, surely, there were plenty of other girls just like her. She'd been a fool to think she was any different.

She leans her head back against the leather seat of the train and tries not to think. The sky is a brilliant blue, so blue she wants to cry. The seat is hot, and she shifts a bit, trying to get comfortable, trying not to think about how good creek water would feel, lapping against her bare skin like silk. She closes her eyes and sees the little silver fish that dart just under the water's surface, quickening in a stream of bubbles. She opens her eyes, breathes deeply, keeps her mind clear and still. A fire, she tells the nursing director when she arrives at the school without her clothes and trunk. There's nothing left. It all burned to the ground.

THE mist is almost gone, and sunlight glints off something tucked in the far corner of the meadow. Gert wanders toward it, taking her time. She spies a black feather lying in the grass ahead, and bends to pick it up. Brown tints its edges, the color of dried earth or blood. She turns it slowly in her hand, letting it brush against her fingertips. In the end, no matter how many years she's spent on this land, she's still a stranger. For a million dollars, she couldn't name the bird that left this feather behind.

She drops the feather and watches as Buddy bounds after it, batting it with his paws. Only when he loses interest does she turn to the structure in the corner of the meadow. Someone's made a little paddock, almost hidden by the swell of land in front. Chicken wire is strung tight between cedar posts, and a small run-in shed sits in the far corner. Gert lays her hand atop the nearest post and gently rocks it. The workmanship is solid—the post doesn't move—but for the life of her she can't figure out what will go in here. The space is too small for cows or horses. Pigs, maybe. Or sheep.

Whatever the beast may be, Gert has a good guess as to who built its home. She's seen that little red pickup truck going back and forth all week. Her niece is surprisingly citified for a girl who once squashed June bugs between her fingers, but Cort is a McCallister down to the dirt on his boots.

Gert's never warmed to Cort's father, Jim. A nosy boy grown into a meddlesome man, in her opinion, always looking like he knew more than was good for him. He was one of the boys Clara hired to modernize the cottage, and Gert can still remember how he'd looked at her when he'd finished insulating the walls. "That's as warm as you can get, alone," he'd said, and smiled right at her as if he knew her thoughts.

But she has to admit that he's held on to his land when others would have given up. More than once she's seen him nod off during church service, his body taking what rest it could find. His features have faded over the years, become weathered like the land he works. It's a fate Gert's glad to have escaped, despite the cost.

Andie may be dating a farmer, but from what Gert knows of her niece, she's no farmer's wife. It's a summer romance, no more. Just the same, Gert decides, she'll speak her mind about the paddock. No matter how firmly they're pounded into the ground, those posts won't last past September. Gert's sure of it.

Frank

IT'S late, past midnight, and the house is quiet. Andie's asleep upstairs, worn out from another day of packing and sorting, as well as other activities. The boy's gone home at last, and it's a relief to be out of the attic for a bit, where I've been confining myself for decency's sake. The hallway is lined with boxes, stacked two and three atop each other. If I concentrate I can sense the contents of each. Clara' favorite yellow sundress, the cloth carrying the faintest fragrance of peaches, too subtle for the living to detect. A stack of Andie's report cards. A pale blue bit of cloth, its ends raggedy and worn. I drift along.

In the kitchen, the cool light of the open refrigerator gives Nina's eyes an unearthly glow. She whines and noses at a foil-wrapped package of chicken.

"I don't think so," I say. "How about a nice piece of beef jerky instead?"

The dog grasps the foil in her mouth and trots off into the dark.

"You realize there could be bones?" I call after her. The only answer is a crunching sound from beneath the kitchen table.

I let the refrigerator door swing shut. Nina's gnawing away, and when I look under the table, she thumps her tail. It's a comforting noise. Maybe Andie won't miss the chicken.

I prowl from room to room, but there is nothing else to see, so I leave Nina to her spoils and head back upstairs, stopping to check on Andie along the way. She sleeps deeply, the way she did as a child, curled into a ball beneath the covers. She stirs, and I think of quiet things, of midnight in the woods when the air is still, and she settles. I listen to her breathing and I remember the first night she spent with us, a tiny wide-eyed toddler afraid of the dark. I spent that night dozing in the armchair next to her bed, scarcely able to sleep myself. To have a child in this house, even if just for the summer, was a gift, a dream we'd all but abandoned. Every time I looked at her that night such a fierce joy rose up I wanted to shout. If it were up to me, I'd have kept her here forever, not just summers but all year long. It took everything I had to shake Richard Murphy's hand and not grab him by the throat when he came to pick up his daughter each September. A whisper of rage fills me even now, remembering, and Andie frowns.

"Sleep, doodlebug," I whisper. "Sleep." And then I leave her be.

The attic is silent, cast in dark and shadow, but I've lost the need for light. I feel for the ring's energy, like a miser surveying his treasure. It throbs when I probe it, the molecules dancing in a mad rhythm of their own, the rhythm of love, of lust and desire, of loss and despair. Could Gert feel it, if I placed this ring upon her finger? Would she understand what's been written on my heart every day since she left me? The ring's energy is intoxicating. It fills me, makes me grow larger, so that my shadow almost spreads upon the wall. If she were here right now, I could force her to see, make her realize what she should have realized all those years ago.

There's a soft whine behind me. The dog has come upstairs. When it sees me, it drops to its belly, cowering, and now I'm certain I see it, the faintest outline of my shape against the wall. I let go, separate from the ring's energy. It's an effort, and when I'm through I feel drained, not recharged as I expected.

"It's all right," I say to the dog. "It's just me." Although what that means, who I am, I cannot begin to guess. The dog doesn't seem to care, though. She scrambles to her feet, plows past me on her way to the far side of the attic. My niece has been painting here, the last few mornings, and there's likely a few crumbs left from her breakfast.

The easel is centered just in front of the porthole window, an empty coffee cup left at its base. The dog pokes her muzzle deep into its depths, comes out disappointed. She grumbles and settles at my feet.

The easel holds a small canvas. The colors are blues and grays, the shades of morning in the meadow. I've stood next to Andie and watched as she captured the mist rising off the land, the dew-slicked grass, the weak early sunlight filtering through the green of the woods, and I've whispered to her of the unseen, just beyond her vision: the hidden nest of the bluejays; the quivering rabbit, safe in the tall grass; the dragonflies warming themselves for flight. These things, too, are there, concealed for the viewer to find.

And what of the figure at the picture's center? The mist swirls about her legs, cloaking and revealing her all at once. Her body is twisted, and it's unclear which way she will turn, toward the observer or away and deeper into the mist. Her face is hidden. My niece has a fine eye and a steady hand, but she cannot see what is not there, and I cannot show her.

The first time I saw Gert again, her eyes were as flat and still as the creek on a summer day. How much of that is my fault I do not know, but if I torture myself with the memories of her leaving, it's the memories of her return I find hardest to bear.

It was summertime and the peaches were late that year. Clara was canning in the kitchen, and the house smelled of summer, hot and sweet and sticky. I'd carried the bushel baskets down for her from the orchard, and was sitting at the kitchen table watching her work. She had quick hands, and was able to slice and peel a whole bushel in almost no time at all. When she was upset or nervous, she kept busy, and it had been an upsetting few weeks.

I remember her back was to me, and while I couldn't

see her hands, I could hear the faint thud of the knife as it sliced through the peaches and hit the cutting board. I was wondering whether I had time to mow the lawn and shower before I headed in to work, or if I should leave it till tomorrow. I hated it when the lawn was untidy, and I figured if I hurried, I could just make it. I stood, drained the glass of lemonade she'd made for me, and turned toward the door when she spoke.

"I talked with Gert today," she said. Her hands didn't stop moving, but I found I was having trouble standing. It was warm, too warm in the kitchen. I sat down again, carefully, and waited. Gert had been gone years by then. In the beginning, I'd dreamed of her walking away, growing smaller and smaller as I watched from the door, as helpless to move in sleep as I'd been in life. The last time I'd had the dream, I'd woken and found Clara next to me, and reminded myself it had all happened a long time ago. Resting in the dark, waiting for my pulse to return to normal, I couldn't even picture her face. Now, after Clara said her name, it was as if she were standing in the kitchen, so close I could reach out and touch her. I could see her long braid, the brown and the gold strands mixed together, and a finger of excitement touched my heart.

But Clara was still talking, her hands still slicing the peaches, the rhythm of the knife never slowing. The simple silver band she wore on her left hand flashed in the light. "We need her here, Frank," she said. "It's time. That baby won't make it without her."

I tried to speak, but my mouth was too dry, and the glass

was empty. I worked my tongue around until the words could come out. "What'd she say?" I asked, listening carefully to the sound of my voice. If it was different, Clara didn't seem to notice. She didn't answer my question. Instead she spoke of the trail she'd followed, the hospitals she'd called, that led, finally, to Gert.

"What'd she say?" I asked again. And at last Clara put the flashing knife down. She turned to me, wiping her hands on the cloth she kept tucked in her apron pocket. The fine strands of hair by her temple were beginning to curl in the heat. "She said she'd come," Clara said simply. "Of course, she'll come."

"Of course," I echoed, and Clara glanced at my face.

"Lord, you look all worn out," she said, and fetched me another glass of lemonade. "Here. Take this and go on up to bed for a bit. I told you it was too hot to be working outside at noon, and it's no cooler in here. I'll get you up in plenty of time for your shift."

At the doorway I stopped. Clara had gone back to her slicing, but when I called her name she put her knife down again. "Did she say when she was coming?"

"Didn't I tell you?" Clara looked at me in surprise. "That's the best part. She'll be here on the Monday afternoon train."

Three days away.

I lay down on the bed in our room, but couldn't sleep. Instead, I found myself on the staircase to the attic, a place I'd rarely visited in the past few years. It was hot, almost stifling, up there, and the air was fragrant with the odor of peaches cooking. I walked to the loose board, bent to lift it, and found what I was looking for—a cloth bundle, mono-grammed with the letter W, and the hard nub of the silver ring within. I brought the bundle to the window and stood looking out, although I couldn't have told you what I saw.

In the days after Abe died, I'd stopped going to church. I'd stopped doing a lot of things: going to school, going out. I'd heard that "that Murphy girl" had simply left town one day, walked all the way to the train station with just the clothes on her back, abandoned her family and returned to school. I'd written her letters, one every day for weeks, but they all came back unopened, so I stopped doing that, too. I worked the farm but didn't have my brother's skill, his talent for coaxing life out of nothing. When it became clear that my efforts weren't enough, not even with Abe's death benefits, I got a job in town. My mother had already spoken to the draft board, pulled on her connections, and I'd been deferred, the farm being the reason. I'd thought about running away and joining to spite her, but I didn't have the energy for it, or for anything else. The fact that I was walking around at eighteen with four good limbs and fine hearing got me some looks in town, so I quit spending time there as well.

It went on like that for the better part of a year: the farm by day, the plant at night, sleeping in snatches between. Until one day my mother, faced with a second corpse on her hands, dragged me to church and plunked herself down in the pew behind the Murphys, or what was left of them. The old man had passed away a few months ago, I'd heard, and Clara and her mother were still in black. The two of them had nursed him till the end, and being Jack Murphy, he hadn't gone easily.

I sat through the service, staring at Clara's hair and trying to remember if the lighter parts in Gert's were the same shade of gold. I was still staring when my mother nudged me in the ribs. The service had ended. People were starting to leave, and my mother fell into step with the Murphys on the way out. She took up with Mrs. Murphy, which left me with Clara.

By rights, she should have cut me dead, walked down the aisle without a word. I expected as much, and thought I'd make it easier on her by staying quiet myself. So when she touched me on the arm and asked how I'd been, it was a surprise.

"All right," I said, and kept walking.

She tried again. "I've missed our rides."

I nodded, said something about work and the farm keeping me busy.

"I know it's been a hard year for you," she said. "I'm so sorry for your loss, Frank." The words made me turn and search her face: no guile or malice waited there. My mother, waiting by the car, saw me look, and that was enough. She waited a few days, just long enough to be decent, and then hired Clara to mend a few of my workshirts. It was a natural-enough request: Clara was known for her skill with a needle, and my mother's sight was starting to fade. Natural enough, too, once she'd seen Clara's talents, that my mother find other work for her, enough to bring her to our home two or three times a week, always on the nights when my shift at the plant started late and I could walk her home on my way into town.

We fell into our old pattern easily enough, although there was a difference: a third person walked between us, silent and unseen. Clara must have felt it, too, and although she chatted easily enough, she never spoke of what I was desperate to hear, not until I'd been walking her home for over a month and had found a way to work it into conversation.

I'd waited until she was at her doorstep. I'd seen Mrs. Murphy's shadow at the window, the dip of her head as she moved away into the kitchen to give us our privacy, and I knew no one would overhear. Clara's hand was touching the knob before I got up the nerve to speak, and my voice sounded false even to my ears, though I'd practiced the words enough at home.

"By the way, how's your sister? I heard she went back to Boston."

"Gert?" Clara turned to me as smoothly as if she'd been waiting for me to speak. "I thought you knew."

"Knew what?"

"Gert's gone, Frank. She enlisted. The government let her finish her coursework with them, and they sent her to Italy a few months ago. We hardly ever hear from her now—half the time we don't even know where she's stationed."

I don't remember how I answered or even if I said good-bye before I left. My mother was in the kitchen, writing out bills, and when she asked what was the matter, I didn't slow a step. I'd planned to throw the ring out, to toss it in the creek or into the ocean when I went to New London, but

I found, once I'd lifted the board and unearthed it from its hiding place, that I couldn't. So I left it there, unseen but not forgotten, until the day Clara told me Gert was coming home. Standing there in the attic that day, fingering the ring, I wondered where the line for too late was, and if I'd crossed it already.

Crazy, I know. I'd been married to Clara for years by then. We'd fallen into the habit of spending our free time together, and then when her mother died and mine took sick, it seemed the most natural thing in the world to have her come here. My mother liked her, and it eased her last days to know I wasn't alone. When the time came to propose, I'd gone up to the attic, lifted the board, then hesitated. Suddenly I couldn't bring myself to touch it. I took the bus into New London—the car was gone by then—and found a simple band at Mallove's. It wasn't fancy, but Clara cried when I slipped it over her finger on the walk back to her place. She cried a lot back then—her mother had just passed away—so I didn't read much into it. Gert hadn't come home for the funeral. When people asked, Clara told them she'd tried, but couldn't get leave. She did send a beautiful wreath of roses, grown in a hothouse and brought all the way from Hartford, the flowers white with just the faintest blush at the tips, like the cheeks of an infant. She didn't come home for our wedding, either, although of course there was no way for her to know about it ahead of time. Clara wanted it simple, and it was, just us, my mother, and Richard. Clara sent a note, after, but didn't get a reply. Not that I'd expected one. She'd made that clear a long time ago.

When the war ended, Clara kept sending letters, and the army must have forwarded them. Eventually we got a Christmas card, and then one a year after with the return address on it. I noticed she moved around a lot—the addresses were never the same two years running—but the last few times the return address has been from the same place, in upstate New York.

Clara wrote to Gert regular like, but Gert never wrote back, besides the one card a year. She did send flowers after Richard's wedding. Richard had got the girl pregnant within weeks of their first date, and then managed to leave town until it was almost too late to do the respectable thing. He'd been living on his own then for a few years, coming round regularly to cadge money off Clara when he thought I wouldn't notice. He had a notion he could make it as a race track trainer, and was always following the ponies, from Plainfield up to Rockingham and then on to the New York circuit. Clara put a stop to that, at least until the baby was born.

The day the girl came to see her, Clara spent the rest of the afternoon banging around in the kitchen, slapping out buttermilk biscuits and roasted chicken with potatoes, fine fare for a Sunday afternoon but unusual for midweek. We'd lost two babies by then, both early on in the pregnancy, and I knew enough to stay out of her way. When she'd finished, she packed the meal up in a wicker basket and asked me to drive her to the train station.

"I'll be back tomorrow or the next day," she said, and kissed me as she got out of the car. It was new—I'd bought it after the war by selling off a few acres, something Abe would never have done—and she shut the door carefully behind her, bumping it gently with her hip. I waited until I saw her board the train to New York before I drove away. The house was quiet, but in a good way, and for the first time in a long while I dreamed of Gert, woke up with my heart pounding in the dark.

When Clara came back, she had her brother in tow, following behind her as meekly as if she'd twisted his ear. The Murphys had spoiled him after the death of his pa, and he reminded me of a bantam rooster, always strutting around and crowing. But Clara got him to marry Lily in a quiet church wedding, and started talking about a honeymoon baby almost as soon as the minister finished the vows.

The baby was born seven months later, a tiny, screaming thing, almost small enough to pass off as early. It was a long labor, Clara said, even for a first time, and Lily was worn out and white at the end of it. I saw her a few days later and she still hadn't recovered, but her smile was luminous, enough to light the room. That's how I see her when I remember: bending over that tiny baby, the child's dark eyes and impossibly long, slender fingers, with Richard grinning from the doorway as if he'd engineered this miracle himself.

It ended less than a week later. Lily woke up in the night with a headache. She collapsed on her way to the bathroom and never spoke again. A vessel in her brain just let go, the doctor said.

Richard took to drinking again, long nights when he'd sit at home with the baby and a bottle of whisky, drinking until he'd pass out on the floor and Clara would find him there the next morning, the baby screaming and the room dank with the smell of soiled diapers and sour milk.

She tried to take the baby to our house, but Richard wouldn't hear of it. To make matters worse, the child was jaundiced, an ugly yellow that started in its eyes and spread all through its skin. I'd offered to go and take the child, Richard be damned, but Clara was afraid to have it so far away from town. In an emergency, the doctor might not make it out to the farm in time. She took it into her head that the baby needed more help than we could give, that she needed a medical professional. That she needed Gert.

And now Gert was returning. In the attic, I stared down the road, as if I could see her there, coming this time instead of leaving. I twisted the ring within the piece of cloth and thought of her face the way I'd seen her last, and of how she must look now, and wondered if she'd find me the same, or if I'd changed to her.

The next three days passed in a haze of memory and longing, anticipation and fear all rolled into one. Clara had a hundred little tasks for me to do—she wanted the car polished until it shone, the mattress in the spare bedroom had to be turned and beaten to get the dust out, a cot found for Richard's house in case Gert decided to stay there—and there were the regular, daily tasks of life on the farm, plus the night shift at work. If Clara had any regrets for what she'd put in motion, she kept them to herself. Except, Sunday night, I woke to find her arms about me, her lips on mine, moving against me with a hunger she'd never shown. When we'd finished, she put her head on my chest and fell asleep. I stared at the ceiling and thought of what had passed, and what might have been, until dawn came through the window.

It all ended, all the dreaming, the moment I saw her on the train platform. If I'd remained the same in time and place, Gert had changed in a way I could not follow. Her figure was the same, the same slight build and proud, fierce carriage she'd always had, but as she walked closer to us, I sensed a difference I could not name, not until she was up close and I could see her face. Clara reached to embrace her first, and Gert allowed her to, but there was a space between them even so. She'd sliced her long braid off, the ends coming to a sharp point just below her chin, and the color had gone to mostly silver. But her eyes were the biggest difference. We'd once called her the ice princess, so cool and smooth she was, but I could see the ice was gone, replaced by a substance that would not shatter or break no matter how hard you beat upon it. She'd turned to steel, forged herself a defense so razor sharp and strong you'd cut yourself if you held her the wrong way. And so I didn't even try, just nodded and smiled and carried her bags to the car, all the while wondering what she'd done and why she'd done it, and if I was to blame.

THE dog stirs in its sleep, a long, slow sigh, and I turn from the window and look at the space about me, my prison and my fortress. And something more. If the sea was built into this house, with its mast-like beams and porthole windows, the shipwrights who worked on it crafted another secret as well. I feel the pull of the ocean from this room, hear the ebb and flow of the tides, and find nightfall and day turning back. Currents crisscross the air, pulling me into a different ending, a different life. I see my grandfather aboard his ship, his face relaxed and dotted with droplets from a fine salt spray. I see his namesake, my brother Abe, alive and whole, sunburnt from working the fields all day. There's a woman in a yellow dress waiting in the shadow of the porch, and he sweeps her into his arms and laughs.

Always, always, I see Gert. Sunlight is on her hair, a small hand tugs at her dress, and when she turns to me, her face is alight with joy. This is how our lives were meant to be, she tells me, and from my distant place in time I can only nod.

Andie

ANDIE wakes craving peaches. She wants to hold one in her hand, bite the rosy flesh, let the juices dribble down her chin. She breathes deeply and inhales their phantom scent, sweet and rich.

Percoca. In Italy, the white peaches are round and heavy, so luscious that eating them in public feels like a lewd act. Maybe because the slang word for peaches also means a ripe young girl. At the grocery store in Hartman, Andie passes them by. Most are tiny and hard, tinged green around the stem. The few ripe ones bear bruise marks.

But peaches stay on her mind. She tastes their sweetness beneath her breakfast of toast and black coffee, feels their juices running down her throat. She thinks about settling for the store-bought variety, placing them on the windowsill to ripen, but knows she'll be disappointed. The fruit will stay hard and unyielding until she throws it out.

It's not till she's finished cleaning up the kitchen that she remembers Aunt Clara's peach jam. Golden with just a hint of blush, like the last rays of a sunset, the jars lined the shelves of Clara's pantry every year. During canning time, the kitchen was steamy and filled with a delicious scent that drew bees to the window screens. Andie never stuck around for the actual canning—that would have involved staying indoors on a summer day, heresy to her teenaged self—but she's almost certain Aunt Clara never purchased a peach in her life.

That means there must be some on the property. The thought of finding them makes her mouth water, though she feels a pang of guilt at the prospect of wasting a morning. But she's earned some time off, she argues with herself. Despite Gert's absence and Cort's presence, she's managed to get much done. Yesterday she spent the whole afternoon rummaging through Frank's desk, throwing away years of neatly filed phone bills, canceled checks, and receipts for everything from shoelaces to lawn mower parts. She'd found curiosities, too: a moth-eaten velvet bag, tucked into one compartment in the back. When she'd untied the string that held the neck closed, cool glass marbles spilled across her hand. An envelope, unsealed, with three squares of fabric—a silky cornflower, a red rough flannel, and a blue cotton square, the color of sky, that looked vaguely familiar. In the very last drawer, she'd found a handkerchief, carefully knotted, containing a faded bouquet of, of all things, lavender and bittersweet. When she'd tried to pick it up, the flowers and berries crumbled into dust. She'd swept up what she could but the fine particles scattered every which way.

She's done enough for now, she decides. Tomorrow she'll tackle the closet in the master bedroom. For one day, the house can wait.

She whistles for Nina, picks up a wicker field basket from beside the front door, and claps on a man's straw boater, both finds from the hall closet. She'll surprise Cort with dinner tonight—cold chicken sandwiches, a green bean salad, and a peach tart. She's already roasted a chicken for Gert, but her aunt won't mind if a few pieces are missing.

IT takes most of the morning to find the peaches. Andie starts with the apple orchard. It's overgrown with grass and Nina twines underfoot, whining and tripping Andie to the point where she wishes she'd left the dog home.

"What's the matter with you?" she says, grabbing a tree branch to avoid falling on her face. The branch is loaded with green fruit, but there are spots on many of the apples.

Nina barks once, then curls up in the grass, her nose on her paws. Andie's about to leave her there when something long and black slithers just beyond her foot. She screams and jumps back. Nina races past her. The dog is a blur of flying fur and white teeth, and the snake doesn't stand a chance. When it rears to strike, Nina darts in, grabs it by the neck, and shakes her head with joyful savageness. Even after the snake stops writhing and goes limp she keeps shaking it, a low growl emitting from between her powerful jaws.

"Good girl. Good girl. Drop it now," Andie says. She realizes she's been holding her breath, and she lets it out in one long exhale. Nina gives the snake one last shake and then lets it go, tossing it in the air. It lands with a soft thud in the grass, and Andie takes a step back. It has to be at least three feet long.

"Good girl," she says again, and Nina trots over, tail high in the air. Andie crouches and runs her hands over the dog's muzzle, neck and body, checking for puncture wounds. To her relief, she finds none. She gives the dog a pat before standing up.

"Aren't you the brave one," she says, and Nina wriggles with pleasure. "I'll have to find a special treat for you when we get home."

She finds a long branch under one of the apple trees and gives the snake a poke to make sure it's really dead. It is. Her heart rate slows to near normal.

For the rest of the morning, she keeps Nina in front of her, and the dog's jaunty tail waves above the grass like a flag promising safe passage. It's silly, Andie knows. Poisonous snakes in Connecticut are few and far between, but still she shudders at the thought of encountering another.

There are no peach trees in the apple orchard proper, nine acres with hundreds of trees packed together in row upon row. Wooden signs mark the beginning of each section. Some of the signs are leaning and others have fallen over; on all the paint is peeling and fading.

A few of the varieties—Red Delicious, Gala, and Cortland—are familiar, but most—Gravenstein, Ashmeads Kernal, Maiden's Blush—Andie's never heard of. She wanders through the orchard of twisted, gnarled trees and wonders how old they are and who planted them. They look ancient, but many are still bearing fruit. A few have split at the trunk, showing rotten wood, and others have lost limbs to disease or storm.

She reaches the end of the orchard and almost passes by the peach trees. It's the buzzing that stops her, a high, almost constant hum that makes her pause and look around. Off to the side, in an untidy cluster of their own, she finds a dozen peach trees swarming with bees, yellow jackets, and wasps.

Even Nina seems to understand that caution is called for. She flops down on the ground, panting in the tall grass, while Andie carefully approaches the trees. The ground is littered with overripe fruit, and the smell is intoxicating. A little cloud of yellow jackets rises when Andie nears the first tree and she halts, but the insects appear almost drunk on sweetness. Moving slowly, she picks as many peaches as the basket will hold.

When she's done, she walks back to Nina, checking the grass carefully before sitting down. The first bite of peach is so good she holds it in her mouth for a moment without swallowing, letting its warm liquid sweetness fill her. She eats the whole peach, bending over so the juices drip down her chin and onto the grass, then licks her fingers.

When she's finished she lies back in the grass for a moment, comfortably warm and full. The sky is so blue it looks solid, punctuated by only a few white streaks of cloud. The heat, the rich scent of the grass, even the buzzing of the insects soothes her. She breathes deeply, closes her eyes. For this exact moment, she could stay here all day. She could stay here for the rest of her life.

THE tart turns out perfectly. There's no cinnamon in the house, only nutmeg, so Andie sprinkles a pinch onto the dough. Butter, sugar, flour, and the nutmeg make a shortbread crust, which Andie presses into the pie plate with her fingers. She bakes it for fifteen minutes, then in a flash of inspiration adds a layer of pine nuts, brought back from Italy in her suitcase. She toasts the nuts before sprinkling them over the surface of the still-warm crust. They'll keep it from getting soggy.

The peaches need almost no help. Andie slips off the skins, slices them, and tosses the slices with nutmeg, a teaspoon of sugar, a little flour, and a dash of cream. She arranges them on top of the crust, and puts the whole thing back in the oven.

While it's baking she boils water for the green beans, trimming the ends and adding salt to the pot. She'll toss them with balsamic vinegar—another item from her personal survival kit—walnuts, and a little blue cheese, and serve them at room temperature.

The timer sounds, and she removes the tart from the oven, placing it on the counter to cool. Nina eyes it hungrily, and Andie nudges her away with her knee.

"Not for you," she tells the dog. She'll give the pup a few bites of chicken later.

But when she opens the refrigerator later that evening, the chicken is gone. Andie's standing there, staring into the shelves, when the phone rings. She reaches for the receiver, stretching the cord so she can talk while continuing her search.

"Hey, it's me," Cort's voice says in her ear, and she glances at the clock. It's 6 p.m.

"Hey, yourself. What's up?"

"Looks like I'm not going to be there for a while. One of the damn goats got out of the crate in the back of the truck, and I had to pull over."

His voice is grim and Andie closes her eyes, picturing goat mayhem on a major highway.

"Where are you?"

"At a rest stop on the Massachusetts border. It'll be a couple of hours, anyway, and then I have to unload the damn things."

"It's fine. Don't worry about it."

"I'll be there as soon as I can."

"See you later," she says, and hangs up. The chicken's still missing, but since her boyfriend is, too, it doesn't seem to matter as much. She closes the refrigerator door. Nina catches her eye and slinks out of the room. Andie looks after her for a second, then shakes her head. The dog's smart, but it's not as if she has thumbs. Maybe Gert stopped by and decided to rummage in the fridge, Andie tells herself, knowing even as she thinks it how unlikely that is.

The missing chicken doesn't affect her dinner plans, at least. She fixes herself a plate of green bean salad and good bread spread with tapenade, pours herself a glass of red wine from the bottle she purchased yesterday, and carries her meal out onto the porch.

It's odd to be eating dinner with the sun still out. In Italy, she and Neal never dined before eight, and almost never alone. But today she skipped lunch, unless you count the peach, and she can't wait to eat any longer.

When she's finished, she pours herself another glass of wine. She considers having a piece of tart, but it looks so pretty she decides to wait for Cort. If he's really late, they can always eat it for breakfast. She places it on top of the refrigerator for safekeeping.

Nina's stretched under the dining room table and heaves to a stand, brown eyes following Andie.

"Settle down, girl," she says, but the dog comes over and butts her head into Andie's thighs. After scratching behind Nina's ears for a bit, Andie finally goes to her bedroom, drags out Frederick Hartt's *History of Italian Renaissance Art*, and carries it to the porch.

She's had the tome since college. It's battered and worn, the pages curling, with notes written in the margins and occasional stains from coffee, espresso, even butter. In the slowly fading light she leafs through the illustrations, all of which she knows by heart, the way others might say the rosary or play with worry beads. It's a mindless occupation, a way to calm herself, although why she needs soothing at this moment, she couldn't say. It could be because her father, in characteristic Richard style, hasn't bothered to call back with an exact date for his arrival. Andie refuses to call him, and the result is a low-level continual anxiety, which ratchets into stomach-twisting agitation whenever she hears tires crunching up the gravel drive.

Richard's unreliability is nothing new. The only schedule he's ever followed has been those of the ponies, as he calls them, and it's one that dragged her across the country and back every year, until the aunts finally put their foot down. She'd been in eighth grade when she'd started boarding school, and when Richard had pulled up to the farm to take her away she'd hidden in the safest place she could think of. Nobody ever went up to the attic. She'd lain there, behind an old rolled-up rug that smelled of cedar, and waited for her father to leave. If he left, they'd have to keep her, not just for the summer but for good. She watched the dust motes drift across the air and listened to her father swear outside. She never heard the attic door open. It was Frank, of all people, who found her. She still remembers the sorrow in his blue eyes when she asked him why she couldn't stay.

It worked out for the best, anyhow. That's what she tells herself when she looks back. She can't picture growing up in Hartman, all family dinners and church on Sundays. By her second year of boarding school, even summers were too much here. She'd spend the first month babysitting for pocket cash, then join her friends with their families at the Cape or on Nantucket. She'd get out of town as fast as she could.

Still, it annoys her how much Richard can affect her

mood. She thought she'd left that behind a long time ago. She takes her wineglass and wanders through the rooms. Outside, the crickets are chirping, and the trees at the edge of the pasture slide into darkness, their leaves whispering secrets in the warm evening wind.

The house itself unsettles her tonight. It's so full, stuffed with the accumulations of the people who lived and married and died here. Most of what Andie owns fits in the single suitcase she brought with her when she'd left Italy. She's grown used to a lifetime of traveling light, of never living long enough in one place to get attached or weighed down. Except in Italy, and even then most of it belonged to Neal.

She looks out at the blackness and sees instead her old apartment. That first time he'd come for dinner, he'd looked around, at the card table she'd covered with a thrift store cloth, at the mismatched chairs and the wine bottles with candles in them, and his eyes had crinkled in amusement.

"I've never known anyone who actually was a starving artist," he'd said. She'd been mortified, but when he picked her up and spun her around the room, she'd felt giddy and safe at the same time. It was Neal who introduced her to comfort: to down pillows and high thread count sheets, to heavy silverware and beautifully embroidered tablecloths and a constantly changing selection of artwork, of etchings and sculptures and paintings. She'd learned not to grow too attached to any one object, because when she'd returned home from class, it might be gone, sold to the highest bidder to finance the next beautiful thing.

When she'd moved in with him, she'd taken almost nothing with her, leaving the bargain furniture and dented pans for the next grad student. She'd known without thinking about it that they had no place in his carefully composed world.

Now she looks around the house, with its overstuffed chairs, fading carpets, and ancient wallpaper, and wonders idly what he'd think of the mishmash. She's lost her place here, too, if she ever had one, and the silence that once seemed so welcoming is oppressive. She returns to the porch and picks up the book, straining to see the illustrations in the fading light.

Whatever the reason for her restlessness, Hartt does his work. One moment she's gazing at her favorite illustration, the tiny Apollo and Daphne, and the next she's blinking, bleary-eyed in the dark, up at Cort.

"Sorry," he says, brushing the hair off her forehead. "Didn't mean to wake you up. I was afraid you'd brain me with that thing." He points to the book, lying next to Andie on the swing.

"S'okay," she mumbles. She pulls herself to a sitting position and yawns. "What time is it?"

"About ten. Unloading the little buggers took longer than I thought," he says. A sudden breeze blows past them, and upstairs the attic door bangs shut. Nina sits up and cocks her head, whines once, then settles down again.

"Yeah, well, just so long as they don't bother Aunt Gert." Andie yawns again, stretching. "God, it feels like midnight."

"That's 'cause you're old."

She swats him.

"Ow."

"That's what you get for disrespecting your elders."

"Well, Granny, any chance of getting those old bones up? I want to show you something."

She lets him tug her off the swing and to the door. Nina tries to come with them, but Cort gently holds her back by the collar and shuts her in.

"Don't want her making the goats any more crazy than they are," he says in response to Andie's questioning look.

They hold hands to the truck. The passenger-side door creaks when Cort opens it. Andie's ready to get in, but he shakes his head and pulls out a large brown paper bag. He tucks the bag under one arm, takes her hand, and leads her toward the meadow.

In the dark the path is almost invisible. Andie's eyes take a few moments to adjust, and she stumbles a few times, leaning on Cort for support.

"I've got a flashlight, but I'd rather not use it yet," he says. "Give it a second and you'll be able to see just fine."

Andie stubs her toe on something and bites back a comment, but already she understands what he means. To the east there's a faint line of light, diffusing into the black sky like milk into chocolate. The west, over the woods, is dark and the stars above are radiant.

They walk slowly, bushes and rocks assuming odd shapes until they come close. The family cemetery looms out at them, white stones glinting in the moonlight.

They're going downhill now. Over the loud chirps of

crickets Andie hears something rustling. She freezes, refusing to move when Cort tugs her on.

"What's wrong?"

She tells him about the snake, and although she can't see his face, she hears amusement in his voice. "Probably a black rat snake. They're not poisonous. Most farmers like them because they're good for keeping pests down. He was probably more scared of you."

"I doubt it," Andie says. She lets Cort lead her on, but she's careful to step where he does.

She hears the rustling again, even louder this time, and sees up ahead the shadowy outline of the paddock. Something snorts, and Cort stops and sets the bag down. He pulls out a flashlight and shines it at the paddock, keeping the beam low. Andie catches movement through the wire, and then a head pops into view over the fence.

"Easy girl," Cort soothes, moving forward. The goat bleats at him. Its face is small, with large eyes and ears so tiny that at first glance Andie doesn't see them.

"It's a LaMancha," Cort says. He gives the head an affectionate pat, and the goat butts his hand.

"A what?"

"A LaMancha. It's a kind of dairy goat. This is Clarabelle. The other one is her daughter, Clarissa."

Andie peers into the pen and sees a tiny goat curled up quietly on the grass.

"Is she okay?"

"I think so—just tired. It's been an exciting day for them," he says, giving Clarabelle another scratch. "They probably miss the rest of the herd. I'll let them settle in for a couple of days before we try milking."

The little goat gets up and walks over to Andie, who dangles her hand over the side of the fence. It gives her fingers a friendly sniff and tries to suck them.

"Hey," Andie says. "Cut that out. Your mother's over there."

"She's just a baby—about three months old, the breeder said. And Mama over there is almost two."

They stand watching the animals until the doe loses interest and settles down in a far corner of the paddock. The kid curls close, making soft bleating sounds.

"Let them sleep," Cort says.

They walk off a little distance. Cort sits down, patting the grass beside him.

"I should've brought a blanket—sorry," he says. When Andie hesitates, he reaches up and pulls her into his lap. "C'mere, you. Still worried about a little snake?"

"It wasn't all that little," Andie says, but she leans her head against his shoulder. They sit quietly, looking up at the stars. After a moment, Cort reaches into the bag and takes out a paper carton of lemonade and a couple plastic cups.

"This should probably be champagne, but the package store was closed by the time I got there." He pours them both a glass. "Happy anniversary."

The words take her by surprise. She's been letting the days here slide by, like beads through her fingers, and she'd hoped Cort would do the same. Quickly, she counts back to their first date. A month, exactly.

"To summer," she hedges, accepting her glass and bumping it against Cort's. He looks at her, starts to say something, then appears to change his mind.

"To summer," he says. He tips the glass back and Andie can see the long, smooth muscles of his throat.

Around them, crickets start to chirp again, lulled into security by how still Andie and Cort are. A mockingbird starts—it sounds as if it's singing from a bush to Andie's right—and in the background there's the low hum of an airplane. She can hear the goats shifting restlessly in their paddock, and when she lets herself lean back, the slow steady throb of Cort's heartbeat.

She's almost asleep when she feels Cort stir.

"What?" she asks.

"It's getting buggy—we should get back." She scrambles out of his lap and Cort rises, brushing the seat of his jeans. She expects him to head straight for the path, but instead he opens up the brown bag and pulls out a large glass jar, the kind Clara used for her preserves. He unscrews the lid, and when he passes it to Andie she can feel that holes have been punched in it.

"What's this for?"

"Watch," he says, and guides her up a little rise. She can smell wild roses, that deep, clove scent. At the top of the hill are the roses themselves, blurry-edged shadows.

She takes a step toward them, but Cort holds her back.

"Wait a sec," he says. She waits, and after a minute she sees a cool flash of light. Then another. And another.

"Lightning bugs!"

"I thought we could catch a few," Cort says. He takes the lid from her and deftly claps it over the most recent flash. Inside, the light from a single beetle twinkles on and off.

Together they fill the jar, cupping the tiny beetles in their hands and scooping them in. When it's full, they turn for home, Andie holding the jar and leading the way. She doesn't stumble once.

BY early morning the lightning bugs have lost their energy, sparking only intermittently from their place on Andie's dresser.

"Worn out," Andie says. "Like us."

Cort lays his leg across hers and nuzzles her ear. "Don't even think it." He rubs her neck and she groans in pleasure.

"Mmm, that feels good." Maybe it's because she's tired, but the next words spill out before she thinks. "God, I wish summer could last forever."

He slides his hands to her shoulders, kneading them gently. "Who says it can't?"

"My bank account, for one." The money she'd deposited when she'd arrived in town is almost gone, and she'll need to find a job soon. The thought of sending out her CV, applying for positions, facing the inevitable rejection, makes her shoulders tense up. She takes a deep breath, flips over on her stomach so that Cort can reach her whole back, and tries to relax.

"Why not look around here?" he says casually. His hands increase their pressure, their rhythm slow and languid, sliding up and down her spine. "There are plenty of museums and schools in the state. You could live at Evenfall, save up some money, and pay off your loans."

"Great plan," she says. "Except for the fact that it's going up for sale."

"Then live with Gert. She could use the company."

"Right," Andie says. "I've already proven I couldn't last a day there."

"Then live with me." His hands stop moving.

She buries her face in the pillow, takes a deep breath before turning over to face him. She'd had a feeling this was coming ever since the lemonade last night. Still, it would be easier if she weren't naked.

"Look, I'm flattered," she says gently. "Really. I am. But there's a bunch of reasons why it wouldn't work."

"Like what?"

"Well, for starters, you live with your folks," she says, trying for humor. "Let's be realistic, okay?"

"Say yes and I'll be out of there tomorrow." Cort's face has such an eager, hopeful expression that Andie has to look away.

"Cort, I'm sorry," she says. Even as she's saying it, she knows the words don't help, not even a little bit. "I thought you understood I was only here for the summer."

"That was before," he says. "I figured things had changed. You're telling me they haven't?"

She reaches out to touch his arm, but he brushes her off. "You don't feel something special here? I know you do."

"Look." She pauses, choosing her words carefully. "I've

had a lot of fun this summer, with you. But we both know this is just a temporary thing. I need to be in a big city, for my career. And there are too many differences between us for this to work long term."

"Name one."

She can't believe he's making her spell it out.

"Well, there's your age, for a start."

"That's it? That's what's got you so upset?" He smiles, and it pisses Andie off a little, that he thinks it's funny. She's a little less careful when she speaks this time.

"That and the fact that we have totally different lives. I mean, I don't see myself living in Hartman for the rest of my life, in the same house I grew up in, but you seem to have no problem with that."

He stops smiling, and is off the bed searching for his jeans before she's finished. "Come on, Cort. Give me a break here. You asked."

"I guess I'm too young, or maybe too dumb for you. I don't have the fancy degree or the big bank account. Is that it?" He pulls his T-shirt over his head. Andie wants to reach out to him, but she feels impossibly exposed. She stays in bed, clutching the sheet up to her chest.

"You know you're not dumb. But young, yes."

"Guess I am, since I didn't pick up this was just a summer fling for you. Glad I could help out. Anything else you need before I leave? Another fuck, maybe?"

"Cort . . ." She stands up, pulling the sheet with her, but he's already at the door. "Where are you going?"

"Home. At least I know where that is." He clatters down

167

the steps. There's a whistle for Nina, the slam of the door, and a few moments later the truck's engine starting. Tires crunch gravel as the truck pulls out of the yard.

There's a tightness in Andie's chest, a heaviness that wasn't there a few minutes ago. She finds her shirt and shorts under the bed, where she'd kicked them last night in her hurry to undress, and pulls them on. Downstairs, the house is too quiet, as if it's holding its breath. She's not really hungry, but when she sees the peach tart, still on top of the refrigerator, she takes it down. She doesn't use a knife, just pulls off a piece of the crust and eats it. It's featherlight and sweet. She takes another bite, then throws the whole tart in the trash.

Gert

IN her dreams, Gert is dancing with the southern boy. He's tall and slender and his legs work perfectly fine, but something's wrong. She can hear their feet tapping on the hard wooden floor of the church hall and realizes the rhythm doesn't match the music the band is playing.

She tries to tell the boy this, but he won't listen. Instead he moves her faster and faster, so that their feet are flying, but the sound they make is still a steady clip-clop, clip-clop, clip-clop.

She moves her head on the pillow, opens her eyes, and squints against the early morning daylight seeping in from beneath the window shade. She lies quietly, letting her body recollect what her brain already knows, that she's not twenty-four anymore. The dream of dancing lingers at the edge of her consciousness, a sharp contrast to the aches and pains that take up familiar residence in her limbs. Which is why it takes her a moment to realize she can still hear the sound of feet on a hardwood floor.

The noise is coming through the open kitchen windows and sounds like a hesitant woman in high heels—a few steps, a pause, then more steps. "Hello?" Gert calls. "Andie?" The footsteps stop.

She rises from bed, irritably brushing her loose hair over her shoulders and pulling on her robe. It's not enough that her dreams are mysterious; now her mornings have to be, too. "I'm coming," she calls, though no one has asked.

She looks through the kitchen window but can't see anyone. A shiver of unease runs down her spine. Gert doesn't believe in ghosts, not anymore, although there was a time in her youth when she hoped, even prayed, to be haunted, would have traded a life's worth of sleep for a single moment of contact with the small creature whose cries filled her dreams. All nonsense, she tells herself, marching across the floor and throwing open the porch door.

She's prepared for almost anything except what she finds—a nanny goat and its kid. The mother gazes calmly at her, yellow eyes unblinking. The kid takes one look at Gert and utters a single bleat, jumps off the porch steps and races in circles of either terror or glee, Gert's not sure which.

The goat surveys her shrewdly for a moment before apparently deciding Gert's no threat. It goes back to eating the few straggly morning glories that deck the porch's railing, unmoved by the kid's bucking and kicking.

"Stop that," Gert scolds, pulling the morning glories from the goat's mouth. It pulls back, then releases the vine to Gert's hold and moves to the next plant.

"Shoo!" Gert lets the screen door bang shut, setting the kid off in a fresh paroxysm of leaping. The goat, surprised, stops in mid-mouthful. Purple and blue flowers dangle from its teeth.

Gert passes her hand over her eyes, draws a deep breath, and tries to remember how her life has come to this, how she, who once lived overseas, who commanded a staff of twenty, who ran an emergency room with surgical precision, has somehow become an old woman on a caved-in porch not five miles from where she once started out. When she looks again, the goat has given up on the flowers and is sampling strips of paint that curl from the cottage's walls. The kid, emboldened by Gert's stillness, has clambered back onto the porch and is nosing inquiringly at her bare legs. When she doesn't move, it takes a mouthful of her robe and sucks on it experimentally.

Gert exhales. She'd call someone to help, but who? She's supposed to pick up Florence Gilbert this morning. It's their turn to collect the altar flowers and bring them to the town's shut-ins, then up to the hospital. But there are limits to what Gert is willing to do, even in the name of Christian charity. Calling Florence to say she's been detained by a goat is one of them.

She tugs the hem of her robe, now a soggy, crumpled mess, out of the kid's mouth. It's clear who's responsible for this, and she's pretty sure where to find him. Cort McCallister is a farmer's son, but he knows nothing about keeping goats. That sorry fencing of his is the reason Gert's standing here with a handful of dead flowers and a wet bathrobe to boot.

Andie may be an adult, and what she does her own business, but enough is enough. Gert's been willing to turn a blind eye to Cort's pickup truck rattling in here at all hours, but no more. This morning the whole charade comes to an end.

She eyes the goats, both of which are now focused on the porch's plastic folding chairs. In the time it will take her to call over to the big house and explain things, the cottage might not be standing, she decides. Best to just bring the problem there and wash her hands of it.

She hurries inside to change, pulling on khaki shorts and a white shirt. Rather than take the time to plait her hair she leaves it down—she's never cared for ponytails on women her age, and if she can't braid it it might as well be free. She slips her feet into canvas sneakers—the left one has a hole cut out for her bunion—and peeks outside, half-hoping she's imagined the last few minutes.

The goats are still there. Gert sighs again and starts to rummage through the cottage for the necessary supplies. Florence Gilbert and the Lord are just going to have to wait.

Frank

IT'S early morning, and Andie's almost out of coffee. When it's gone, she'll leave the attic. She'll run the vacuum so loud my whispers will be lost in the din. She'll heave boxes so heavy that to distract her could cause injury. I don't have much time, so when she looks out the window and bites her lip, I take my chances.

"I saw him this morning," I say, conversationally. "Before dawn. I tried to wake you." Andie swats irritably at the air, as if she's shooing away a mosquito or a fly, then picks up her brush. She stares at the painting in front of her. It's been more than a week since the sound of hollering brought me down from the attic, and the boy's gone to ground, rolling in at odd hours of the day and night to care for the goats. My niece spends her mornings painting and her afternoons rearranging the dust of this house. Evenings, she creates a stack of fancy documents, each so thick they take three stamps apiece to mail. They've got addresses as far away as Tokyo. The girl's got running in her blood, and he's got the McCallister stubbornness, all right. It's not looking good.

"You could call him," I say. "Just pick up the phone."

My niece narrows her eyes, takes another sip of coffee. She's lost weight, and it shows in her face. "You're as obstinate as your aunt, and liable to end up just like her."

She swats the air again, spattering paint. I sigh. "How about more green? Right there."

Andie feathers a little green at the edge of the canvas. The green is the exact color of the fringe of trees along the front pasture, the green of heat and of summer and of discontent. I glance out the window to compare, and then I see it. If I had eyes I'd rub them: Gert Murphy is leading two goats down my driveway, her hair loose and flowing, dirt streaked down one cheek and wrath in her eyes. One look at her and it's almost a relief to be dead, because it's clear she has murder on her mind.

Andie stands back, looking at her painting. From what I can tell, it's nearly done, but this is no time for woolgathering. "Andie," I say, loud as I can. "We've got company."

It doesn't work, at least not the first time. I try whispering it, right next to her ear, and whether that does it or whether it's just coincidence, she glances out the window and her eyes widen.

"Shit," she says. "Shit, shit, shit."

I couldn't agree more.

Andie rushes through the open attic door and clatters down the steps. I hear her on the second-floor landing, but I've got time, so I linger, studying her painting. She's added the cat, who floats along the ground like a black plume of smoke, all mysteriousness and stealth. Then I hear her in the front hall, and picture her there, and we both wind up at the front door at the same moment.

"Aunt Gert?" Andie calls from behind the screen.

Gert doesn't reply, just keeps on with the goats until she's standing right outside the front steps. She's got a man's belt I recognize as mine looped around the bigger goat's neck like a leash, and a small red box of raisins in her free hand, and she looks like fury herself. When she stops, the big goat bleats at her, and she shoves a raisin in its mouth. The little one's been walking free, trotting alongside its mama. It bleats and gets a raisin, too.

"Aunt Gert?" Andie says again. "What happened?"

"Strange," Gert says, and I long to brush the dirt from her cheek. "That's exactly what I was going to ask you."

"Oh, crap." Andie opens the screen, steps out onto the stone landing, and lets the door bang shut behind her, causing both goats to jump. "Look, I can explain. They're Cort's, but . . ."

"The wretched creatures certainly aren't mine," Gert says. "Now, since we've established ownership, and you've already commented on their bodily functions, perhaps you would be so good as to ask your friend Mr. McCallister to join us so we can discuss the matter of damages."

"Cort's not here, Aunt Gert."

Gert looks at her, and I can tell she's taking in the circles under Andie's eyes, the way her hair's still uncombed at a quarter past nine in the morning. "I see," she says, and it's clear from her tone that she does. But Gert's never let a broken heart stop her from doing what needs to be done, and I can tell she's not about to start now.

"Well then, perhaps you could call him and suggest he come over immediately," she says. When Andie doesn't move, she adds, "Unless of course, you'd like to hold on to these two while I do it."

Andie sighs and steps away from the screen. Her voice floats back as she vanishes into the house. "Yes, Aunt Gert."

I stand there with Gert, looking after the nearest thing to a child we'll ever have. I come closer, close enough to see the lock of hair that's fallen across her forehead. I want to touch it, to move it gently, piece by piece, out of her eyes, but my longing overwhelms me, swirls up the wind near our feet, kicks up bits of dust that cause Gert to cover her face and turn away. The goats sense me and sidestep, small hooves moving restlessly as they seek to put distance between themselves and a presence they can't see. The kid butts Gert hard in the back of the knees, almost bowling her over, and receives a sharp slap on the nose. It blinks and maahs a protest.

"Stand still then," Gert says, holding the belt more firmly.

The mama goat pulls and shuffles in her desire to be away, yellow eyes rolling.

"Stand still, I say."

Gert, I say. *Gert*.

"What is the matter with you?" she scolds, giving the belt a shake. Along her hairline, tiny drops of perspiration appear. "Andie," she calls. "What's taking so long? If he's not there, then come lend a hand."

There's an ocean of longing welling up in me. I don't try to speak again. The desire, the frustration of the last fifty years, is too big for words, so I simply let it be, let it wash over and out of me. I'm reaching her this time, I can sense it. Her thoughts scurry away from me like field mice, but they're there, I can feel them, just below the surface, and I'm on the verge of breaking through . . .

Gert calls out again and Andie appears. She's changed from her paint-splattered shirt into a black tank top and shorts, and when she comes through the doorway her expression shifts from annoyance to concern.

"Aunt Gert! Are you all right?" she says, and just like that our connection breaks, is shattered, I'm flying in a thousand directions, into the air, the wind, the earth itself. It's a struggle to pull myself back, to piece myself together again, and I'm gone for a bit. When I return, when I can focus my energies, I see Gert's pale face, the pulse in her throat fluttering like a trapped wren. Andie has taken the belt from her, but when she tries to guide her to the porch, Gert resists.

"I'm waiting right here, thank you very much. He may be your beau, but he's getting a piece of my mind all the same."

"Aunt Gert, he's not . . ."

Gert flaps her hand. "Spare me the details. All I want to know is whether you reached him."

"Yes. He's on his way."

"Fine."

I try to connect with her again but I'm weak, I can't. We wait in silence, the only sound the calls of the birds and the rustling of the goats, until Cort's red pickup bounces into view. It brakes to a stop a good distance from the house, as if Cort wants to ensure a speedy getaway. Cort steps out and behind him comes Nina, bounding and frisking like a puppy. She freezes when she sees the goats, then charges forward, causing the kid to flee in terror and the mother to struggle and twist against the leather holding her in place.

An angry huff escapes from Gert, like a smoker exhaling. She advances on Nina with a vengeance in mind, but Cort intercepts her.

"Sorry, Miss Gert," he says, slipping his fingers under the dog's collar and pulling her backward toward his truck. He rolls down the window and leaves her in the cab.

With Nina gone, Andie, who hasn't looked up since Cort stepped from the truck, gets the goats under control. They cast a wary eye in my direction occasionally, but they're happy to crop grass and sample whatever else they can find.

"Here, let me take her," Cort says, and his hands brush Andie's as she relinquishes the belt. They look at each other and my niece's face flames red and the two of them stand there, catching sparks off each other, until Gert interrupts.

"These worthless creatures belong to you?" she snaps, and they break apart with a jolt.

"Yes, Miss Gert," Cort says. "And I'm awfully sorry about any trouble they may have caused."

"You should be. They ate half my porch before I was able to catch them. Not to mention what they did to my flowers. Did you know that morning glories are poisonous to goats? If I were a vengeful person, I'd have let them eat their fill. As it is, you're liable to have loose goat droppings for some time."

"I didn't know that," Cort says. He voice is strained—the mother goat has dug in her heels and is ignoring his tugs on the lead. The kid has circled back and is chewing the raisin box Gert dropped.

"What you don't know about goats would fill several books, I expect," Gert informs him. "What I want to know is, what are they doing here in the first place?"

"Well, ahhh—" Cort says, but Andie interrupts.

"That's my fault, Aunt Gert. I told him it was okay if they stayed here for a while."

"Really? And what on earth made you think that? I don't believe I've ever indicated a fondness for goats."

"No, ma'am. I'll get them out of here right now." Cort gives another ineffectual tug on the lead, and Andie leans over to help him. Her shoulder bumps against his.

"Sorry," she says sweetly, and gives him that Murphy smile, the one that's worth waiting a lifetime for. Just like that, the boy's gone again, hook, line, and sinker. I can tell, having had some experience myself. But then Andie's smile fades. She's staring at something over his shoulder, and when I follow her gaze I see a cloud of dust rising from the driveway. A baby blue convertible is purring down the gravel, kicking up dirt as it comes. As it passes Cort's truck, Nina's head pops out of the partially open window. The dog gives a single bark.

"Lord, what now?" Gert says, watching it come. The car brakes to a stop just in front of her, and the driver gets out. He's a large fellow with reddish gold hair, tawny, like a lion in *National Geographic*. Handsome, in a movie star kind of way. He wears a short-sleeved blue shirt, tight across the biceps, and khaki shorts creased so fine they could cut bread. Black sunglasses, the type movie stars wear, hide his eyes. He moves them to the top of his head when he spies Andie.

"Babe," he says.

My niece's mouth is open so wide she looks like a trout. She shuts it, then opens it again, but no words come out.

"Neal?" she finally manages.

"Surprised?" The stranger has a pleased look, as if he's pulled off an especially daring stunt.

"You have no idea," Andie says. "What the hell are you doing here?"

"I'm here to talk to you, of course. In person, since I can't seem to get you on the phone." He turns and reaches into the car, pulls out the largest bouquet of red roses I've ever seen. He moves to hand it to Andie, but she backs away, crossing her arms in front of her. The fellow's left holding the flowers by his side.

"Sorry they're not wildflowers, but the florist was all out," he says, as if that's why my niece rejected them. "And chocolate gelato wouldn't survive the plane ride. So I brought you a different present." With his free hand he points to the car, and for the first time I notice there's another person sitting inside it.

"I thought that was my line," the man in the car says. He disentangles himself from the bucket seat, swings open the passenger door and crosses the yard, bussing first Gert, then Andie, on the cheek.

"Richard?" Gert says.

"Daddy?" Andie echoes.

Time hasn't been kind to Gert's brother. He's got the weathered face of a man who's done hard living. He's still a natty dresser, though, just like in the old days. His pants are pressed, he's wearing a clean shirt, and despite the heat he's got a sweater-vest on top. He took off his baseball cap before he kissed the girls, and now he's turning it in his hands, his bald head glistening in the sun.

"Hey now," he says. "I told you I had something special for Andie, didn't I?"

"No, I don't believe you did," Gert says. "And I distinctly recall you saying you were coming next week." She's got that look on her face, and I can tell it's making him nervous. With good reason. It's been my general experience that Murphy women don't care for surprises. He does a little shuffle step, catches himself, and pretends he was stepping back to look at Andie.

"Well, you know, I just couldn't wait. Hard to believe my little girl's so grown up," he says to no one in particular. Andie's face takes on the same look as Gert's, and Dick almost trips over himself in his haste to move back toward the car.

"So, ahh, Andie, aren't you going to introduce your fellow?" Dick turns to Gert. "He flew in all the way from Italy just to surprise her."

"He's not my fellow," Andie says. "We broke up, in case he didn't mention it. Shit."

"You broke up with me," Neal says. "I don't recall agreeing to it."

"Yeah, well, who hasn't had a lover's spat or two, eh, Gert?" Dick says. "The trick is to make it up before too much time passes. Never let the sun set on a quarrel, is what I say. Of course, the ladies usually say something different." He gives out a dry little chuckle that dies on the wind. "So, anyhow, when he called a few weeks ago looking for Andie, I told him I was heading out to see her myself. Thought I might as well bring him along."

The man straightens up from against the car where he's been leaning and offers his free hand to Gert. "She's right, you know, about the lover's quarrel, but I hope you won't hold it against me. I'm Neal. Neal Roberts. It's a pleasure to finally meet you. Andie's told me so much about you."

Oh, he's smooth, that one.

"Likewise, I'm sure," Gert murmurs, casting a sidelong glance at our niece.

There's a pause. While everyone's busy figuring out what not to say, the fellow catches sight of the goats.

"Hey, look," he says, striding over to them. He gives the mother goat a pat on the ribs that almost fells her. "Andie never told me you kept animals here."

"Generally speaking, we don't," Gert informs him. But

Neal has finally noticed Cort, who is gripping the goat's belt so tightly his knuckles are white.

"Neal Roberts," he says, pumping Cort's hand vigorously. "You a friend of Andie's?"

"Something like that," Cort says, and he looks at Andie, who looks away. Neal sees this and looks puzzled, then surprised, as if the harmless garter snake he'd just picked up turned out to be a rattler. The two men stand there, staring at each other, and the testosterone level is so high even the goats are getting randy.

"How long do you plan on staying?" Gert says to Dick, who's been watching the standoff with interest.

"What?" Dick says, then follows her gaze to the car, which is laden with suitcases. "Ah, no. I'm heading to the city for a few days. Got a lady friend there. We're going to take in a few shows, some shopping, the works. I just thought I'd swing by, see Andie, and drop Neal off at the old Murphy homestead."

I snort. The Murphy homestead was a three-room shack long since torn down for firewood, but Gert just raises an eyebrow. Dick sees it and hurries on.

"Right, well, you know what I mean. Show him the house, anyhow. The boy's got an eye for real estate. Who knows how long it will be here? And, I, um, figured Andie wouldn't want her old dad getting in the way of the big reunion, so I was planning to head out after lunch. Me and the lady friend have tickets to a show tonight."

"You have got to be kidding me," Andie says.

"I don't know what you're talking about, babe," Neal says.

183

He abandons the staring match and comes to stand in front of her, still clutching the roses. "All I know is, I missed you. I came halfway round the world to tell you that I love you and I miss you. That's got to count for something, right?"

"I cannot believe this," Andie says. She looks at him, at her father, then turns and heads toward the house. Neal goes after her, and Cort is left holding the goats and watching Andie walk away. My vision telescopes, and suddenly it's Andie and it's not, it's Gert, and it's August, and the peaches are ripe and Gert is coming home and she's leaving and from my place at the attic window I'm watching her walk away. I'm in the kitchen and I see Andie coming toward me, the fellow in hot pursuit, and then I'm outside again and Gert has crossed to stand in front of Cort. She puts her hand out, as if to lay it against his arm, but then thinks the better of it. She brushes the hair out of her eyes instead, but there's a softness to the gesture that makes me want to weep, and when I call her name this time, I could swear she hears me.

"Come on, Gertie. You can't be keeping goats. You've always hated them," Dick is saying. "They're the last thing you need right now. I thought you were trying to unload this place."

"Hmmm?" Gert says, and it's as if she's pulling her thoughts back from a long ways away. She gives her head a little shake, and the strand of hair falls back again. This time she leaves it there. "Nonsense. We're just having a little problem keeping them in their pasture, and you remember what a nuisance escaped goats can be, Richard. But you must be tired after the drive. Why don't you go up to the big house for a cold drink, and make sure you stop by the cottage before you leave."

"Aren't you coming in?"

"No," Gert says thoughtfully. "No, I don't believe I am."

Cort tugs on the belt, but the mother goat digs in her heels. I can see amusement twitching the corner of Dick's mouth, and all at once I've had enough.

I shift so that I'm between the goats and the driveway, and with all my energy I think of winter, of the coyotes of my youth, of want and fire and famine. The goats' eyes bulge with terror and they take off at a run toward the pasture, towing Cort behind.

Andie

THE faucet is cool beneath Andie's touch. She runs the water, letting it stream over her wrists and hands, then fills the pot for coffee. From the window over the sink she can just glimpse a curve of driveway, and she lingers there, staring, pretending to herself it's because she wants to see the sun rise, not because she knows it's early yet, and if Cort's driving in to check the goats he'll have his headlights on.

She's overfilled the pot, so she pours the excess water out, then changes the filter and puts in fresh grounds. She's running on coffee and sugar these days, and that, plus a lack of sleep, must be why she's on edge. Every creak and groan from the floorboards makes her jump. She'd like nothing more than to go up to the attic, close the door, and take a nap. It's quiet there, peaceful, and when she paints she feels herself falling into a trance, as if she's dreaming the scene rather than painting it. When she puts her brush down and looks at it, it's as if it's someone else's work entirely.

But if she goes upstairs she risks Neal following. He's a bulldozer, knocking down all objections with the strength of his will, and her painting is so new, so fragile, she's not ready to share it yet. She feels as if her whole body is bruised and exhausted from yesterday, although only his words touched her, trailing her throughout the rooms and the fields until she could scarcely think straight, until it was so late and so dark that she'd agreed to let him spend the night in the spare room she'd cleaned out for her father, who'd long since left for the city, taking the rental car with him.

She has to admit, it's heady stuff, this devotion. Neal's the type of man anyone would swoon over. He's so handsome women steal looks at him, then blush when he returns their gaze. They cluster round him at parties, drawn by his laugh, by his easy way of talking, and when he grins they blush again. And now she's the center of his attention, just where she's always longed to be, with no distractions, no sidelong glances at what else is in the room or on the table. And yet it doesn't feel quite like she thought it would.

She opens the cabinet and takes down a cup, waiting for the coffee to brew. It's one of a set she gave Frank for Father's Day a few years ago, fine black ceramic she sent from Italy. It cost more than she could really afford, but she loved the way her hands curved around the mug in the store, the way she imagined coffee would look against the smooth ebony. Frank took his coffee black, just as she has since she was sixteen, and they shared a private joke that it's why, at five foot eight, she's not closer to six feet tall. She traces the lip of the mug with her index finger, and wonders idly what she gave her father that year.

The thought of Richard makes her shoulders tighten until they're almost at her ears, and she takes a conscious breath, then blows it out as if she's extinguishing a candle. She'd been a fool to think he'd stay the night at Evenfall. Aside from dropping her off and picking her up during school vacations, she can't remember him ever spending time here. Even then, if he could have let her out with the car still moving and not been arrested, she suspects he would have done so. The fact that he came at all yesterday speaks more about Neal's determination to win her back than about any filial bonds.

In the four years she spent in Italy, her father visited her exactly once, for one day last summer, before disappearing with his latest girlfriend, who had blonde hair piled high atop her head, a tight black tank top sporting boobs harder than apples, and a bank account she was perfectly willing to empty on a trip for two to Italy. When Andie and Neal took them to a gelato stand, she'd recoiled as if they were offering her antifreeze to taste.

"Oh no, honey," she'd drawled through the smoke from her cigarette. "That stuff's poison after a certain age. Don't tell me you still eat it?"

They'd left the next day for Venice because Marilyn— that was her name, Andie remembers ("like Monroe, get it?")—had read in her guidebook that Venice was for lovers and honeymooners. It had been no great loss, although if she's honest, she'd hoped her father would come alone. But Richard's never been one for father-daughter bonding. At the train station in Rome, he'd put his arm around her, and she'd been sure he was going to congratulate her on the life she'd made for herself, on how far she'd come on her own.

"I'm going to tell you one thing, kid," he'd said. "In a relationship, somebody always loves the other person a little bit more. Make sure you're that person, and not the somebody."

Thinking about that day, her face flushes. She'd been showing him her success, but he'd seen something else entirely, something to which Andie, with all her degrees and intelligence, had been blind.

And yet, it's not as if he disliked Neal, as another father might have. On the contrary. On the rare occasions when Richard called—usually for her birthday, and always a few days late—it was Neal he spoke with the longest. Part of that was simply Neal's gift for smoothing over social situations. But part of it, too, was an easy rapport the two shared, a connection, as if it were they who were related, not Andie and Richard. If she'd thought about it, she'd have assumed that connection would have ended when Neal fucked his secretary. But apparently not.

The coffee's ready. She pours herself a cup and takes a sip, and when she burns the tip of her tongue it's a welcome distraction.

"Hey, coffee. Just what I need." Neal stumbles into the kitchen, yawning and scratching his chest. He's got drawstring paisley pajama bottoms on with no top. The bottoms are new since Andie left Italy.

"Help yourself," Andie says. Let him get his own damn coffee.

Neal waits a beat. When she doesn't move, he goes through the cabinets until he finds the cups. "Hey, I remember these," he says. "We got them at that little kitchen shop, the one in Lucca. It had all those weird cooking tools, remember?"

Andie does. They'd wandered through the store hand-in-hand, whispering invented uses for the rubber and wooden implements, giggling like teenagers at the basting brushes and syringes. Neal found an ornate silver juicer, bulbous and heavy, and when he picked it up and brandished it suggestively, Andie had laughed out loud. The woman behind the counter looked up, suspicious, rattling the pages of her newspaper to let them know she'd seen and did not approve.

"No," Andie says, and turns away to gaze out the window again. "I don't."

Neal sighs. He pours himself a cup, takes a sip and makes a face.

"Jesus, what is this stuff?"

"Maxwell House. Coffee of champions. That and Folger's is all you'll find at the grocery store."

"You should've told me. I would've brought over some dark roast."

"I didn't know you were coming, remember?"

"Yeah, well." He takes another swallow before setting the cup in the sink. "I thought Connecticut was supposed to be some kind of outpost of good taste. What happened?"

"You've got Hartman confused with the other end of the state," Andie says, sipping her coffee. "Up here all you'll find are dairy farms, submarines, and wetlands. That and some Native Americans growing hydroponic lettuce and talking about starting a casino."

"In Connecticut?" He snorts. "That'll be a big money-maker."

Andie stares out the window, willing Cort to appear. She can't shake the sensation that she owes him an apology, though for what she couldn't say. It's not as if she knew Neal was planning to show up. And even if she had, she doesn't owe Cort anything. He's the one who started this stupid fight by stomping out the door. Over what? Nothing, that's what. Over the fact that their lives weren't going in the same direction, which is nothing but the truth. So far as Andie's concerned, the fact that Cort can't handle it shows how immature he really is.

"Andie, come on. Have you heard anything I've said?"

She turns from the window to see Neal looking at her. He's leaning against the counter with his arms crossed, and he has that maddeningly patient look that makes her crazy, as if he's dealing with an unruly toddler.

"Look, I know you left under bad conditions. What I'm trying to say is that I'm sorry, okay? I didn't mean for it to go that way. But you didn't exactly stick around and let me explain."

She puts down her coffee cup. She crossed an ocean to avoid this conversation again, and now they're having it right here in this kitchen. The muscles of her shoulders are tight, and she shrugs one, then the other, trying to release the tension.

"What's to explain? It seems pretty straightforward to me," she says. "The only thing left to talk about is how you're getting to the airport."

"Come on, Andie. It doesn't have to be this way. I screwed up, okay? I admit it. But it wasn't as bad as it looked. Nothing really happened, I swear."

She remembers how his head had been bent to the crook of her neck, lips nuzzling the flesh there. He'd had one hand at the buttons of her white blouse, undone just enough to show the lacy ribbon at the top of her bra. Italian lingerie costs a fortune. Andie wore—still wears—simple cotton Hanes bras, devoid of decoration. She can't remember the woman's face or even the party they were at, but she can still see that lacy black ribbon.

"I don't really want the details, Neal." There's an icy weight in her stomach, and she's having a hard time breathing. She takes a step toward the kitchen door but Neal moves to block her way.

"Look, babe. I know you're mad," he says. "And I don't blame you. But I came all this way to say I'm sorry—doesn't that count for something?"

She thinks of the nights she spent waiting for Neal to come home, watching the sun rise over the ancient buildings, wondering how many other women were awake and watching by their windows with her, how many had watched over the years. She wonders how many of those nights he'd spent with someone else. She shakes her head.

He puts an arm gently around her shoulder, pulls her close.

"I'll make it up to you, I promise," he whispers in her ear. He drapes his other arm around her, enclosing her in his embrace. She stands stiffly, willing herself not to dissolve against him. His beard brushes her cheek, carrying with it a faint trace of his cologne, a scent so familiar it takes her by surprise. She sees his face coming closer, the pores and wrinkles, and she closes her eyes. He kisses her, and her eyes are closed so tight she sees stars, spreading out against the black into constellations, into galaxies, dazzling her so much that she's left blinded, has to open her eyes, and is just in time to see, through the kitchen window, the stand of birch trees illuminated by the bouncing headlights of a small red truck.

august

Gert

GERT'S made a lifetime out of walking away, out of keeping herself to herself and avoiding other people's troubles.
Stick your nose out, get involved, and you'll only get hurt.
Yet for the past few days she's been haunted by the look in
Cort's eyes when Andie's beau showed up. She'd like to swat
her niece's behind for playing with the boy's heart when she
had no right to it in the first place. She tells herself it's not
her problem, that the boy's well-being is no concern of hers.

And yet. The memory of that look stays with her throughout the day and into the next. It's not till she catches sight
of her face in the mirror beside the cottage door that she
recognizes where she's seen it before.

When she first returned to Hartman, she'd thought she
was over him. It had been years, after all. She'd survived a

war, made a career out of the skills she'd practiced on the dead and dying. She'd had lovers, men who could be—or needed to be—discreet. If they didn't touch her heart, it was easier that way. When Clara called, she'd just ended her latest liaison, a doctor who'd become too attached.

July in the hospital was a hot, sticky affair. The window in the break room looked out over an air shaft, and a fly was buzzing against the pane, desperate to get out. She threaded the telephone cord through her fingers. In her sister's voice she heard the rippling waters of the creek, dark shot through with gold, calling her home.

"I'll come," she said, staring out the window.

She'd thought she had something to offer. She wasn't that girl anymore, the daughter with something to prove. She was grown, a woman, and she'd gone farther than any of them ever would. She'd meant to help, of course, but to show them, too, a bit of what they'd missed.

Clothes were something she thought little about, but she'd dressed carefully for this trip. She'd bought a blue silk suit that she knew brightened her eyes and a soft gray cloche that accented the sharp angles of her hair. When she'd boarded the station at New York, the conductor had whistled, long and slow. She'd had his admiring attention throughout the ride, and when she stepped onto the platform she felt only pity for the sister who greeted her. Clara was thinner than she remembered; she'd lost the girlish roundness that had made her so attractive.

"You look like a million dollars," Clara said, half laughing, half crying. "I'm afraid to touch you, you're so fine." But she did, leaning in for the careful hug Gert permitted. Up close, worry lines cobwebbed out from the corners of her sister's eyes, and a furrow creased the space between them.

It was over Clara's shoulder that she caught her first glimpse of him. He stood just off the platform, arms crossed, leaning against the car. When Clara released her, he came forward, and she saw how the same lines that marked Clara spread across his face. She thought, with satisfaction and a bit of regret, that she'd made the right choice. He didn't offer to hug her, just smiled and said it was good to see her again, then picked up the bags at her feet, turned, and walked away, leaving her with the distinct impression that she'd been judged as well and found somehow wanting.

They didn't speak again. On the car ride to Richard's, where Gert insisted she be taken first, Clara filled the silence with talk of the new baby and Richard. Gert remembered her little brother as a scrawny, fearful child, one they'd tried to protect from their father. She'd been fifteen when he was born, her mother's change of life baby, and she'd pitied him. He'd been barely six when she'd left home for good. She could not reconcile the image of that small boy with the cursing man who met her at the door and barred her way.

She thought Frank would knock him down. There was rage there, but at what she couldn't yet say. She told Clara to stop wringing her hands, stepped between the men, backed Richard off with the tone of voice she'd used on soldiers twice her size. When Frank brought her bags in, she sent him and Clara home. Despair was her vocation, and she was practiced enough in it not to need help.

She found the infant in the back bedroom of Richard's house. When she picked it up it mewled. The cloth diaper was overflowing with soft yellow stools, and she had a moment's regret for the fine blue suit.

She cleaned the child up, stripped the sheets and left them in a corner until she could attend to them. She took the baby with her into the bathroom and laid it on the mat while she scrubbed the tub and ran a bath. She ignored Richard, who stood in the doorway, watching, and studied the child. It was small, and the yellow had spread to its limbs, but it wasn't the worst case she had seen.

She found a stack of clean diapers on the floor next to the bed, carefully pinned one on the baby, then left it on the bare mattress of the crib while she went to prepare a bottle.

Her brother followed her.

"What's it's name?" she asked.

"Andrea," he muttered. "Will it live?"

"Yes." She heard his exhale, then the scratch of a match being struck. "Outside," she told him without looking up, and he didn't protest.

She spent the next four days there. The living room received the most light, so she cleaned the windows and dragged the crib in. When her brother staggered back in, he saw the infant, still naked except for its diaper, sleeping peacefully in sunlight.

"Catch its death," he slurred, but she didn't bother to answer, and he collapsed on his bed, shoes still on. She left him there.

She knew all the hiding places: the tank of the toilet, the

wedge of space behind the furnace, the shoe box at the top of the closet. She'd taken his wallet and secreted it among her sanitary napkins at the top of her suitcase. When he raged through the house, he overturned the box but looked no further. His hands shook so badly he couldn't unlock the door.

She stayed beside the child the entire time, leaving it only to prepare a bottle or make coffee. When the dry heaves started, she pointed to the bathroom and told him that if he missed, he'd clean it up himself. The coffee cup he threw went wide, smashing at her feet on the wooden floor.

On the third day, when he began to weep and cry for the dead wife, she ceased making coffee and switched to chamomile tea. She laced his cup with a mild narcotic she'd been prescribed after the war to help her sleep, and only when he'd closed his eyes did she lock herself inside the baby's room and let herself doze. She made herself wake every hour to check on them both.

At midnight, she'd turned over to find the baby staring at her, dark eyes opened wide. She'd reached over, brushed a finger across its brow to check for fever, and it smiled at her. A reflex to gas or air bubbles. Gert withdrew her hand, but it continued to smile.

"Don't," she heard herself say. "I'm not your mother, you hear me?" She heard the exhaustion in her own voice. She left the room, checked to make sure her brother was still breathing. When she came back, the child was fussing. She changed it, carried it downstairs with her to the kitchen. She'd scalded the bottles earlier and left them to cool on the counter. Now she opened the icebox, took out the milk she'd had Clara pick up from McCallister's farm, and mixed it in a pan with blackstrap molasses. When it was warm enough, she poured it into the bottle—tricky, one-handed—and took the bottle and the child upstairs. She'd had the idea of putting it back in the crib, but each time she tried to put it down it fussed. At last she settled herself on the floor, the babe in her lap, wide dark eyes staring. She plopped the nipple in its mouth and it sucked immediately, tiny starfish fingers splayed against her hand. When the bottle was three-fourths empty, it fell asleep. She tried to rouse it to burp but it wouldn't wake, a warm limp weight against her shoulder. It smelled of milk, and of the molasses, and beneath that a soft damp scent all its own. She found it hard to put down, even though it was sleeping, and sat for some time, its head tucked beneath her chin.

By the fourth day, Richard's hands were steady enough to hold the plate of toast she brought him, and when the first bite didn't send him retching to the toilet she packed him and the babe up in a taxi and brought them to the big house. Richard needed nourishment, and she needed rest.

She'd told Clara to settle the child on a blanket in the late afternoon sunshine and taken her brother up the stairs to one of the spare rooms on the second floor. She'd helped him to bathe and shave, his hands still not steady enough to trust with a razor. She'd put him to bed in a clean pair of pajamas, his hands scuttling like nervous crabs over the top of the quilt.

"Stay a moment," he'd said, and she'd sat on a chair beside him. She'd heard the same words a thousand times, but she listened anyhow. They liked it when you listened, she'd found. It made them more pliable later, that they thought you cared. When he reached the part in the words where he thanked her, she stood up.

"You'll be all right," she said. "You've got the babe to live for."

"Ah, but who do you have, Gertie girl?" he asked, and she turned to the door without answering.

The light was starting to fade when she started down the stairs. The house was redolent with the scent of peaches; she'd forgotten what fresh peaches smelled like. She went to the kitchen, meaning to ask Clara for some clear broth for their brother and perhaps a bite for herself. A peach, maybe. A bit of bread with real butter.

But she heard humming in the front room and followed it, curious. She stopped in the doorway. He was holding the child, its dark head tucked under his chin, and when he looked up the cat-shaped blue eyes met hers, and she was gone, drowning. He reached a hand toward her and said something, but the words vanished as he spoke them. She thought she'd lost the capacity to feel like this, but now she was all feeling, no rational thought at all. If he'd touched her then, she would have walked out the front door with him, taken the child and nothing else. The three of them, the way it had been supposed to be.

There's a noise behind her, a footstep. Someone is gasping for breath. She raises her eyes, and sees in the mirror above the fireplace mantel her sister, ashen, and her own white face.

*　*　*

SHE turns away from the mirror. "Mind your business," she says aloud, but there's nobody but Buddy to hear. He purrs and twines beneath her feet, batting at her ankles with his oversized paws. She picks up the phone book, puts it down again. The cat is driving her to distraction. When she picks up the phone book for the second time, he jumps on the table, swatting the pages as she flips them.

"Enough of you," she says, and carries him out to the porch. She doesn't run him off, though, and he stretches out in a patch of sun, boneless and content in its warmth.

She watches him from the window as she dials the number, absently curling the phone cord through fingers thickened by age and arthritis. She's still thinking of what to say when Catherine McCallister answers the phone. Her voice, amplified by years of scolding schoolchildren back into their bus seats, booms through the receiver into Gert's ear. They exchange pleasantries about the state of the weather (good) and the size of the collection plate at church last Sunday (poor) before Catherine gets down to business.

"Well, hey, Miss Gert, what can we do for you?" she says. "Tell me my Cortie's not being too much of a pest. He's up there so much I'm surprised you haven't run him off before this."

"Not at all," Gert says. "Actually, your son's been quite helpful."

Catherine snorts. "I'll bet. I've raised five boys, Miss Gert, and despite what they think, I'm no fool. If one of them is off busting his butt for free, it ain't you he's looking to impress. No offense."

"None taken," Gert says.

Catherine lowers her voice. "To tell you the truth, I don't know what's gotten into him. We've hardly seen him all summer, and suddenly he's moping around the house like a cat with its tail run over. I made my roast beef for dinner last night—the one I bring to the church picnic every year—and he hardly touched it."

"Really," Gert says, but Catherine's not listening.

"Now he's talking some fool nonsense about goats. I tell you, Jim just about had a heart attack. We had a buck growing up, and the smell alone is enough to put you off them. I'm not saying dairy cows are fresh as a daisy, but goats? No, thank you. Not to mention the trouble they get into."

Gert looks out the kitchen window. There are gnaw marks on the porch banister and tiny hoofprints all over her lawn.

"I understand perfectly," she says. The glimmer of an idea has occurred to her, and it takes shape as she listens. When Catherine pauses to draw breath, Gert jumps in before she can change her mind.

"Actually, Catherine, I have a problem," she says. "And I was hoping Cort could help."

"Well, of course, Miss Gert. Just say the word—what do you need?"

Gert picks her next words carefully. She knows how Catherine has raised those boys, and while she's always been in favor of a stern hand and a strict approach, in this case it could work against her. If she reveals too much, Cort might not make it over to the farm again in her lifetime. Too little, and he might not be motivated enough to return while there's still time to make a difference.

"It seems some visitors here made quite a mess of my front porch," she begins. "Not to mention my front lawn."

"These visitors—they wouldn't happen to be friends of my son's, would they?" Catherine says shrewdly.

"Not exactly," Gert hedges. "More like acquaintances. Anyhow, what with the mess and the fact that it's high time the cottage was painted, I was hoping you might be able to persuade Cort to help me fix the place up."

They spend the next fifteen minutes negotiating time and rates. Catherine's all for giving her son into slavery, but Gert thinks a little money might sweeten her trap, so she holds out for giving Cort a fair rate. Once that's decided, she has to persuade Catherine to let the boy come in from the dairy barn for lunch before sending him over.

The extra time gives Gert the opportunity to prepare her attack. And so it is that when Cort arrives, he finds her sitting on the porch, cool and fresh in clean khaki shorts and a white shirt. She's fanning herself with yesterday's edition of the newspaper, a pitcher of lemonade by her side.

"Lemonade?" she offers, waving him to the other chair. She pours him a glass without waiting for an answer. She passes a plate of oatmeal cookies, and he takes one and sniffs at it suspiciously. She doesn't blame him—they look like hockey pucks. She never did learn how to cook, but she sees how it could come in handy.

Cort takes a bite of the cookie. To his credit, he doesn't

spit it out; just places the remainder on the armrest of his chair and swigs some lemonade.

She judges him to be sufficiently softened up, and begins the attack. "I assume your mother told you about our conversation," she says.

Cort nods.

"I'll have you know I didn't mention the abominations you're keeping up on the hill."

Another nod.

"Nor did I mention the fact that they tore up my lawn and damaged my porch." She waves her hand around in the general direction of the gnaw marks and hoofprints.

When the boy still doesn't say anything—just sits there looking glum—Gert's small reserve of patience runs out. This is another reason she doesn't meddle—it takes too much energy.

"Well?" she says. "Do you have anything to say for yourself?"

"Begging your pardon, Miss Gert, but your cottage was in tough shape way before my goats came along."

Gert exhales a great gust of air through her nose. It is times like these that she misses her sister the most. Clara could take the most recalcitrant man and sweet talk him into doing her bidding, all the while making it seem it was his idea in the first place.

"I admit, the cottage needed some work," she concedes. "But your animals didn't help matters. And I saw on my walk this morning that you've still got them corralled on my property."

Cort shifts in his chair. "I'm working on moving them," he says.

"Maybe you don't have to. I have an idea we could help each other."

The boy doesn't say a word, just sits there, looking at her. Gert ignores his lack of enthusiasm and carries on.

"I need someone to perform some general chores. Nothing too difficult—painting, landscaping, that sort of thing. In exchange for your help, I'd be willing to let those goats stay here—and give you some much-needed advice about their care."

"I don't know, Miss Gert."

"I'd also pay you a fair wage," she adds. "And you could work at your own schedule, provided we agree upon the tasks to be completed each week."

"I don't know," he says again. He looks into his lemonade glass as if he expects to find an answer there.

"Of course, I'd need some help with the big house, too," she says, playing her trump card. "There's quite a bit of work to be done there. I can guarantee through the end of summer—say, September first? That's four weeks. It should give you plenty of time to accomplish what you need to do."

He looks at her straight on for the first time. His eyes are brown and guileless, and it's clear he knows what she's thinking. "That's a long time just for some handyman work," he says.

"September first," she repeats.

He takes a sip of lemonade, and she can see him working through the idea of having a legitimate excuse to be on the property every day. She counts to ten, then counts again. On the third count, she decides she's waited long enough.

"Well?" she says.

"What the hell—heck, I mean." He sets his empty glass down beside his chair. "You've got a deal."

"Good. You can start today."

"I thought you said I could work at my own schedule?"

"I spoke with your mother, Cort. You have no schedule. I'll expect you back here in an hour, no less. You can start by scraping the cottage. You'll find a ladder behind the garage." She stands, collects their glasses and tray of cookies, and walks inside to the kitchen. As she's rinsing the plates, she listens. There's only silence outside. She moves to the screen door and sees Cort sitting where she left him, morosely contemplating the few morning glories that escaped the goats' rampage.

"You'd better get going," she tells him. "With all you've got to do, why are you still sitting there?"

"I'm just wondering if your cookies are as poisonous as your flowers are."

"Shoo, you," she says, opening the door to flap her dishtowel at him. He gives her a small smile, the first she's gotten out of him today, before he stands, stretches, and clatters down the steps.

"Mind you're back here in an hour—no less," she calls after him, and he waves a hand in response. She finishes washing the dishes, and when she takes the kitchen towel outside to dry in the sun, she walks past the mirror without a glance.

Frank

NEAL Roberts smokes. Slender brown cigarettes he keeps in a leather case. The tobacco has an earthy sweetness to it, and combined with the leather it's a heady scent. He wears cologne, too. It's subtle, spiced with the warmth of distant places I'll never see. He splashes it on and then smokes a cigarette out the bathroom window.

The day I died, the only things I could smell were rubbing alcohol, medicinal and harsh, and lemon cleaner. Now, scents that were lost to me—the salty tang of sweat, the cool richness of creek mud, the dry, leathery odor of a dog's paw—come easily. Like changing stations on the radio, it's a simple matter of tuning in to the right frequency.

Neal's cologne, for example. The scent's not sharp-edged, like the grapes ripening outside; it's made up of soft, rounded bits that float to all corners of the house and yard. If I concentrate hard enough, I can move them to a place of my choosing, batting them like bubbles through the air.

In the week he's been here, I've discovered I most like to concentrate them over Neal's head, a homing beacon of sorts for the mosquitoes and wasps that roam the air searching for their next landing spot. It's nothing personal, I tell myself, or at least not much. Neal's pleasant enough. He's handsome, I suppose, with a kind of sophisticated charm you don't see much in these parts. Andie's probably brought home worse. But there's something there, just beneath the surface, that I don't care for. It shows in his eyes sometimes, a shrewd, calculating glance that weighs the value of Evenfall and everything in it, even Andie.

He's calling to her now, his voice carrying throughout the house. It reaches me in the attic, and when she doesn't answer I find him and tag along behind. She's outside, pulling weeds from between the bricks in the front walk. The cloud of fragrance hangs above his head as he stoops to kiss her. His clothes are clean and neat, unmarked by any stain, and for some reason this annoys me.

"Morning, babe."

"Morning. You were out early." Already there's a faint sheen of sweat on Andie's forehead, and she wipes it away with the back of her hand before she goes back to work. Andie smells like dirt and sunshine, like the sharp bitter tang of bruised weeds.

Neal watches her for a minute. "Want to take a break and come for a ride with me?"

"Where to?" Andie doesn't look up.

"The guys at the feed store said some teenager a town over is trying to unload a cache of fireworks. I thought we could pick some up."

"You went to Baxter's?" Andie stops working and rocks back on her heels to look up at him.

"Is that what it's called? Man, it's a crazy place. Did you know they sell everything from donuts to live ducklings there?"

On a slow Saturday afternoon, I've known Henry Baxter to take a tipple or two from the flask he keeps under the counter. He also likes to put a mousetrap in the donut box, to discourage sampling.

"The donuts are only on weekends. And make sure you pay before you reach in to grab one," Andie says.

"I bought these for your aunt." Neal holds up a brown paper bag, and pulls out a glass jar filled with golden peach halves. "Seems like the kind of old-timey thing she'd like."

"Thanks," Andie says. "But what's with the fireworks?"

"I don't know. I just thought, we missed the Fourth, so maybe we should try and do a little something. We could have a barbecue, set some off, and invite your aunt and maybe your dad."

Richard coming to Evenfall again is as likely as my rising from the dead, and by the snort Andie gives I'd say she agrees. She stands and stretches, then takes the peaches from him.

"Whatever. But if you light so much as a sparkler on the property, Aunt Gert's liable to have you arrested. She's not big on the whole burning-down-the-house thing."

Andie's not just talking. The woods are dry enough this time of year that they'd go up like kindling.

"Yeah, well, I'm not sure that would be a bad thing," he says, looking around. "Might save a developer some bucks, you know? Your dad didn't tell me how much work the house needed. Of course, he didn't tell me about all the antiques, either. The place is loaded."

"I guess," Andie says. "I've never thought about it that way—as antiques. It's just stuff that's always been here." She looks down at the peaches in her hands, then back up at Neal. "I didn't know you and Richard had talked about Evenfall at all."

While Andie and Neal talk, I try my hand at redirecting a yellow jacket. I've just gotten it aimed right when Neal jumps. At first I think I've been successful, but the bee is just buzzing a confused figure eight pattern over his head. I look again and see that a shadow has detached itself from the house and is heading toward Neal, who takes a step back and trips over Andie's trowel.

"Jesus." He staggers but doesn't fall down.

"Relax, it's just Nina," Andie says. The dog steps forward, wagging her tail, and grazes against Neal's shorts. He pushes her away and brushes at his clothes with his free hand.

"Nice of you to show up," I say. She whines and rolls over on her back, muddy paws in the air.

If Nina's here, it's likely that Cort's around, too, a thought that's clearly occurred to Andie. She stands and turns in a slow circle, searching the surrounding woods. Two days ago, Cort was weed-whacking around the grapevines just after sunrise, but by the time Andie got dressed and downstairs, he was gone. Yesterday, the sound of hammering echoed from the woods shortly after dawn, and the noise kept up for over an hour. Both times, Cort's truck was nowhere to be seen. I've a thought as to where it may be, and I wonder if the same thought's occurred to Andie.

"These shorts are Italian linen, for christsakes," Neal is saying, still trying to fend off Nina, who has risen and is trying to rub her face against him.

"She's just trying to say hi," Andie says, grabbing Nina by the collar with her free hand and dragging her back. Neal opens his mouth to respond, but I've finally brought the yellow jacket in for a landing, right where his chest hair peeks out of his pink collared shirt.

"Shit!" Neal slaps at his chest, but the insect is already in the air and happily heading toward the grape vines, its mission accomplished.

"It probably thought you were a flower," Andie says. "I think there's a nest of them up in the attic. I keep hearing this humming."

"Jesus Christ." He scrunches his neck, trying to see the sting.

"It's just a little sting," she says. Her face softens and she comes closer to him, pokes a finger at the swelling. "Come in the house and I'll put some ice on it."

He brushes her hand away. "Forget it. Look, there's a big antique depot on the way—I thought we could stop in and shoot the shit with them for a while. Get some prices for things, so you know what you're dealing with."

She shakes her head. "I think I'll finish up here. You go and I'll see you later."

"The damn dog of yours is right in front of my car," he says.

"It's not my dog," Andie says, but whistles anyways, and Nina slowly crosses the yard to her. My niece gives him a kiss before he stomps off, and a moment later his car is roaring down the driveway.

The second he's gone, Andie turns her attention to Nina, who slinks onto her belly.

"All right, you," she says. "Where is he?"

The dog squirms until Andie relents and stoops to pat her head. Beads of water glisten in her fur, and she has a damp, earthy smell.

"At the creek, hey?" Andie says, but she doesn't take the path that leads toward the water. Instead, she looks thoughtfully at the woods before she walks toward Gert's cottage. She carries the peaches in their brown paper sack, Nina trailing behind.

I consider. Leaving the farm requires more energy than I like. For days after, I'm reduced, an echo of an echo. But if Gert's up to something, as both my niece and I seem to think, I'm curious to see what it is, so I drift along behind.

Andie walks at a quick pace, head down, and in no time we're at the cottage. Gert's standing on the front porch, a watering can in her hand. She looks up, and it is as if she's been waiting for us.

The sun's behind her, and I can see the outline of her body through the white shirt she wears. She's thinner than

I like, and when she moves I'm overcome by the memory of the warmth of her skin, the sharpness of her hip bones beneath me.

Andie's said something, but I've missed it. I follow her gaze and realize that my first impression—the cottage is more run-down than usual—is wrong. It's been scraped clean in preparation for painting. And judging by the shingles that litter the ground, the hammering yesterday was somebody working on the roof. Cort's truck parked at the top of the driveway pretty much eliminates any question of who the somebody is.

A rise in Andie's pitch catches my attention, and I focus on the conversation. "And I'm just asking why all of a sudden it's okay for Cort to be outside my bedroom window at six a.m.," she's saying. She puts the paper sack down on the porch.

Gert pours water on the morning glories that twine around the cottage's front railings, ignoring Andie's impatient exhale. "I have no control over when the boy does his work, Andrea," she says. "He's taken on the project as a favor to his mother, and I'm paying him quite a bit less than his labor is worth."

"Crusty McCallister, the bus driver?" Andie says. "Please. Since when have you been friends with her?"

"Catherine has organized the altar flowers for the past two years, and we've struck up a relationship. Of course, if you'd come to church with me on a Sunday, you'd know that."

"The point of this conversation is not my church attendance," Andie says. "The point is that you are interfering in my life."

"And exactly how am I doing that?" Gert asks, turning to face her. "You told me, quite clearly, that Cort wasn't your boyfriend—that you weren't interested in him romantically. Or did I misunderstand?"

"Oh no—you understand exactly, Aunt Gert. And all I'm telling you is, butt out."

"And I'm simply trying to get the property in shape. If Cort is willing to do it, at a price I can afford, then Cort is whom I will hire," Gert says. "Of course, if I'm missing something, you're welcome to take it up with him."

"Fine. That's just fine," Andie says. "Just tell me where he is, then—at the creek?"

"I should hope not. I'm certainly not paying him to spend his time fishing."

If Gert is paying money to the boy, she knows not only where he is, but what he had for breakfast and how many fillings are in his teeth. I can tell Andie would like to call her aunt a liar, but she's not that mad. Not yet.

"Fine," Andie says again. "Then I'll find him myself."

"Go right ahead," Gert says. "But I daresay you'll have plenty of chances to talk with him. There's still quite a bit of work to be done, you know."

Andie stares at her aunt. She opens her mouth, closes it, and then turns on her heel and marches back through the woods without a word. She brushes against the sack as she goes, and the glass jar of peaches rolls out and comes to a stop just in front of me.

Her leaving doesn't seem to upset Gert, who goes back to watering. But then I see that the container is empty; she's tilting air over the last few plants as she stares at the spot where I'm standing. If I close my eyes I can see it; a rush of silver, ghostly water raining down.

Gert

WHEN Gert comes downstairs from settling the baby, her sister is sitting at the table. Evening is coming; the light from the windows is dim. Even at this hour the kitchen is uncomfortably warm. A row of canned peaches stretches across the countertop. The curve of the fruit reminds Gert of an infant's cheek, and she looks away and thinks about dinner. It's been a long few days.

"Frank will be down soon," Clara says, but she doesn't stand up. Her hands are folded in her lap, and when she shifts, the cracked and roughened skin of her fingers catches on her blue dress. She catches Gert's eyes and smoothes the material carefully.

"I've saved the extra," she says. "I'll use it for a quilt for the baby."

The material's the wrong color for a girl, but Gert doesn't say that. She just nods. But Clara answers as if Gert has contradicted her. "It's good, soft cloth. I'll back it with a cambric lining the baby can snuggle into."

Others might scoff at such frugal ways, but Gert understands. There's always a reason to save what you can. Most times, you'll need it later.

These past few days, she's seen how there are women in Hartman who still envy her sister, all these years later. Women who whisper behind gloved hands at how the daughter of a drunkard could be sitting in the finest house in town. They don't see how Clara's own hands aren't fit to take out of her apron pockets when they come asking for donations for the hospital or the library. They think she's reached above her place when she doesn't invite them in for a cool drink or a cup of tea. But Gert's seen how hard her sister works. She knows you get just as hungry eating air off china as you do off tin. Not that anyone's going hungry these days. A few chickens, a garden that grows more than flowers, a willingness to dine on leftovers and stretch one dollar six ways to Sunday has seen to that. No one, not even Gert, could have done the job her sister has done here.

Clara smoothes her dress again. "It's funny seeing you here, dressed like that. When I pictured you, you were always dressed in white, standing over some poor body with its innards cut open."

Gert's own skirt is blotchy with the infant's spit up, stained from her first day at Richard's house, and it sticks to her with the heat. She lifts it away from her, considers.

"That's near enough, I suppose. Though it never seems to stay white for long."

Clara eyes the blue silk critically. "The skirt's as good as ruined, you know. It's not enough by itself, but if you give it to me, I'll use it with the leftovers from the baby blanket to make one for you, too. I've got a few old workshirts of Frank's, red ones, that would look real pretty with it."

"Thank you," Gert says carefully. "That would be nice."

Neither of them speaks for a bit. And then, in the moment just before day turns into darkness, Clara stands. She doesn't look at Gert, but rather through the window over the kitchen sink. The view is of the driveway, and beyond it the tree line that divides the property from the road. She points.

"There's a cabin of a sorts, that way. They used to use it for the farm workers who came through. There's no electricity, but it could be put in. And there's good water. With a little bit of work, it could be fixed up nice."

"For Richard? It's a thought," Gert says. "Keeping him nearby will make it easier for you after I've gone."

Clara shakes her head. "I meant for you. You'll be coming back, won't you? For the baby."

It's possible, then, for Gert to believe her sister has seen it all. The first day of school, Frank's eyes following her down the aisle. The two of them bumping shoulders, both faces flushed red. A mud-stained dress. She wonders if a fragment of memory ever breaks free and draws blood from Clara's conscience.

But her eyes tell the story. Memories might tumble round Clara's head all day, but by nightfall they're always worn smooth. This is a gift, and nothing more.

And perhaps she's right. It's likely, Gert thinks, she would have regretted it in the end. They hear Frank stirring overhead. Clara turns, cups the lid of the nearest glass jar with her hand. In a moment, she knows, her sister will offer her some, and Gert will refuse. She finds she can't abide the fruit, with its soft, fuzzy skin, but Frank loves them.

Andie

THE inside of Neal's rented Saab convertible is hot, even parked in the shade at seven p.m., and the white leather seat burns the back of Andie's thighs. She pulls her skirt down. A bead of sweat drips down her nose, and she can feel a damp patch on the back of her shirt.

She starts the engine, then presses the button that folds back the roof. There's a whirring sound, and the black top slowly and smoothly rises up, then disappears from view into a space behind the backseat. A neat trick. In Rome, Neal tooled around the streets in a cherry red leased Fiat, a car Andie thinks fits his personality much better. He tried driving Frank's Nova, but each time he stepped on the gas, the car spluttered, then died. Neal claims it's the car, but Andie knows he likes to accelerate in a rush, and the Nova needs to be babied. He took the train to Hartford last week to see what was available, and this black Saab was the flashiest thing he could find. It reminds Andie of a boxy, oversized beetle.

She shifts, trying to get comfortable, and the toe of her shoe brushes something. She reaches down and finds Neal's cigarette case. It's calfskin leather, monogrammed with his initials: NGR. She'd given it to him two Christmases ago, when his smoking still seemed like a charming foible, one she could easily fix. Holding the case in her hand, she feels her heartbeat slow, and she realizes she'd been worried about what she'd find when she reached under the driver's seat.

Enough of this. She taps the horn until Neal's head appears in the upstairs bedroom window. "I'm coming," he shouts, and Andie sits back, not satisfied, exactly, but pleased at the thought that she's maybe pissed him off a little.

She knows she's being bitchy, but she can't help herself. A year ago she would have given anything for proof of Neal's love—and if flying across the world to be with her at his busiest time of the year isn't proof, what is?—but lately she's not so sure love is what she wants.

She pulls her bag across the seat and searches inside it for her lipstick. The bag, lime green, is a make-up gift from Neal, a prototype of the ones that models will be carrying down the catwalks this fall. She'd simplified a little when she'd explained his job to her aunt; Neal's not a designer, not exactly. He's more an opportunist with a good eye, seizing on trends of the day and manufacturing them at a lower price. Her bag could be the real thing—an authentic designer sample—or it could be a cheap knockoff. Andie's found she prefers not to know.

She locates the lipstick and swipes it across her mouth, where it immediately starts to melt. She thinks longingly of the house's dirt basement, its dark, windowless walls cool no matter what the weather. She'd love to bring a beach towel and a book down there and hide until this heat breaks.

Instead, she's going out to dinner. At least a restaurant will be air-conditioned. She lifts her ponytail higher with one hand and fans the back of her neck with the other. She's about to honk the horn again when Neal comes out the front door.

"Sorry," he says. When he's close enough, Andie gets out of the car and walks around to the passenger seat. Neal rushes to get there first and open the door for her. He's wearing a charcoal T-shirt, stretched tight across his chest, a pair of olive green shorts, and leather moccasins Andie's never seen before. He looks like he just stepped out of a catalog for country living. But there are drawbacks to living with a man who cares more about his appearance than you do, as Andie's discovered. One of which is that he's never ready on time.

"So," he says, accelerating as they pull out of the driveway, "where do you want to go? I know you're the tour guide, but I got a couple of recommendations from the guys at the feed store."

I'll bet you did, Andie thinks. In Italy, Neal's gift for blending into the local scene, for discovering the best trattorias and the coolest bars, was both enviable and irritating.

It's a bit disconcerting to watch the same skill at work on her home turf.

"What'd they say?" she asks.

"Well, there's a new place one town over that's getting good reviews. Apparently the chef's some kind of fanatic who will only cook with native ingredients. If it's not from around here, he won't serve it."

Oh god. She sinks lower in her seat. "I don't know, it sounds kind of trendy. I thought you wanted some local color."

"Right you are." He turns the wheel, heading the car toward the center of town. "Well, we've got Lena's Pizza or Johnny's Bar and Grill. Your pick?"

Andie thinks fast. Lena's has edible food, but on a Friday night half of Hartman—including Cort or his parents—will be there. Johnny's is a case of food poisoning waiting to happen, but most of the locals only go there to drink. With luck, she can get Neal in and out before the bar gets busy.

"Well, if it's atmosphere you want, Johnny's is the place to be," she tells him. She leaves out the part about food poisoning.

"Johnny's it is," he says. She has to admit, he's been endearingly agreeable since he's been here. She knows the country isn't his thing, but he spent last week walking the property with her, listening to her stories of growing up here and scouting the boundaries as if he really cared. He's taken on the task of getting the assessor out to the house, too, a job Gert's been avoiding for far too long.

He's even helping with the cleanup, a bit. Neal has a

knack for beauty, for finding the dross in overlooked objects and spinning them into gold. Some days, she's felt he views her the same way. She'd been sorting objects in the sitting room, starting a pile for the Salvation Army and another for the trash, and he'd all but had a heart attack when he saw what she was letting go.

"You've no idea of the value of things, do you?" he'd said, rescuing an old, water-stained globe with misnamed countries and an obscene ashtray made from an elephant's foot. "My little starving artist still. Why don't you let me sort it out for you? You've got a great opportunity to make some easy money here."

"Knock yourself out," she'd said, stung by the starving artist comment. If Neal wanted to paw through two centuries' worth of junk, fine with her.

Unlike the old days, though, he'd sensed she was hurt. That night, he'd surprised her with a wicker hamper filled with the things she'd missed since leaving Italy: biscotti, green olives stuffed with herbs, sun-dried tomatoes, cheese and good bread, even fig cookies. They'd picnicked out in the pasture, complete with a bottle of Prosecco and real glass flutes, and Andie had tried hard to keep any comparisons of a different picnic out of her mind.

She owes it to him to try, so on the drive over, she points out local landmarks—the barn with beams dating from the seventeen hundreds, the church built over an Indian tribe's graveyard, the field behind the library where all the kids used to party. She lets the McCallister farm roll past without a mention.

The parking lot at Johnny's isn't close to full, and when Neal pulls in, the Saab is the only foreign car. Cort's pickup isn't there, though, and Andie offers a quick prayer of gratitude. She'd searched for him for a good half hour the day before, her temper rising with every mosquito bite, until she finally gave up and stomped back to the house.

Thinking about it now, she gives the mosquito bite on her elbow a quick scratch. She's still wondering where Cort could have been when Neal opens the door to the lounge for her. The blast of spilled beer, stale smoke, and staler air almost makes her take a step back. But the room is comfortably dark and the air-conditioning is cranked, so she leads the way to a red vinyl booth, Neal following, and they slide in. Neal's looking around with a dubious expression, and Andie gets the feeling it's not the kind of atmosphere he was expecting.

She can't really blame him. There's a large strip of silvery duct-tape running along the back of his seat, gray stuffing oozing from around the edges. When the room's sole waitress drops off their menus, the plastic covers are smudged and sticky.

"So what's good?" Neal says. The waitress, an older blonde, looks at him as if he's joking.

"The beer," she says.

Neal smiles at her. "Oh, come on now," he says, and Andie can see her relent.

"Anything fried is probably safe," she says and walks away. Andie can tell Neal thinks she's kidding, until he looks at the menu and his eyebrows go up.

When the waitress comes back, Andie orders a platter of buffalo wings and a pitcher of beer. Neal gets a house salad, a cheeseburger, and fries.

The television above the bar is showing the game, and a cheer goes up when a Red Sox player rounds second base, dreadlocks bouncing above his shoulders. The bartender stops wiping glasses and turns to watch, and the waitress pauses on her trip back to the kitchen.

"Slow night," Neal says. Andie just nods. It's hard to talk over the noise at the bar, so they watch the game until the waitress comes back, carrying Neal's salad in one hand and the beer and glasses in the other. She pours them each a drink, tilting the glasses expertly so there's only a slight head of foam atop each one.

Neal waits until the waitress leaves before clinking his glass with Andie's.

He leans forward, puts his hand on Andie's, and gives her his best full-watt smile, then tucks a damp strand of hair behind her ear with his other hand. "You are so lovely," he says softly.

For just a moment, the noise of the bar recedes. She shifts in her seat. A buzz starts in her middle, spreads up, making it hard to concentrate. Neal knows the value of a thing, can judge its worth with a fingertip, and it's clear, the way he's looking at her now, that he's rediscovered her appeal. There's not a woman in this room who wouldn't change spots with her right now, and so long as Neal's looking at her this way, Andie's not giving her seat up.

The guys at the bar groan and shout, and they both look

up, startled. The Sox have struck out and the game is over. The bartender snaps off the television, shaking his head.

"Lazy bums," the waitress mutters. She slides their food onto the table. "For a million bucks even I could hit better than that guy. You two want anything else?"

"No, I think we're good," Neal says, and she walks away, still muttering under her breath.

"Well, it's not Cafe Mondo, but it'll do," Neal says. He releases her hand.

Cafe Mondo was just a block from their apartment. The last time Andie ate there, she had antipasto and braised lamb, with baby potatoes and a carafe of the house red wine. Neal was twenty minutes late meeting her, and when he came in he was wearing a shirt she'd never seen before. Now, it occurs to her that his affair had probably already begun. She takes a swig of her beer. The glow she's been feeling recedes. She decides not to warn him about eating the salad.

She looks at her food. The wings are glistening with fat, and there's a pool of blue cheese in the center of the plate. What the hell, she decides. She picks up a wing, dunks it in the sauce, takes a huge bite, and swallows. The hot sauce burns her tongue, so she washes the rest of the wing down with a gulp of beer.

"Not eating?" she asks Neal, who's stabbing a piece of lettuce with his fork.

"I'm just not a fan of iceberg, I guess. Maybe we could still make it to that other restaurant, get a late table. What do you think?"

"On a Friday night? It would never happen," she says.

"Besides, it's been a long time since I've had fried food and beer, and I'm not planning on depriving myself now."

"To calories, then," he says, and clinks her glass with his again.

The room is beginning to fill up, but Andie's had enough beer to take the edge off, and she no longer checks the door every time it opens. There's a jukebox on the far side of the room, and now that the game is over, somebody's put a quarter in. John Prine's froggy voice fills the room, paired with Bonnie Raitt's melancholy alto.

"Good tune," Neal says. The jukebox sits in the corner of the room, and Andie can tell when he spots it by the way his eyes widen. It's a Wurlitzer 1015, with the rounded top and bubble tubes. It still plays on quarters, and on nights when the bar is too rowdy, the owner shuts it down and throws a cover over it.

"It's all that's left of the original Johnny," Andie says. "It's been here since I was a little girl."

"You actually came in here as a little girl?"

"Not with my aunt or uncle. My dad sometimes brought me down," she says. "It was Richard's idea of a bonding experience."

Bonnie's singing about dreams being thunder and lightning desire, but Andie can tell Neal's no longer listening. She's seen the signs before.

"Jesus, that thing's gotta be worth a fortune," he says. "What do you think the chances are they'd sell it? I know a couple of people who would pay big money for it. That guy over at the antique depot, for one."

"No chance," Andie says. Johnny was a fat man who died young of a heart attack, but she can still remember how light he was on his feet, grooving in the late afternoon gloom of the bar to an old blues song on the jukebox. There's a handful of classic rock records in the stack, but most of the music is blues, pure and simple.

"I gotta ask anyhow—I'd kill myself if somebody else bought it. Do you know the owner?"

When Johnny died, the bar passed to his son Jake, a close-clipped, ex-Marine who frowned on his dad's habit of passing out free beers to his old buddies. Cynical teenager that she was, she remembers feeling vaguely amused by her father's outrage when he'd had to pay for his own drinks on his annual trip to the farm.

"Mark my words, the place won't last a year," he'd said.

She'd long since lost the habit of paying attention to anything Richard said, but she made it a point to update him on how Johnny's was faring in the summer missives Clara insisted she write. And over the years, it had fared rather well. About the only change—besides the wide-screen television above the bar and the repaved parking lot outside—was the large sign on the wall behind the jukebox. She'd heard Jake added it after a drunken pool player busted a stick over the machine's top. The sign read: "Management not responsible for damage." The pool player went to the hospital that night with two broken ribs and stitches to his lip, and the jukebox has remained untouched ever since.

A couple of guys are cueing up at the table now, and Andie can see Jake standing behind them, framed in the doorway of the back room. It's been a while since she's seen him, and his crew-cut is going gray, but the muscles in his arms look as tight as ever from here. She nods and points him out with her chin to Neal.

"That's the owner, over there."

He swivels to take a look. "The guy in the black T-shirt? Think he'd remember you?"

Between her father and the time he busted her trying to use a fake ID, Andie's pretty sure Jake remembers her. And since he's the kind of guy who keeps pretty close tabs on his customers, it's likely he'll realize she's here soon enough. So there's no good reason to say no, yet she finds herself shaking her head.

"I doubt it. It was all a long time ago."

"Too bad. Still, a guy's got to try, right? Want to come over with me?"

"I'm not so good with the sales thing, you know that."

"I keep telling you, you're looking at it wrong. It's not sales, it's opportunity," he says. He leans across the table and kisses the top of her head before sliding out of the booth. "Back in a bit."

She watches him go. She can't help but observe that the shorts stretch nicely across his ass. There's a sudden flurry of activity in the booth of women across from her, and she knows she's not the only one to have noticed. One of them elbows her seat mate and whispers something, and they all giggle. She feels a quick flare of the old jealousy, and she looks away from them.

Across the room, Neal's all hearty smiles and handshakes,

just one of the guys. Jake sends a flicker of a glance her way, enough to tell her that Neal's dropped her name. The guy closest to Neal says something, he answers, and the crowd laughs, a few of the men nodding appreciatively. She can tell Neal's just warming them up. Already, he fits in here in a way she never has. If she wanted to, she could walk through the crowd, past the women who admired his ass, and stand next to him. He'd place an arm around her, draw her to his side without even thinking about it, and just like that it would be clear that they were together, that whatever mantle of charm he had extended to cover her as well. In Italy, the slipstream of his allure had carried her all the way to belonging. She's tempted, for a moment. Then some guy in a Springsteen shirt stops to listen, blocking her view.

She drains the last of her glass, stands and threads her way carefully through the crowd to what her father used to call "the ladies." It's a tiny room, cornered off at the far end of the bar, with an alcove that hides it from view. The air-conditioning isn't on as high in here, and the room smells strongly of disinfectant. She takes her time, reading the graffiti scrawls as she washes her hands. She doesn't recognize any of the names, although there's no reason she should. "Joleen is a skanky whore," one reads, and she wonders who Joleen pissed off.

She reapplies her lipstick, brushes back a few stray wisps of hair that have escaped her ponytail. When Neal comes back to the table, they'll go. Heat outside be damned.

Outside the bathroom's alcove, she stands for a moment to get her bearings. She's pleasantly lightheaded, and she sees from the way the bar floor is filling up that she's not the only one. A few couples are swaying in place to the music, arms wrapped around each other, as the jukebox pumps out another tale of true love gone wrong. She looks toward the booth but doesn't see Neal.

"Searching for your boyfriend?" a voice asks, and the buzz she's been cultivating vanishes. Cort's leaning up against the alcove wall, arms folded against his white T-shirt. He's got a few days' worth of stubble on his cheeks, and his hair's standing on end, as if he rolled out of bed this morning and hasn't given it another thought. She'd like to smooth it down for him, and finds herself tucking wisps of her own hair behind her ears instead.

"What?" he says, pushing off from against the wall. "No quick answer? No snappy comeback? I'm disappointed."

It's the way he slurs the last word that tips her off. Even with her own brain cells doing happy little high dives to their deaths, she can tell he's had a few—a good many few— more beers tonight than she has. She scrutinizes him. True, he's standing straight, but he's also not moving much, and as if to prove her point he uses her silence as an excuse to collapse back against the wall.

"What?" he says again, but this time the words are defensive.

"How drunk are you?"

"Drunk enough to dance," he says. "Or is that not what you're looking for tonight?"

"What I'm not looking for is a fight. Okay?" She tries to move past him, but he sticks an arm out and blocks her way.

"That's it? That's all you got for me?"

"I never, ever, meant to hurt you, Cort," she says, and wishes he knew how much that were true. "When I came here, I thought Neal and I were through. I didn't know he'd show up."

"And when he did, you told him it was over, right? That you were with somebody else? Because from where I stand, it looks like he didn't get that message."

"Look," she says. She's so, so tired suddenly. "What Neal and I have, what we had . . . We've been together for a long time. There are things between us. That doesn't just go away overnight."

"You're telling me? Christ, Andie, I've been chasing after you with my heart in my hand since I was six years old, and you act like I'm the one who's in the way here. Like I'm the newcomer." He pushes off the wall and stands closer, so that he's towering over her. "But there's always going to be some guy, isn't there? Some other guy who's older or richer, with a nicer car or a bigger house or a trust fund. It doesn't matter, just so long as it's some other guy who's not me. You don't even see what's in front of you, not until it's walking away."

He sways a little bit, so that his hip brushes hers and for a second in her drunken haze she thinks he really means for them to dance, but then he straightens up.

"Well, take a good look then, Andie, because I'm going. I'm gone."

He pivots away and pushes through the crowd, disappearing in the general direction of the door. She's still standing there, waiting for her breathing to settle, when Neal finds her.

"Hey there, looking for a partner?" he says, grabbing her around the waist.

She tries to smile. "How did it go with Jake?"

"Well, he remembers you. But he's not what I'd call a chatty guy, although he's fond of a few select words. Like no, for example."

"He won't sell?"

"Doesn't look like it, at least not this time. Interesting guy, though. I may try him again later."

"Sorry," Andie says, though she's secretly glad. She can't imagine Johnny's without the jukebox.

"No worries. You know me—there's always another opportunity around the corner."

He spins Andie once, twice, three times, and as the room blurs past she tries hard not to think about the opportunities she's missed, the chances that just walk away.

Gert

IT occurs to Gert, not for the first time, that she's come full circle. The worthless animal bleating in front of her could be a great-great-granddaughter of those her family kept, for all its fancy pedigree and funny-looking ears. She prods its kid gently with her foot, and it maas in response.

She'd found the kid sprawled on the ground just past dawn this morning and walked back to the cottage to call Cort and fetch a bottle of mineral oil. Then she'd returned here, but she'd be damned if she was going to be the one to wrestle the oil down the animal's throat. Although if Cort doesn't get here soon, she might have to.

At last she sees his pickup truck bouncing up the hill. He's got that ridiculous animal with him, sticking its head out the passenger-side window and grinning. Why it can't ride in the truck bed like a normal farm dog is beyond her.

The truck rolls to a stop, and Cort hurries out, the dog bounding down behind him. They both skid to a stop in front of the fence.

"Is she up yet?"

Gert shakes her head. Cort glances down over the fence, then swings the gate open and comes in, gently closing it against the dog's inquiring face.

"Keep her out. This kid is in no shape to be harassed," Gert warns. But Cort, now that he's up close, is slowly turning an interesting green color. Gert, who'd taken the precaution of putting some Vicks VapoRub under her nose when she'd stopped at the cottage, is without sympathy.

"Holy shit," Cort says.

"Exactly," Gert agrees. She starts to hand him the mineral oil but he waves it off.

"I, ah, I left the syringe in the truck," he says, and hurries outside the paddock. It's a reasonable excuse, and while it takes him a few moments longer to retrieve it than Gert thinks is strictly necessary for a farmer's son, when he returns his color is normal.

"What do you think she got into?" Cort says. His words are a little strained, and Gert guesses it's because he's trying to breathe through his mouth.

Gert opens the bottle of mineral oil and hands it to him. "If I had to guess, I'd say chokecherry. There's some on the other side of the fence. That, combined with worms, could do it. You've been worming her regularly?"

He nods. "Every four weeks, just like the schedule you made says. But when I checked the label last time, the batch had expired. I was heading in town today to pick up some more. Think we need to call the vet?"

The kid is still on the ground, but its breathing isn't as laborious, and when Cort kneels to press its gums, the color stays pink. The mother goat bleats anxiously, and Gert gives it an absentminded pat as Cort fills the syringe with the oil and squirts it down the kid's throat.

"Let's wait a bit," she decides. "I'll make some tea—that'll help."

Cort looks up. "I've got coffee in the truck, but thanks."

"Not for you, fool. The tea acts as a stimulant, and the tannins in it can help counteract the poison if you drench her with it."

"Oh."

"And do you have any electrolytes? They'll help with the dehydration from the diarrhea."

Cort nods. "I brought some from the barn. I'll need to mix it with water, though."

"Well, let's get a move on. Take me back to the cottage and you can get some there."

She gives the doe a final pat and slips out of the gate, the dog twisting and twining in front of her. "Move along, you," she says. "Shoo." But the dog simply sits and whines.

She opens the cab door and is boosting herself in when Cort jogs over. "No, no, I can do it," she says, waving him away.

He shakes his head. "You Murphy women kill me. Although at least your niece likes the dog."

"It's her taste in men that's questionable," Gert says before she can stop herself. She's out of breath and irritable from the struggle into the truck. The second she's settled, the dog bounds up and tries to push its way into her lap. "Shoo, I said!"

"Back, girl," Cort says, and the dog scrambles into cargo space. It twists around so that its head rests on the back of the seat, breathing hot doggy breath into Gert's ear.

"See, she likes you," Cort says, starting the truck.

"Then her taste is questionable as well," Gert says, but she lets the beast's head stay where it is.

They bump along the pasture's track, scaring up bobwhite and the occasional oriole. When they pass the big house, the dog's breathing quickens and it whines softly, thumping its tail behind the seat. There's movement at the attic window. The lace curtain moves sideways, and Gert's fairly certain she sees her niece's form at the glass.

"Just passing through, girl," Cort says, and the dog falls silent.

They bounce down the driveway and onto the road, then turn just a few hundred feet later onto the cottage's own driveway. The little house looks tidy for the first time in years, with a fresh coat of yellow paint and powder blue shutters framing each window. The morning glories, mowed down in their prime, have been replanted, along with climbing roses and clematis, stretching their new leaves toward the sky. There's even a wicker rocker on the front porch, a little worn but respectable again in a fresh coat of white paint. Cort found it in the shed when he was hauling junk to the dump and fixed it up over Gert's protests. Now, it's her favorite spot in the evening.

He kills the engine and they sit in silence for a second. "It's looking pretty good, don't you think?" he says.

"Not bad," Gert agrees. "But there's plenty more to be done." In truth, once he paints the big house, she'll be hard-pressed to find enough work to keep Cort around. She'd counted on the fact that proximity to Andie would be enough to bring the two of them together, but it seems she'd misjudged the boy's spirit. Or perhaps their relationship was doomed to a quiet death, slated to end with the fall's first chill even without the appearance of Neal.

"Miss Gert?"

The boy's standing at her door side, and she has to blink to bring herself back to the present.

"You need a hand?"

"Just gathering my strength—fending off your animal has sucked the energy right out of me," she says.

She climbs carefully out of the truck, ignoring his outstretched hand, and takes her time up the steps to the cottage. Buddy's curled in a small puddle of sun in the porch corner. When the dog sniffs him, he yawns, stretches, and twists onto his back, luring the dog in closer.

"Watch him," Gert warns, but it's too late. The cat's paw snakes out like lightning, scratching the dog's nose. The dog yelps in surprise, and the cat scrambles for the porch railing, its back arched, hissing. Another bark and it jumps off the railing and stalks toward the woods.

"Jesus. Nice pet you've got there, Miss Gert," Cort says, shaking his head. He kneels to inspect the dog's nose.

"It's not mine—just a stray who stops by sometimes," Gert says. "And if you'd control your animal, none of it would have happened."

Inside, she washes her hands and puts the kettle on. While it heats, she fills a metal bowl that she keeps for the cat with cold water, then searches the bathroom cabinet for a tube of antibacterial cream and some cotton swabs.

She brings the water outside and sets it on the porch floor. "Don't think you're coming inside," she warns the dog, which thumps its tail enthusiastically at her voice. Cort's sitting on the floor next to it, rubbing its ears. She hands the tube and the swabs to him.

"Use this on its nose. Cat scratches can be nasty."

The kettle is starting its metallic shriek, so she heads back inside, shaking her head at the steadfast optimism of dogs. Scold or shove them and they'll lick your hands, confident your ire is just a misunderstanding between friends. Simply look at a cat the wrong way and it'll take offense. She can't decide which outlook is better.

She reaches into the top shelf of the cupboard for her tea, takes two bags down, and puts them into a clean glass jar. She pours the hot water in slowly, watching for breaks in the glass. When it's full, the mild, dusty odor of tea makes her decide to brew a cup for herself. She lets the cup steep on the counter as she goes outside to check on the boy.

He's sitting in the same spot, one arm around the dog's

neck, the other engaged in pulling a cotton swab out of its mouth.

"The cream is for the outside of the animal. I make no guarantees about the inside."

"I don't think she ate much—it's just a game to her," he says, retrieving the swab. "And the scratch doesn't look deep."

"Well, I suppose that's something," Gert says. She pats the dog on the head. "Keep your nose where it belongs next time," she tells it, and it thumps its tail.

"The tea should be about ready," she says. "If you'll give me the electrolytes, I'll mix them in water."

He shakes his head. "Let me get a bucket from the truck. I don't want to mess up any of your stuff."

She watches as he walks to the truck. There's a slowness to him that she doesn't like. His hair looks as if it hasn't seen a comb in days, and whatever Catherine's feeding the boy, it isn't enough. She's seen the boys at the market with their pants falling down around their hips, their underwear on display, but on Cort it's not a fashion statement—it's disinterest.

"You're looking a bit peaked," she informs him when he returns.

"Is that so," he says. "This bucket should be big enough. The ratio is on the package. Okay if I come in to mix it?"

"It is not. You can sit your fanny down in that rocker. I'm making you a sandwich and some tea."

"I don't drink tea."

"You do now," she says, pointing to the rocker. He gives her a look but does what she says.

Inside, she scours the fridge for food. There's not much. She settles on a turkey sandwich, white bread, a generous smear of mayonnaise. The tea in the jar is too strong, but the cup she poured for herself should be about right. She hesitates for a moment, then drags over a chair and rummages in the cupboard above the refrigerator. In the way back, behind the mixing bowls and glass pie plates, she finds a bottle of Irish whiskey that's two-thirds empty. She uncaps it, and as the smell of alcohol rises, her stomach rolls uneasily. Gert's not a drinker, never has been. She thanks her father for that. But the day Frank died, the pastor pressed a small tumbler on her and left behind the bottle. She'd called Andie, left a message for her brother, then sat at the table, not moving, the afternoon shadows growing longer and longer. Somewhere a dog or a coyote howled, and the sound clawed at her insides. She uncapped the bottle, poured a shot into her glass, and drank it. She studied how she felt. Not that different, really. A burning in her midsection somewhere, a faint fuzziness in her head that was rather pleasant. She didn't see what all the fuss was about. She poured the next shot to muffle the animal's howling, which was so loud, so close, it was tearing her apart. She took the third shot to bed, burying her face in the pillow to muffle the noise, but the howling wouldn't go away. It raged through her, and in the morning her throat was as sore as her head.

Standing in the kitchen now, she takes the bottle down, pours a healthy tot into Cort's cup, recaps the bottle and puts it away. After a moment's reflection, she adds a spoonful of honey.

She brings the sandwich and tea out on a tray and hands

it to him, so that he can balance it on his lap. "Uh, thanks, but really, I'm fine."

"Eat," she says in her best charge nurse voice, and it works. He takes a bite of the sandwich, chews, swallows, and reaches for the tea. It's halfway to his mouth when the fumes stop him. "What's in this?" he asks suspiciously.

"Nothing. A bit of honey, is all."

He takes a cautious sip. "Jesus, what is this, hundred proof?"

"I have no idea what you're talking about," she says firmly. "Drink up."

"Miss Gert, do you have designs on me?" he jokes, but he downs about a third of the cup. After the sandwich is gone and the tea is mostly drunk, she can see him relax. It's like he's setting down a weight he's been carrying for too long. "I ought to get back to Clarabelle," he says, but makes no move to get up.

Naming farm animals is a mistake—when it comes time to eat them or put them down, you're emotionally invested, and it clouds your thinking. Gert's about to tell him this, but it occurs to her he must already know. Growing up on the McCallister farm, he's breakfasted on plenty of animals he tended to the night before. She forgets sometimes, because he's so young, that he knows how the world works in a way that her niece does not.

"She'll be fine for a bit."

"How do you know so much about goats?" he asks.

"A misspent youth," she says.

"Yeah, well, to misspent youth." He raises the cup in a toast. "To a youth misspent."

She didn't pour that much whiskey. Unless, of course, the sandwich is his first meal of the day. In which case, she poured more than enough. She looks at him, and he grins happily back.

"You haven't had a bite to eat all day, have you?" she says, shaking her head. This is her punishment, for meddling. But if she's going to hell, she could do worse than spend her last remaining hours in the presence of Cort.

It's unfortunate that her niece can't see that. In some ways, Gert blames herself. She's always held that family comes before all, and now she's wondering if she's been wrong all these years, pushing Richard on Andie. Gert's no fool. She's watched Oprah, she's listened to Dr. Phil, and while she thinks most of what is said on those shows is claptrap, she knows how important a father's influence can be on a young girl. All summer, Richard's been calling her, checking on the progress of the big house, pushing her to put it on the market. He's worried about her, he says. It's too much for her, she should let him help, but Gert sees right through him. In all these calls, he's never once mentioned his daughter.

It makes her uneasy, this sudden attention from her brother. There's a current beneath his words, a subtext she can't quite read. They've grown apart, and she's lost the key to him. Her fault, she supposes, although if what she did cost him, it cost her just as much. And it was for the best, she's sure of it.

Even now, looking back, she can't say it was wrong. She'd been watching Andie on her summer visits, had seen the girl's quickness despite her spotty attendance at school. She'd taken her for long weekends over the winter break, showed her the city and all its possibilities, prospects Andie would never have if she stayed in Hartman.

She'd seen, too, the way the girl lingered over the hidden spots of Evenfall, the way she rose early to say her farewells to the farm in the privacy of the predawn air. There was an attachment there it would be best to end quickly. So at the start of summer, when Gert found her brother alone at the kitchen table, waiting for Andie to come in and say good-bye, she'd laid her groundwork carefully.

"Junior high is the time when her grades start to matter. Think of what she can do. The brochure shows classes in Latin, Greek, even Chinese," she'd said, spreading the glossy pages in front of him.

He'd glanced at them, then set his coffee cup down on the centerfold, the one that showed smiling coeds on a brilliantly green lawn. "She don't need all that," he said. "The school in Hartman's good enough, and she's got her heart set on living here. Clara's got it all arranged."

"But this school has a full art studio, too," she'd said, playing her trump card. "She has potential, Richard, potential even I can see, and it will be wasted if she stays here." Her brother, who studied the breeding notes of his horses as carefully as other men studied the stock market, believed in potential. Wasting it was the only sin he recognized.

He was silent a long moment. Shifted his coffee cup off the brochure and took a sip. "Even if that's true, I don't have the money to pay for it," he said at last.

"But I do," she said. "I make good money as a nurse, and

I've got plenty saved with no one to spend it on. I'd be honored if you'd let me use it for Andie."

She'd already filled out the application form, and only needed his signature to send it in. When she placed it in front of him, he gave a sardonic smile, and she saw that he knew the other reason she was doing this. It shocked her, that her brother of all people could see past the facade she'd spent so much time erecting. She had to go cautiously, now.

"I think it might be best if the news came from you," she said carefully. "Clara doesn't see the benefit of an education the way we do, she'd think I was just meddling, and Andie . . ." She let it hang.

"You want someone else to break the girl's heart," he finished. "And you figure it might as well be me."

She didn't answer, just handed him the pen. He touched it to the paper, then paused. "It occurs to me—how am I supposed to be paying for this, again? A big run on the ponies and I'd have the cash to flash."

She'd prepared for this, too. She pulled the envelope from her purse and held it just out of reach. He signed and she passed it to him. He didn't open it, just hefted it in his hand.

"Ah, Gertie," he said. "You never cease to surprise."

If she'd never answered Clara's call that day in July, if she'd told the nurse at the duty desk to say she wasn't there, who knows what might have happened? But she did. Now she can't imagine life without Andie. She remembers, even now, the sweet, salty scent of her head after a day at play, the limp heaviness of her in sleep, the chubby folds at her elbows and knees.

But she remembers, too, the fierce, hot covetousness, the

pain of being close, but never close enough. She wonders if Richard ever felt this way. Clara—and Gert, too, if she's honest—clutched Andie so tightly, he must have seen there was no room for him. By walking away, instead of staying and fighting for her, he simply declared the distance between them his choice.

She sighs. There's enough she'd do differently, God knows. But no amount of compunction will help the boy sitting in front of her, and it's unlikely at this late date to help her niece. All she can do is go forward and fix what she can.

"You think it's time to give up," she says. "Let me tell you. You think you won't get over it, but you do. And somehow, the getting over it is worse."

The boy doesn't say a word, just stares at her, then drains the teacup. He sets it down and wipes his mouth. "I'd better go check on the kid."

She wants to warn him to be careful, but there's not much he can hit between here and the pasture. She stands instead, takes the tray away, and returns with the tea and electrolytes.

He takes the bucket and glass jar from her. "Thanks. For the sandwich and all."

"You're welcome."

He whistles once for the dog, and she bounds up from her corner. Gert watches them go. There's more she could say, but it wouldn't make a difference. When your heart is breaking, it's a solitary pain, and words are just the background noise, a fuzzy interference that reaches you only sporadically. This much she remembers. This much she wishes she could forget.

Frank

ANDIE'S sitting on the front steps, a cup of coffee clasped in her hands. It's early yet—the grass in the shade is dew-flecked—and the rough-hewn stone of the steps must feel cool against the back of her legs. Most days my niece runs about the front yard barefoot, heedless of the yellow jackets poised to sting or the splinters lurking just out of sight. Today, though, she has on sneakers, and keeps her feet tucked beneath her. She takes a sip of coffee and contemplates the lawn, where the reason for her caution rests.

It's a snapping turtle, about as wide around as a hubcap. Mud and a solitary leech mark its back. Behind it, a trail of flattened grass shows a path to the woods and, I suppose, the creek beyond, from whence it came. Now it waits, motionless, eyes trained on Andie, who stares back over the rim of her cup.

The door behind her opens and Neal comes out. "Hey, babe," he says, stooping to kiss the back of her neck. "Where's the . . ." He catches sight of the turtle and his eyes widen. "Jesus Christ, what the hell is that?"

"That," she says, "is a turtle. Probably a snapper."

"What's it doing here?"

"I don't know. Looking for a place to lay eggs, I guess."

"You mean it wants to make more of the ugly little fuckers?" He starts backing slowly down the side lawn, his eyes fixed on the turtle.

"Where are you going?" Andie asks.

"To get a shovel."

"A shovel?"

"Yeah. To whack its head off with."

I decide it's time to intervene. I conjure an image of the creek, cool and mossy, its water as inviting as I can manage, and mentally urge the turtle to return there. But the turtle resists. I can feel it, a hard, dark block of stone, a sense of age and weight and general annoyance. Instead of heading toward the creek, it turns toward the house and clicks its toothless jaws together. To Andie, it must look as if the creature is snapping at nonexistent flies, and she shifts uneasily in her seat, tucking her feet further beneath her.

I probe at it, idly, and feel a strength that surprises me. I try to move it again, but it's obstinate, so I try something else. I concentrate on seeing the creature, the way I see the glass of the windows or the wood of the door, and then the level below, and suddenly my view changes and I'm staring up at Andie's feet. The angle is off: her feet are enormous, and the house behind her a giant's. The house flickers, and then Andie is gone. A child runs across the lawn and a woman calls out the window to her. Clara. I let go of the turtle, and the world around me wavers, then snaps into focus again. "Leave it," my niece is saying. "It's not bothering anything."

"It's bothering me," Neal says. "At least let me move it back to the woods or the creek or wherever the hell it came from."

She shakes her head. "It'll go when it's ready. Just leave it alone."

Neal tiptoes slowly back to the house, giving the turtle a wide berth. He's just passing in front of it when the turtle hisses and he jumps.

"Jesus," he says to Andie. "I can't believe you're defending this thing."

The turtle clacks its gums again. It ignores Neal the way a cat ignores a piece of food it's discarded.

How long do turtles live? I've no idea, but I'd guess this one to be ancient. Once more I slide into it, unfolding its memories as gently as I can. This time, the house flickers immediately, is replaced by the same house, subtly different. From the distance of the woods, I see a couple make their way up the steps, and recognize my younger self with Clara, the child Andie between us. The sky darkens, the sun goes down, and candlelight flickers on the porch. There's a faint noise from across the yard, and the picture shifts, changes. A woman stands just on the edge of the side lawn. The trail to the cottage is behind her, but she makes no move to take it, just stands in the dark, looking up at the lights of the house, her yearning so great I can see it even through this imperfect view, see it the way I never could in life.

The picture shudders, disappears. The connection breaks altogether and I'm back to myself again. The turtle has pulled into its shell. The ground vibrates, and Gert's station wagon sputters up the driveway and stops in front of the house. As she steps out I'm struck, as always, by the sheer force of will at the heart of her beauty: the fierce, intelligent gray eyes; her strong mouth, thinner-lipped than it used to be; the sharp bones that jut just beneath the skin. She's traded her standard khakis and white shirt for a dress in a smart black and white print, and when she stands in front of me she looks for all the world like my heart's desire at eighteen.

"Hi, Aunt Gert," Andie says. "What's up?"

"Hey, Aunt Gert," Neal echoes, and I see Gert's struggle not to visibly recoil at such familiarity.

"Andrea, Neal," she says, then pauses, noticing the turtle for the first time.

"A monster, isn't it?" Neal says. "Andie found it out here this morning. I think we should get rid of it before it bites someone."

In one long second Gert looks at him and reads the whole scenario, coming down firmly on Andie's side just for spite.

"Oh, I don't think so," she says sweetly. "After all, it's one of the charms of the country, isn't it? The ability to see wildlife up close? Speaking of which, did you hear the coyotes howling last night?"

Neal gives an almost imperceptible shudder. "Is that what that was?"

Andie gives her aunt a look. "Is there something I can help you with, Aunt Gert?"

"As a matter of fact, there is. I'm expecting a load of mulch for the front garden," Gert says. "I was hoping Cort could be here to supervise, but regrettably, he has other plans."

"How unfortunate," Andie says drily.

"I'd like you to remind the driver to dump it on the drive, not the lawn," Gert says, ignoring her. "Catherine McCallister told me that when they delivered it to her house, they killed a patch of lawn as wide as her car."

"Sure, no problem," Andie says. "Where are you heading off to?"

"Town. I have some appointments there."

"Any chance I could hitch a ride? I need to do some shopping, and there's no point taking two cars."

Gert hesitates. "I'm going to be there for quite some time, Andrea. You might not want to wait."

"I don't mind."

"All right. But I need to leave soon, so if you're coming, you'll have to be quick."

"Just let me get my bag," Andie says. "Maybe we could grab lunch, too. Where are you going, anyhow?"

Gert hesitates again. "To the hospital," she says finally. "I have an appointment there."

A flicker of alarm runs through me. I look at Gert again, and notice for the first time the ways shadows have pressed themselves like thumbprints into the flesh beneath her eyes. I telegraph my concern to Andie, practically shouting in her ear. But there's no need.

"Just a regular check-up," Gert's saying. "If I'm leaving too soon . . ."

"No, no, I'd like to come." Andie stands, finishes her coffee in one gulp. "Just give me a minute. What time is your appointment?"

"At ten." Gert checks her watch. "That gives you just under half an hour to get dressed and ready."

"I'm set now," Andie says. She's wearing a white tank top that's seen better days and paint-splattered shorts. Gert doesn't move, just eyeballs her until Andie sighs and goes inside the house.

Neal smiles at her. His teeth are perfect.

"Beautiful morning," he says, putting his hands inside his short pockets.

"Indeed."

"It's a great place you have here. The area's charming, really. Andie's description of it didn't do it justice."

"I can imagine," Gert says.

"It must be hard for you to sell, but what a terrific opportunity," he says. "You must have developers pounding down the door. Why not move on that? You know, I've done some real estate. It's not really my field, but I still have connections. Just say the word, and I'd be glad to hook you up. Your brother thinks . . ."

Gert makes a dismissive motion, as if she's swatting a mosquito. "Thank you, but no."

"But . . ."

"Mr. Roberts, let me be candid," she says, and I brace myself. "It may surprise you, but I'm not interested in what my brother thinks. Whether I take two or twenty years to sell is not his concern. Besides which, Evenfall is a family matter, and you are not family."

"Well, not yet, anyways. And please, call me Neal."

Gert gives him a sharp look. He smiles at her and rocks back and forth on his heels. They don't speak, and I focus my energy on willing him to leave, but he's a stubborn cuss. He stands there in the silence for another five minutes. At last he turns to go inside.

"Well, I suppose I'd better go see what's keeping Andie," he says, and without offering her so much as a cup of cold water, he goes inside my home and shuts the door behind him, insolent bounder that he is.

At least he's left me alone with Gert, who has abandoned her usual perfect posture and is slumped against the car. Through the liquid air between us I can hear her heart beating, as rapid and quiet as a hummingbird's wings. I want nothing more than to hold her, and so I do. My love. This time, she doesn't run, just lets me envelop her, my whole being wrapped around her the way it should have been every day in life.

We stand that way, Gert's head just where my shoulder would be, her eyes closed, until her breathing slows and I can feel her heart calm. If you could see us both, we'd look for all the world like a couple of old coots at the end of a long run together. Or so I tell myself.

It's the reptile who reminds me of the truth. I'm so focused, so drawn to Gert, that when she straightens and steps away, it's as if she's cut off my oxygen supply. I gasp, struggle to reclaim myself from the air and earth, and while I'm floundering I see what's caught her attention.

I'd forgotten the turtle in Gert's presence, but now it's moving from the lawn to the woods with surprising speed, tracing back its path of flattened grass.

Come back, I call to it. I'd like to probe through its memories again. But the turtle doesn't obey, just increases its pace. I drop a small limb from one of the outlying trees into its path, but it turns and avoids it so neatly I wonder if it sensed the branch even as I sent it hurtling down.

Come back!

But the turtle won't stop, just keeps trundling toward the woods. I chance one last encounter with it, sink beneath the layers of its outer being until I'm looking through its eyes. At first I see nothing but the grass and mud of the trail, the indistinct canopy of the trees above. I probe deeper, and the image changes, becomes blurrier. I see a shadow reaching down, its edges wavy and dark, and it takes me a moment to understand that I'm looking up through water. I see four long limbs entwined, crushing the moss beneath them. Two torsos, locked together. The printed pattern of a dress, hastily discarded. The corner of a white handkerchief, pressed into the mud. I want to look away, but of course I can't, caught in a trap of my own making. I'm seeing with the turtle's eyes some fifty years ago, and I hear the clacking of its gums as it shows me what I've tried so hard to forget: the slick of wet skin, the taste of salt, the throbbing, frenzied pulse of life.

Andie

IT'S eighty-nine degrees out and climbing, and Andie's trying to find something to wear to the hospital. She'd like to be comfortable, which means cotton, and as little of it as possible. Unfortunately, her aunt, who appears to be working on some kind of a nervous breakdown, disagrees.

Five minutes ago, when Andie went outside in perfectly respectable black shorts and a T-shirt, Gert startled as though she'd been sleeping, although as far as Andie could tell her eyes were wide open.

"Well?" Gert snapped, as if she'd asked a question and Andie had failed to answer.

"I'm set."

Gert eyed her outfit. "We're not going to the supermarket, Andrea. Nor are we attending my funeral. Not yet, at least. I'd appreciate it if you'd put on something more appropriate, preferably in a color."

Which is why Andie is standing in front of her closet for the second time this morning, stripped to her underwear, contemplating the few choices that aren't black. She's having a hard time choosing something, made more difficult by the fact that Neal is circling behind her like a shark coming in for the kill. When he moves in and nuzzles her neck, she swats him away. "Quit it."

"I don't think your aunt likes me very much," he says, sitting on the bed. He has the pouty look of a little boy who has just been scolded, and normally Andie would find this adorable, but today she doesn't have time. She pulls out a blue T-shirt and slips it over her head. "Aunt Gert doesn't like anyone these days, me included. Just don't forget to remind the driver about the mulch and you'll be fine," she says, examining her image in the mirror.

The shirt has a small stain just at the neckline. She wonders what it is, and then heat floods her face as she remembers a night on the porch with Cort that involved a bottle of red wine and the slow removal of clothing. She must not have noticed the stain when she'd tossed the shirt in the washing machine. She takes it off, throws it on the bed, and starts again.

"How about if you show me how much you like me, so I feel better?" Neal says, ignoring her comment about the mulch. He grabs her around the waist and pulls her to him, so that she's standing between his knees.

"Neal, I'm not kidding. I do not have time for this,"

Andie says. He tries to kiss her and she lets him, for a second, feels a quick frisson of excitement. But when she opens her eyes and sees the rose-covered walls, the feeling vanishes.

The problem is, it's the kind of sex they would have had in Italy: quick and dirty, up against a wall in a bathroom or somebody else's bedroom while the party went on just outside the door. The thrill of reapplying her lipstick, of walking out of the door on Neal's arm to take a glass of wine from a handsome stranger made her feel both a part of something and an outsider at the same time. But she's not that girl here, not with her aunt just below the window. She resists, pushing against his chest until he lets her go.

"You never have time anymore."

"That's not true." She turns back to the closet so she won't have to meet his eyes. She pulls out a white camisole trimmed with lace and a calf-length, shell pink skirt. It's dotted with green flowers and is possibly the least sexy item she owns, bought on sale just in case Gert ever dragged her to church. She searches for her pearl earrings among the change, receipts, and other detritus that litters the dresser top, finds them, and puts them on. She slides on her white flip-flops, takes a final look in the mirror, and picks up her bag. At the door she turns back. Neal's still sitting on the bed, staring moodily at his reflection.

"Look, I'll see you when I get home," she says.

"That assumes I'll still be here," he says sulkily, and she feels the familiar twist in her stomach, the cold plunging panic his moods always bring. She takes a deep breath. "Suit yourself," she says. "But I forgot, you always do."

She can hear him calling after her as she walks down the stairs. She doesn't turn around, just walks through the front door and closes it carefully behind her.

Gert is waiting in the driver's seat, the air-conditioning on and the windows up, and the cold air seems to have revived her. She gives Andie the once-over, but mercifully all she says is, "About time. Though I must say, you look quite nice."

"Yeah, well, glad you approve," Andie says, and then is horrified by how fast she's regressed to her teenage self. To make amends, she offers to drive.

"No, thank you," Gert says. "Perhaps on the way back."

Her voice is so calm, so unlike this morning, that Andie wonders if she imagined it. She sneaks a sideways glance as she fastens her seatbelt. Gert's color isn't great, it's true, but she's always been on the pale side. She looks tired, a bit hollow around the eyes, and Andie realizes she has no idea how her aunt has been spending her days lately. Just because she hasn't been helping to empty out Evenfall doesn't mean she's been taking it easy. Knowing Aunt Gert, she could be working right alongside Cort on this crazy home improvement project of hers, but getting her to admit it is something else, and the only other person who would know is Cort himself. The coffee from this morning bubbles like acid in her stomach when she remembers their last meeting. The thought of calling him, even to talk about Gert, makes it worse, so she resolves to wait until after the doctor's appointment to decide. The dilemma must show on her face, though, because Gert lets go of the steering wheel long enough to pat her hand.

"Goodness, Andrea, cheer up," she says. "I can't promise, but I'm fairly certain I'm not going to die before we get to the doctor's office."

"That would be good. Especially since you're driving."

"I assume my well-being is the reason for the long face?"

Andie's not about to get sucked into that conversation, not when she's Gert's captive for the next twenty minutes. "Of course," she says, then flicks on the radio and fiddles with the dial. The college station from New London is playing some unintelligible world music, but the drums drown out any chance for conversation, so Andie leaves it on.

When they pull into the hospital parking lot, they have to circle twice around before they find a free space. "Mondays," Gert says, shaking her head before she carefully backs the station wagon into the spot. "Everyone always waits until after the weekend to be seen."

On the walk from the parking lot, the hospital looms over them, a brick and glass structure that casts a cool shadow. The doctor's office is attached to the main building, so they walk through the lobby on their way. They're almost at the elevators when quick, rubber-soled footsteps echo faintly off the walls. Gert glances back just as a nurse turns the corner, a wide smile stretched across her face.

"Gert? Gert Murphy? I knew it was you!" the woman exclaims, wrapping Gert in a hug.

"Doris, such a nice surprise," Gert says, gently disentangling herself.

"Surprise my foot. Where else would I be?" The woman

eyes Andie expectantly, so Gert makes the introductions, adding "Doris is the charge nurse here."

"Thanks to you." The woman turns to Andie. "If it weren't for your aunt, I'd still be a nurse's aide."

"You would have done just fine on your own," Gert says. "Besides, that was all a very long time ago."

"I can still hear her voice in my head sometimes," Doris says to Andie. "I think everybody was a little afraid of her, but boy, did we learn."

"I know what you mean," Andie says. It is likely that she's met Doris before, although her face isn't familiar. As a child, Andie spent plenty of time visiting Gert at work at the hospital. Clara would bring her over at lunchtime, and as a treat they'd usually make a meal of the sloppy joes and red Jell-O the cafeteria served. There was almost always a group of serious young women clustered around Gert, speaking in hushed tones about stomas and amputations and other unappetizing conditions. Her aunt, graced with a natural authority, also had the distinction of working during the school term at a teaching hospital in upstate New York, where she saw more emergencies in a weekend than Hartman encountered all year. Summers, the administration was more than happy to have the illustrious Gert Murphy fill in for vacationing staff.

"Not much of the old crowd is left," Doris is saying. "Mary's still down in neonatal, and Anne works as a floater during the school year, but that's about it. You should have called me, I would have gotten everybody together for lunch."

"Yes, well, perhaps next time," Gert says, and takes a step closer to the elevator.

"You know Dr. Thompson retired last year, right?" Doris says, moving right along with her. Gert nods. Andie remembers Thompson as a bear of a man with a delicate touch. For years, even after he was promoted to chief, he did her back-to-school checkups as a favor to Gert. "The guy they found to replace him is okay. They brought him in from New York, and he has all these big ideas about how a hospital should be run. I tell you, I'm counting the days until retirement. The fun's gone out of it for me."

"You're a very capable administrator, Doris. Don't let anyone tell you differently." Gert pats her on the shoulder, then steals a glance at her watch.

"Yeah, well, enough about me," Doris says, looking pleased. "What about you? Not here for anything serious, I hope?"

"When you get to be my age, everything is serious," Gert says. She reaches the elevator call button and pushes it. "But no, just a routine checkup."

"Well, I hope you get a good report. Who are you seeing?"

"Dr. Littleman," says Gert. The elevator dings and the doors open.

"Littleman? He's not a GP," Doris says, then looks at Andie.

"I hate to rush, but I'm going to be late if I don't hurry," Gert says, stepping into the elevator. She holds the door open for Andie, who has no choice but to follow. "It was wonderful to see you again, Doris."

"You, too. Stop by the nurse's station on the way out if you get a chance," Doris calls as the doors slide shut.

Andie waits until the elevator has started its ascent before she turns to her aunt. "What did she mean, Littleman isn't a GP? I thought this was just a checkup."

"It is, of a sort. Dr. Littleman is a cardiologist," Gert says. She gives an odd little smile. A grimace, really. "It appears, Andrea, that there's something wrong with my heart."

GETTING to Dr. Littleman's office requires wandering through the internal maze of the hospital. Andie follows her aunt to the third floor, across the glass-filled, sunlit bridge to the new building, where doctors have their private practices, and down again to the warren of individual rooms on the lower level.

At last they reach their destination, the second to last door on a nondescript corridor in the bottom of the building. Gert pushes it open. The waiting room has half a dozen plastic chairs, two round tables filled with magazines, and a poster illustrating the inner workings of the heart.

While Gert checks in with the receptionist, Andie finds two vacant seats together and sits down. She picks up a women's magazine and leafs through it. "How to Tell If He's Cheating—Again!" blares the headline. She turns the page. "Sex Secrets Younger Men Know" is the next story. She's reading, openmouthed, when Gert plops into the seat next to her.

"Ridiculous—the amount of time it takes simply to check in these days," her aunt grumbles.

"Un-huh," Andie says without looking up.

"Interesting article?" Gert asks, leaning over to see. Andie hastily flips the page.

"'Why Comfort Foods Are Making a Comeback,'" Gert reads aloud. "Nothing wrong with meat loaf and mashed potatoes, is what I've always said."

"Here, take it, I'm done," Andie says. She thrusts the magazine at her aunt and takes the next magazine on the pile. It's about financial planning, and she spends the next forty-five minutes reading about index funds, stock options, and IRAs, which allows her to worry about the fact that she has virtually no savings, no income, and no job on the immediate horizon. It's enough to distract her, mostly, from memories of what she's found young men to be particularly adept at. That doesn't keep her from noticing that when Gert's name is finally called, it's with reluctance that her aunt puts down her magazine.

"About time," Gert grumbles as an aide leads them down the hall and into a small examining room painted seafoam green. Andie parks herself on a chair in the corner.

"Please strip to your underpants and put on the gown," the woman says. "The doctor will be in to see you in a minute."

There's an uncomfortable silence after the door closes. Andie's not sure she's ever seen her aunt naked before. She averts her eyes, but when Gert asks for help tying the strings on her gown she can't help but look. Her aunt's back is smooth, surprisingly unwrinkled. There are age spots freckled across her shoulders. Andie ties the gown at waist and neck, and when she accidentally brushes the skin there Gert reaches up and squeezes her hand. Her fingers are cold. Andie squeezes back, and they stand that way, holding hands, until there's a light rap on the door.

"All set?" a male voice calls. The door opens and the doctor bustles in before they can respond. He's not much taller than Andie, with dark-rimmed glasses and a head of full, curly hair. He's clutching a manila folder in one hand.

"Sooo, Mrs. Murphy," he says, skimming through the paperwork. "How are we today?"

"About the same, thank you," Gert says. She releases Andie's hand.

"Meaning?" The doctor closes the folder and leans forward.

"On a day-to-day basis, I'm fine. It's just these . . ." She waves a hand. ". . . little spells."

"Hmmm. Had any recently?" He unfurls his stethoscope from around his neck and steps next to her.

"One or two," Gert admits. The doctor presses the stethoscope against Gert's chest and listens for what seems like an eternity to Andie, then moves it around to her back and listens there.

"And we have you on, what?" He removes the stethoscope from his ears, checks Gert's file, and scribbles a note in it. "Metoprolol?"

Gert nods.

"And are you finding yourself fatigued while on it?"

"A little," she says. "But it's manageable."

"Good. I'd like you to continue to take it, but frankly, I

think we need to take additional steps here. I'm not comfortable with the fact that you're still having these episodes, and I'd really like to get to the root of the problem."

Andie steps forward. "I'm sorry, but I'm a little lost here. What's going on?"

The doctor glances at Gert, and she gives a slight nod.

"Okay, your, uhhh, . . ."

"Aunt," Andie supplies.

"Right. Your aunt came to see me . . . ," he glances at the file, "approximately eight months ago, complaining of heart palpitations, dizziness, and shortness of breath. We did an EKG to see what was going on, and it came back normal. An X-ray showed no fluid in the lungs. She refused further testing, so we started her on a beta blocker, which was supposed to help control the problem, but it sounds like it's not working."

"So what do we do?" Andie asks. Behind her, Gert snorts at her use of the pronoun, but Andie keeps her eyes focused on the doctor.

"Well, frankly, I'm at a bit of a loss," he says. He rests his foot on the chair again. "Afib isn't all that uncommon in someone your aunt's age. But the medicine should be controlling the symptoms. The fact that it's not is a bit worrisome."

Andie shakes her head. "I'm sorry, I don't know what you're talking about."

"Afib—atrial fibrillation—simply means that the atrial part of the heart is beating too fast. If that's what she has, the medicine should control it. The fact that it's not . . ." He trails

269

off, stroking his chin. "What I'd like to do—what I wanted to do in the beginning—is order some more tests. But your aunt, as you probably know, can be difficult to persuade."

"I'm sitting right here," Gert says irritably.

"I'll persuade her," Andie says. "What kind of tests are we talking about?"

"Well, I'd like to do another EKG, and an echocardiogram to check heart function. And maybe some bloodwork, to look for anemia, or thyroid problems." He ticks them off on his fingers.

"Okay," Andie says.

"Ideally, I'd like to admit her. Then we could monitor her over a twenty-four- to forty-eight-hour period, and have a better idea of what's going on."

"Absolutely not," Gert says.

The doctor sighs. "Well, these tests should at least help us rule some more things out. I'll see if we can get you in today, so you don't have to come back." He scribbles another note in the file, stands, and heads for the door. He pauses with one hand on the knob. "So, any questions?"

"Any idea what it is, if it's not the afib thing?" Andie asks.

"None that I'd like to speculate on just now."

"But you must have some idea."

The doctor looks at Andie. "If I had to bet money—and I'm not a betting man—I'd put my stake on a dropped heart beat. For some reason, it's just not showing up."

"Well," Andie says. "That doesn't sound too bad. Right?" She looks at Gert, still sitting quietly behind her, then back at the doctor.

"Let me put it this way," he says, lowering his voice. "If you can't persuade your aunt to listen to reason, the next time she faints, she might not wake up."

THE afternoon passes by in a slow blur. Andie traipses with her aunt from department to department, the sharp smells of alcohol and disinfectant lodged in her nostrils. Her aunt submits to the tests, grumbling only once, when the technician fails to find a vein on her second try. She tells the unfortunate woman to go practice on an orange.

By the time they're finished, Andie has no problem persuading Gert to let her drive home. The spot where her aunt had blood drawn is starting to bruise, an ugly, purple mark. When they're on the highway Andie glances over. Gert's eyes are closed, her shoes slipped off. Andie lets her be as the miles tick by, but when they get off at the exit, the McCallister farm spread beneath them like a quilt, she clears her throat.

"I'm resting, not dead," Gert says, keeping her eyes closed.

"Yeah, well, that can change if you don't start listening to the doctor," Andie says.

"Doctors," Gert says irritably. She shifts in her seat, sits up, opens her eyes. "Just because they have penises, they think they have all the answers."

"Aunt Gert!"

"Oh, don't look at me as if you've never heard the word. Most of the men I worked with thought that their getting out of bed each day was enough to hang the moon. And I'm sure the women doctors of today are just the same."

"Okay, fine," Andie says. "But he's worried about you, and so am I. Why didn't you tell me about this before?"

"Why?" Gert asks. "What difference would it have made?"

Andie's about to protest, but the words sit uneasily in her throat. She thinks of her life eight months ago, the hours spent at cafe tables, the markets, the dust motes drifting down through the palazzo. Neal's affair had not begun eight months ago. Or maybe it had, but not for Andie.

"You should have told me," is what she says instead. "I should have known."

They've reached the cottage's driveway, and as they bump over the pitted gravel lane, wild rose branches and forsythia reach out to scrape against the car's side. Just ahead of the car, a turkey stops in the middle of the driveway, perfectly still. Eight babies muddle around her, darting this way and that, until she turns and leads them off into the undergrowth.

The two women watch until the last chick has disappeared, and then Andie takes her foot off the brake and they creep their way to the house.

"Well, thank you for coming," Gert says. "I hope it wasn't too trying."

"Want me to come in and help you get settled?" Andie asks.

Gert snorts. "Please. Despite what that young cub of a doctor seems to think, I am perfectly capable of getting myself inside."

"Just take it easy, okay? I know you think he's an idiot, but he really seemed worried that you have this dropped heartbeat thing."

"I don't," Gert says. "I'm fine, so please don't worry, Andrea."

"Aunt Gert, a few weeks ago you fainted practically on top of me. You look—no offense—exhausted. Something's not right," Andie says. She never contradicts her aunt, but since she's started, she might as well keep going. "If you don't think it's a dropped heartbeat, okay, but tell me what you think it is, please. Because you know something is wrong."

Gert's already opened the car door and swung her legs to the ground, but now she leans back against the seat. The two women sit for a long time, listening to the start of the evening sounds around them: the rustle of the tall grass in the cooling wind, the slowing of the crickets' song, the long, liquid silences that run beneath everything else. Gert rubs her eyes, and just when Andie thinks she'll never speak, she does.

"It's regret, mostly," she says, before turning and gazing out again through the open car door.

Andie waits patiently, but when Gert doesn't say anything more, she reaches across the console and touches her on the shoulder.

"Aunt Gert?" she says, and when her aunt turns it's as if she's coming back from some far-off place, a distant voyage. She looks at Andie's face. "Oh, it's not so bad as all that, Andrea," she says, patting Andie's hand. "I've had a fine life, don't get me wrong. And you have always been the best part of it. But there are things I've left undone, and now, when it's far too late, I find it . . . difficult . . . to live with that lack."

Andie doesn't know what to say, so she says nothing.

"Take it from me. There's not always time to go back and fix things the way you should, so you need to get it right the first time. You need to pay attention."

"To what?" Andie asks. Her aunt smiles, but it's a sad smile. She lets go of Andie's hand, leans over, and kisses her niece on the forehead as if she's a child.

"It's not to what, Andie. It's never to what. It's to whom."

Frank

FROM my window in the attic I watch the station wagon as it winds its way along the dusty track of the driveway. I follow its path to the road, watch it dip and rise and finally be lost to sight on its journey to the hospital. I can hear Neal Roberts moving about in the rooms beneath me. He's in the spare bedroom now, looking, no doubt, for something small and precious he can slip into his pockets. The silver snuff-box that sat on my grandfather's desk in the living room is missing, as is the small oil landscape that graced the parlor's mantel. I have an idea as to where they have gone.

In the distance, thunderclouds gather and roil. It's a ways off yet, but a storm is coming, tonight or tomorrow at the latest. I think of Nina, hope that wherever she is, she'll take shelter. The fool dog's petrified of thunder.

The air snaps and sparks around me, white hot. I feed off the energy of the coming tempest, feel my anger burn and grow. A hairline crack appears in the window, spreads into a diamond pattern. Neal Roberts is coming up the stairs. I hear him talking on his sleek black phone, barely larger than a book of matches. "Yeah, yeah," he says. "I think we should move fast on it. It's not going to happen otherwise, and it's a once-in-a-lifetime opportunity."

A pause.

"Well, once she sees the size of the check I don't think that will be a problem. The place is an albatross anyways."

I bar the door to him, make the molecules of wood swell until it jams tight against the doorframe. He tugs at it, braces himself, and pulls on the handle with all his might. When he's straining his hardest, I let the wood go back to its natural shape. The door flies open and he falls against the wall, cursing.

I wait, like a spider in its web, and soon enough his head peers cautiously around the corner. He's watchful in a way I didn't expect, until I remember Andie warning him about a hive. My energy reaches a fever pitch, so high even Neal can hear the humming, but he doesn't turn back.

He pokes about, peering into corners, lifting dust sheets to see what's beneath. Andie's painting rates only a cursory glance, but he combs through my grandfather's ship's log. A maple tea caddy catches his eye. A silver berry spoon makes its way into his pocket. I wait all the while, until he's close, so close I can feel him breathing. He notices the crack in the windowpane and stoops to peer at it. I set the molecules of the glass to vibrate in time with my humming. The window shatters, spraying the room with ice-sharp particles.

"Jesus Christ," he says, backing away. Drops of blood slowly ooze from his face. Bits of glass sparkle at his shoulders and cuffs. I let the humming grow louder so that it fills the room. I have never been this strong, this angry, and I am drunk with it, with the power I command. As he stands and scrambles toward the door, I cause his cigarette case to fall from his pocket. It bounces once and pops open, spraying cigarettes across the floor.

It must be instinct, but he makes a mad grab for them, scooping them up in fistfuls as they roll beneath his feet. He's reaching for the last one when it lands in a crevice, a tiny indentation between two boards. I see him look at it, considering, and then he slips his index finger into the hole and pulls up.

No, I roar. I mean to breathe wind and fire, but what comes out are little puffs of smoke. They swirl about the room and disappear. Neal reaches down, pulls out the dirty gray bundle, and unwraps it. He holds his discovery up to the light. His bare fingers touch the metal as he turns it this way and that, and suddenly I'm gasping, fighting to stay. The blackness overwhelms me, blots everything out, and I'm on the verge of disappearing when Neal wraps the ring back in its cloth and stuffs it in his pocket.

My fire has burned away. I'm barely a spark, a single red-hot ember struggling not to be extinguished. Neal looks around at the mess, at the glass that shines in the sunlight, then clatters down the steps. I want to weep, to curse his name, but all I can do is watch him go.

Andie

WALKING home from the cottage, Andie hears Gert's voice over and over again in her head. *It's never to what, Andie. It's to whom.* The hours at the hospital and the conversation with her aunt have left her in a kind of daze, the kind she gets when she wakes from a nap. She wants to take a cool shower, to slip into some fresh clothes and curl up on the porch with a glass of lemonade and Hartt's *History of Italian Renaissance Art*. She wants to lose herself in its pages of frescoes and marble sculptures, stone palazzos and quiet courtyards, until she drifts off to sleep.

What she does not want to do is talk with Neal. He comes bounding down the hall stairs as soon as she opens the door. She'd forgotten about their fight until now, and she braces herself for the inevitable aftermath. But he surprises her.

"Hey, there!" he says, giving her an enthusiastic hug. "How'd it go?"

She winces at the sound of his voice so close to her ear. When he releases her, she leans against the front door and rubs her forehead.

"That bad, huh?"

"No, it went all right. I just have a headache."

"I'll bet," he says. "Look, I'm sorry I was such a dick this morning. I don't know what got into me."

"It's okay." Neal apologetic is so far from what she expected, she's willing to let the whole episode go, but he keeps talking.

"No, it's not. Here you are all worried about your aunt, and I'm just thinking about me. It's just that since I got here, you've been so distant, baby. You're making me crazy." If she's ever going to tell him about Cort, now is the time, but then he leans in and starts to nuzzle her ear and she finds she just can't do it.

"I've just had a lot on my mind, I guess," she says instead.

"I know, I know, and from now on I'm going to help," he says, letting her go. "You look wiped. Why don't I order us a pizza and bring it back here. We can eat and you can tell me all about how it went."

"That would be great," Andie says. She looks more closely at him. There are tiny scratches on his face. When he moves, a piece of glass falls from his hair.

"What happened to you?"

Neal shrugs. "The damnedest thing. I was up in the attic, looking for that hive of bees, when the window blew out. I was lucky it missed my eyes."

"It just blew?"

"All over the place," Neal says. "It made kind of a mess, so watch your step if you go up there." Andie sighs, picturing the spray of glass slivers across the floor. Her uncle Frank would have picked up each piece with tweezers, if necessary, but Neal's more like her father, whose talents run more toward creating chaos than controlling it.

"The forecast says we're due for a hell of a storm, so maybe the old glass just couldn't take the pressure," he's saying. "I'll try to tape some plastic or something over it later."

The house does have that heavy, oppressive aura that comes before a storm. While Neal calls in their order, Andie rummages around in the refrigerator until she finds a can of Coke. She pops the top, takes a gulp, then looks around for her purse, where she keeps a bottle of extra-strength Tylenol. It's not on the kitchen table, and when she checks the bench in the entryway, it's not there either.

She's still looking when Neal comes back.

"I got us a half pepperoni, half plain," he says. "Do you have any cash? I'm all out."

"I think I left my bag in Gert's car," she tells him.

"Oh. Well, hey, I can pick it up for you on my way into town."

Andie's about to say that's fine when she thinks of her aunt, who should be resting, and her reaction if Neal wakes her up.

"You know, I kind of wanted to check on her again anyhow. I think I'll walk over and see how she's doing."

"Want me to drop you off?"

She shakes her head, stopping immediately when it feels as if it is going to detach from her neck. "No. I could use the fresh air."

"All right then," he says. "I'll just grab some cash at the bank." As they walk out the door, he laces his fingers through hers. "So, I really want to hear the details when I get back, but overall, she checked okay?"

"Pretty much," Andie says. She tells him briefly about the doctor's visit, leaving out Gert's words in the car. When she gets to the part about Gert refusing to be admitted, he frowns.

"And he didn't push the issue?"

"You know Gert," she says. "Besides, I think he was able to do most of the tests he wanted to today."

"Yeah, but, if he says she ought to be admitted for observation, don't you think she should go along with it? She's a nurse, for God's sake."

"Was," Andie corrects. "She's been retired for a while."

"I'm just saying, if he's worried enough that he wants to admit her, and she won't go in, it makes me wonder . . ." He stops.

"Wonder what?"

"Look, I don't want you to get mad at me again or anything, okay? But your father asked me to keep an eye on her. And I gotta say, she's like, what, close to eighty years old? I'm just wondering if the old girl is still qualified to be making these kinds of decisions."

Andie frowns. "Why would Richard ask you?"

"Well, you know your dad. I think he's just more comfortable with the man-to-man thing." He gives her a playful tap on the shoulder, and Andie winces. "And plus, he knows how close you are to her. Sometimes, when you're looking at something you know, you don't see it the way it really is. You see it the way you want it to be."

"What are you saying? That Aunt Gert needs help and I don't see it?" She rubs her forehead with the heel of her hand.

"Look, forget I said anything, okay? I'm sure she's fine."

They're at the car and Neal opens the driver's side door. "Are you sure you don't want me to drop you off?"

"I'm sure."

"All right. I'll be back in a few. And maybe your head will feel better and we can talk a little bit. I've got an idea I want to run by you." He kisses her gently on the forehead and slides into the driver's seat. The top is down, and before Neal can start the car, a swarm of dragonflies begins to buzz about him, so close Andie can hear the clicking of their wings. Their eyes are enormous, and they dive at his head repeatedly, like miniature fighter pilots, until he's forced to raise the top and seal himself in, a few doomed bugs accompanying him as he bumps down the driveway.

Andie waits until the car is out of sight before turning and walking into the woods. The path between the main house and the cottage is more beaten down than it was when she arrived here three months ago. It looks like it did when she was a child and spent her days running between the two houses, always in search of something she couldn't quite find at either one.

The sun is just starting to set, and if she turns and looks back there are brilliant streaks of pink in the sky above Evenfall. It's the time of day when Clara would have been standing on the front steps, calling her in. If it was getting dark, her aunt would send Frank to look for her. On nights when she'd been at Gert's, he'd stand at the top of the path and call her name, never venturing more than a few feet into the woods.

She watches the sun sink lower. The dragonflies seemed to have mostly disappeared when Neal did; a lone blue one swoops in circles above the drive, chasing the evening's first mosquitoes. She thinks of Frank and how much he loved this time of day, the space between light and darkness. He'd been a quiet man, caught between the two aunts, but with a subtle strength of his own. If he ever regretted the time and attention the sisters devoted to a child not of his blood, he never let it show.

She turns again toward the cottage. It's cooler here in the woods, and after the heat of the day the goose bumps on her bare arms are welcome. In the dim light her headache improves. She takes a deep breath and lets it out slowly, testing. There's just the memory of a dull ache at the back of her head.

A slight breeze tousles her hair. She closes her eyes, stands still for a moment, and listens. The rustle of the leaves seems to call her name: *Andie, Andie, Andie.* She opens her eyes. As she walks along the path she thinks of regret, of how one mistake can change your life, make you forever look backward. But if you aren't watching where you're going, if you can't look ahead, you'll stumble again and again, crash right past the opportunities that are waiting for you. Sometimes, Andie thinks, you just have to let go.

When the cottage appears at the end of the path, it's so neat and tidy it looks like something from a children's story. The morning glories have closed up for the day, their white throats gleaming in the evening light. The smell of pink roses perfumes the air, rich and spicy, and Andie's not at all surprised to see a black cat staring at her from the porch railing. When she climbs the steps, it licks its front paw once, then jumps off and disappears into the dark of the woods.

Andie eases the screen door open, but she needn't have worried—it doesn't squeak once. Someone has oiled the hinges and rehung it so that it is perfectly balanced. "Aunt Gert?" she calls softly. "It's just me." But there's no reply. The cottage is so still it's as if it is holding its breath, and Andie tiptoes through the rooms until she reaches Gert's bedroom. Her aunt is curled beneath a faded quilt, a corner of it clutched in her hand. In the dusk, the lines around her mouth and forehead have been erased, and her face is still and lovely, as though she's dreaming of something beautiful. Andie doesn't touch her. She backs out of the room quietly, but she's not ready to go home yet. She pours herself a glass of lemonade from the pitcher in the refrigerator, takes it onto the porch, and settles herself in the white wicker rocker that someone has painted and placed there.

It seems perfectly natural that after a few moments, the black cat returns. It walks along the railing until it reaches her chair, then jumps into her lap. Although she's never cared for cats, she lets it stay, stroking the spot between its eyes gently.

It's almost dark when what she's been waiting for happens. A red pickup truck bumps down the driveway and brakes to a stop. Andie and the cat watch as Cort gets out, followed by the dog. The slam of the truck door seems unnaturally loud in the stillness, and she worries that it will wake her aunt, but when she cocks an ear toward the inside of the cottage, she doesn't hear a sound.

Cort walks around to the truck bed and starts removing potted plants. There's at least a dozen of them, and he carries them two by two to the walkway leading to the cottage steps. He works backward, starting at the end nearest the truck, and it's not until he's almost finished that he notices Andie.

"Hey," she says.

"Hey, yourself." He goes back to the truck and returns with a shovel and begins to dig just next to where he's placed the first plant. Nina walks down the pathway, brushing against the pots as she goes, and climbs the stairs, wagging her tail. She sits heavily, leaning into Andie's knee, and the cat gives a low warning hiss before settling back under Andie's hand. A woody, sweet scent rises from Nina, and it takes Andie a moment to place it, but when she does she closes her eyes and breathes deeply. Lavender. Now that she knows what it is, she recognizes the plant's spiky shape in the pots closest to her. As Cort removes each plant from its pot, the bruised leaves release their scent to the air, until it's all Andie can smell, a secret message written on the breeze.

It could be that she's drunk on the perfume, that that's why she rises from the rocker, dumping the black cat unceremoniously from her lap and letting it land with an undignified thud on the porch floor. It's the scent that draws her down the steps, leads her to stop so close to Cort that they might as well be touching, even though they're not, even though he still hasn't given her more than a single glance.

"She'll like that a lot," Andie says.

Cort squats down next to the hole, flips the lavender out of the pot with a practiced twist, and plops it into the ground, molding dirt around it with his bare hands.

"I took her to the doctor today," Andie says.

"Yeah, I heard she was going." He keeps his eyes on the plant, positioning it just so. Andie takes a deep, lavender-filled breath and tells him about the day. She keeps talking—anything to fill the silence and make it seem less like he's ignoring her—and eventually, the question that's been on her mind slips out.

"Cort, do you think Aunt Gert is crazy?"

She's finally gotten him to look at her, at least. He stands up, brushes the dirt from his hands, and starts to pick up the plastic pots that litter the walkway. "Don't ask me. I'm obviously no judge of character."

"You spend more time with her lately than anyone else does," Andie persists. "Don't you think she should have listened to the doctor when he wanted to admit her?"

Cort walks away from her toward the truck. He throws the pots in the back, and Andie trails after him.

"You're a Murphy," he says finally. "When was the last

time you did something you didn't want to, just because somebody said you should? Doesn't make you crazy. Just stubborn as hell."

He whistles for Nina, and the dog comes loping off the porch. She brushes against the lavender on her way to the truck, releasing another cloud of fragrance into the air. Andie thinks about Gert's words to her, about how long a span it is from six to twenty-two, about seeing things the way they are. She leans forward and gently kisses Cort on the lips.

"Then I must really have wanted to do that, right?" she says. He looks at her, just stands and looks, as she walks past him and onto the path leading to the main house. It's dark now, and her progress is slow. Behind her she hears the truck rumble to life. She's halfway home before she remembers her purse.

Gert

FOR the first time in close to a year, Gert sleeps through the night. She sleeps soundly and quietly, and if she dreams, her dreams are not of war, of boys without legs, or of Frank. When she awakens her mind is clear, as if she has not dreamed at all.

Buddy's waiting for her on the porch when she's finished breakfast, curled up in a rocking chair, looking for all the world as if he's a civilized cat and not a half-wild animal who spooks if a stranger glances too hard at him. There's an empty glass next to the chair and a dozen lavender plants lined tidily along the front walk, their flower wands as erect as soldiers.

Gert stands on the porch and breathes deeply. There's no note, no calling card, not even a bill, but she knows who did this work. A feeling of well-being stays with her the rest of the morning, while she washes the glass, braids her hair, and writes out a check for the property taxes. When she gets in the car, she finds Andie's purse, a lime green leather bag that doesn't seem like her niece's taste at all. But it's a built-in excuse for stopping by the main house, not that Gert needs one to see her niece. She resolves that today she will make it inside, that the foolishness that's kept her from walking up the front path and through the door for the past few weeks will end. Just as soon as she pays the property tax.

The tax collector's office is located in town hall, which is across from the Hartman library and next door to the elementary school. The motley collection of buildings is a town center, of sorts. Blink twice on your way through and you'll miss it.

Gert doesn't blink, just steers the car carefully into the parking lot and brakes to a stop. She could mail the check in, but three years ago, when Frank first started getting sick, Edna Menay, the tax collector, swore up and down she'd never received his payment. There were doctors appointments and chemo treatments and trips to Yale, where Gert had called in favors with specialists she knew, but the only thing that had seemed to matter to Frank was that damn bill. One day Gert just drove down to town hall unannounced, marched into Edna's office, and started going through the piles of paper on her desk. Edna had been on the verge of calling the resident state trooper to throw her out when Gert found Frank's envelope stuck in the folds of a tractor parts catalogue.

Edna hasn't shared a pew with her at church since, but it's not like Gert cares. Knowing he'd paid the bill let Frank sleep easier those last few months, and even if she'd been arrested, it would have been worth it.

Edna's on the phone when Gert comes in. "I'll call you back," she says when she sees Gert, and quickly hangs up. There's a long counter that runs the length of the room and a cluster of desks behind it. The tax collector shares an office with the town's treasurer and assessor, but the latter are part-time positions, so Edna's made the space her own. Pictures of her bulldogs line the front of the counter, and there's a sign on the wall behind her desk that reads: "I can only help one person at a time. Today's not your day, and tomorrow doesn't look good either."

Edna takes her time coming to the front of the room, and when Gert hands over the check, her nose wrinkles, as if the paper smells bad.

"I keep telling you, you can mail these in," Edna says. She folds the check in half without looking at it. Edna has run for her position four times unopposed, and to Gert's way of thinking, that's half her problem. The other half is her natural disposition, but not much can be done about that.

"I'd like a receipt, please."

"Of course," Edna snaps. "Just hold your horses." She bangs open a drawer below the counter and paws through it, emerging with a pad and pen.

While she's waiting, Gert's eyes settle on a picture of a particularly small and wrinkled dog.

"New puppy?" she asks, pointing to the picture.

Edna nods.

"Nice," Gert says, although she knows nothing about dogs and finds this one particularly odious. But an idea is flickering at the back of her mind, and she wants to follow it and see how far it goes.

"She is," Edna says, softening. "She's Misty Kennel's Achy Breaky Baby, and she got best of opposite in her very first show! She is just the cutest little bitch."

"I'll bet," Gert says. She admires the picture a bit more. "It must be difficult for you to find time to show, given your job."

"You know, I've been saying that to my husband for years. Of course, we do have Mondays off here, but even so, getting the girls ready for a big show can take me a whole day." She leans forward and drops her voice. "People can be so unsympathetic. It's okay to miss work because of your kid's dance recital, but if I ask for time off for the girls . . ." She shakes her head.

Gert makes sympathetic noises and waits until she has the receipt in her hands. Then, on her way out the door, she stops and turns back. "Maybe it's time to give somebody else a shot at the job," she says. "I mean, if your heart's not really in it anymore, it's not really fair, is it? To you or to the . . . girls."

"I don't think so," Edna says. "It's a very difficult job, you know, and people aren't ready to see someone else in my place. They want someone reliable, someone they can trust."

"Exactly," Gert agrees. "That's why I'm thinking about running." She waits a second, to catch the full expression that crosses Edna's face, and then she breezes out with a wave. If nothing else, it'll give the old biddy something to think about, but Gert just might do it. She needs something to keep her occupied these days; that's half her problem. She's always had a good head for numbers, she's organized, and she's nursed enough people around these parts that getting elected shouldn't be too hard, even if Edna does decide to run again.

Gert's almost at the exit, still musing over Edna, when a man's voice calls to her. "Hey, Gert. You got a second?" It's Walter Kawalski, the first selectman. Unlike Edna, he's run against stiff opposition for the last two terms and beaten both contenders handily. He has the thin wrists and delicate fingers of a surgeon, but Gert's never seen him hold anything sharper than a pencil.

When she turns, he beckons her into his office and shuts the door. "I heard the news. So I guess congratulations are in order, huh?" he says. He motions her to take a seat, then goes around to the other side of his desk and sits down.

Walter and Gert were assigned to the same room at the church's cleanup day last spring. He painted the trim in slow, careful strokes, making sure he covered even the hard-to-reach places. She thinks they'd make a good team, and Walt must, too, otherwise he wouldn't have made a point of bringing her in here so fast. He must have overheard her talking with Edna. Gert shudders when she thinks of what he must put up with, working with that old harridan. Still, it's not a sure thing, and it's not right to let him think it is.

"I haven't made my mind up yet," she cautions him. "It'll be a big change for me, and I need to think it over a bit."

"So you haven't signed anything yet?" he says. "It's not official?"

"Goodness, no. I've hardly had time to make it official. The idea just came to me this morning," she says.

"Well, that's great. That's good news," he says. He leans back in his chair. "The way your niece's fiancé was talking down at Baxter's, it sounded like a done deal."

The word "fiancé" strikes Gert like a fist. All the air seems to have been sucked out of the room, and her unreliable heart goes galloping off at a most unseemly pace. Steady, she tells herself. Steady now.

When she can take in air, she realizes Walt is still talking, and that none of what he's saying seems to have anything to do with the position of tax collector.

"Walter," she says, taking a deep breath. "You'd better start again."

"Sorry," he says, a little sheepishly. "I tend to get a little too into the details of a situation like this. Hey, you want some water or something? You look a little pale."

Gert nods, and Walter springs up from his desk. There's a water dispenser in the corner of the room, and he fills a paper cup and hands it to her. Her hands are trembling when she takes it, but she holds it carefully and manages not to spill.

When she finishes, Walter takes the cup. "Do you need some more?" he asks.

She shakes her head. "No, thank you." He's watching her closely, and she manages a small smile. "I'm fine," she says. "Really. Now, explain to me again what you were saying."

"Right." Walter goes back around to his chair, although

he doesn't sit so much as perch. "Well, basically, the bottom line is that we can't afford to match the price that the developer is offering you. I mean, two and a half million dollars buys a lot of schoolbooks, you know? Even when it's not an election year."

"Indeed," Gert says. She'd no idea the property was worth so much, although someone clearly did. It occurs to her for the first time to wonder what happened to the assessor's report.

"But—and it's a big but—I've been looking into the state's conservation program, and I think there's a chance we could get you a pretty fair percentage for the development rights. If you want to sell them, that is."

"The development rights?" That clear, sharp-headed feeling Gert woke up with has long since vanished. Her head feels like it's filled with cotton.

"You sell the state—if I can convince them it's worth it, which I think I can—the rights to develop the farm," he explains. "The state keep the rights, so the land can't be developed, and you get a nice chunk of change, plus the land."

"Hmmm," Gert says. This is all too much. She waits a moment. When Walter doesn't say anything else, she asks, "And why would I want to do that?"

"I don't know. Maybe you don't," Walter says. "But you strike me as a woman who likes to know all the options, and this is one of them. Maybe."

"I'm too old to start farming," she says. "And too tired." The foolishness of her interchange with Edna is apparent now. The woman is at least fifteen years younger. Even if Gert had the energy for such a job, which she doesn't, who would want her? She's been kidding herself. The word "fiancé" keeps buzzing in her head like an angry black fly.

"Gert, I have no doubt you'll be here long after the rest of us are nothing but fertilizer," Walter says. "But that land may not be. Did you know Scotty McPhearson sold his place to a developer, and twenty houses are going up there next spring?"

Gert nods. She'd heard the McPhearsons were moving to Florida. They'd let it slip during the reception after church that their new condo came complete with a hot tub, wall-to-wall carpeting, and a walk-in wine cellar.

"From the time I could walk I spent every summer fishing on that river," Walt says. "Now . . . " He shrugs. "As an elected official, I'm supposed to be happy we're growing the tax base."

They sit in silence and contemplate what progress looks like from the other side. "Look," Walter says finally. "It's not a definite, but even so, I'd appreciate it if you'd think it over."

"I'll do that," Gert says, and rises to leave.

"Oh, and tell your brother hello for me," Walter says. He comes around the desk to open the door for her. "He's quite the character, isn't he?"

"My brother?" Gert asks. "How do you know Richard?"

Walter gives her a look, the same one she's seen him use on Edna when she's come to church wearing a necklace made of bronzed puppy teeth. Clearly, Gert is missing something. She grips the back of the chair for balance.

"He's the one who brought in the developer," Walter says carefully, enunciating every word. "I think your niece's fiancé is the one who knew him, to start, but Richard's the one who was walking him through the land records at town hall."

Gert sits back down. The room doesn't seem to be holding still anymore, so it's just as well she's off her feet.

"Gert?" she can hear Walter say, but it seems like a long ways away. "Gert?"

It's only when he starts calling for Edna that she manages to come to. "Water, please," she says, and takes a sip from the cup he offers her. "Now, tell me everything again. From the very beginning," she says, and he does.

Andie

THERE'S something off about the living room. Each time Andie passes through, the difference nags at her. It's not until well after lunch, when she's carrying a load of laundry to the kitchen to fold, that she realizes what's wrong. The map that normally hangs above the couch is gone.

It's an old seafaring map, one that Frank's grandfather used. Water stained and marked with dirt, Clara had it framed as a birthday present from her and Andie one year. It has the Wildermuth name written in careful, ancient long-hand in one corner, and in the center of the frame, a gold plaque reads, "From the Murphy Girls."

"Well, we can't let him have it all his own way," Clara had said when Andie had asked about the plaque. "The Wilder-muth name is most everywhere else—seeing Murphy here won't hurt him none. Besides, it's not like the map's telling him where to go. They're places his family's already been." The dark spot on the wallpaper where it usually hangs gapes at Andie like a missing tooth.

She puts the basket down, checks behind the couch to see if the picture has fallen there. Nothing. She considers asking Neal if he's seen it, but just as she's about to call to him, she hears the clang of the shower pipes from the upstairs bathroom. He'll be in there at least half an hour, fussing with the temperature. She decides it's just as well. Since yesterday at Gert's, every time she looks at Neal she gets a sick feeling in the pit of her stomach. They need to talk. But somehow she can't seem to bring herself to it. Last night after her walk home from the cottage, she went directly to the spare bedroom, blaming her headache. He's been romping around her this morning like an overeager puppy, all in her space and wanting to chat, but she's managed to put it off. She needs to be prepared, needs to find the words he won't argue with, so he can't convince her to change her mind again. There's a power to believing you're irresistible, and Andie's come up against it often enough to respect its force.

She's standing there, rehearsing what to say for the billionth time, when the doorbell rings. She picks up the laundry basket and walks into the entryway to answer the door. It's Cort, standing on the steps with Nina beside him. As soon as Andie opens the door a crack, the dog pushes it wide and wiggles through.

"Hey," Andie says, but with the laundry basket in her

hand she can't grab Nina's collar. She hears the dog clattering down the hall and then up the stairs.

"Shit," Andie says. "Nina, come back here." But Cort pays no attention.

"We've got to talk," he says. He takes the laundry basket from her, sets it on the floor, then pulls her into the living room.

"If it's about last night, I was out of my mind," Andie says, but just standing this close to him is making her light-headed. The house seems too warm, suddenly. She looks at Cort's lips, at the shape they make when they say her name, and has to stop herself from reaching out to trace them with her finger. There's a buzzing in her ears that won't let her concentrate on anything but his face. It's as if she's under a spell.

"Are you listening to me?" he says. She nods, even though she has no idea what he's talking about. She can hear the clicking of Nina's nails on the second flight of stairs, the ones to the attic. She wants to warn Cort about the broken window, but he interrupts before she can get the words out.

"It's all over town. Chris heard Edna talking down at Baxter's."

"About what?" she says. Andie's standing close enough to him that she could count his eyelashes, if she wanted to, but the way Cort's looking at her isn't particularly affectionate.

"About your fiancé's latest deal. The jukebox didn't work out, huh? So now he's going to sell Evenfall."

"What?" Andie says, finally paying attention. "That's crazy."

"Really? You tell me, then, how come he's got a developer ready to sign for two million bucks?"

"That's crazy," she says again. "Aunt Gert would have said something to me."

"That's just my point," Cort says. "I don't think she knows."

"But Aunt Gert has to sign any deal. She's the one who owns the property. And for the record, he's not my fiancé." It's not until she says this that the muscles around Cort's mouth relax. For some reason, that makes her happy.

"Yeah, well, that's not what he's saying."

"Neal says a lot of things. He likes to talk," Andie says. She's having a hard time making eye contact and fixes her gaze on the wall instead. "He's good at it. It's part of his job, making connections. Some guy he met probably mentioned he was in real estate and Neal thought it would be a great opportunity . . ." Her words trail off. She's staring at the blank spot on the wall, and suddenly it all clicks. She's seeing things the way they really are.

Just to be sure, she crosses the room and opens the desk against the far wall. Two months ago the top compartment was filled with a host of treasures she'd placed there for safekeeping: An ivory letter opener. A crystal inkwell. A moth-eaten velvet bag filled with the cool weight of marbles. They're all gone.

If she walked through the house, if she looked in every room, she'd never remember all that she's lost, all that she's carelessly given away. The water has stopped upstairs, and she can no longer hear the dog's footsteps padding through the rooms.

"I think you need to go now," she says to Cort, ready at last. "I have something I need to do."

"So do I," he says, and when he pulls her to him, it's enough, almost, to make up for what she's been missing.

Gert and Frank

GERT doesn't make it to Evenfall until it's almost dark. After she leaves town hall, she has to talk herself out of heading directly to the big house's cemetery and stretching out across its graves. It's what she deserves, after all, for being a foolish old woman who has outlived her usefulness. This way, she'd at least save Andie the cost of a burial.

Instead she drives to the cottage, makes a cup of tea, and stretches out across the bed, not bothering to remove her shoes or even pull down the coverlet. She stays there for at least an hour, motionless, until the cat begins to claw at the screen door. Gert ignores the sound of nails on metal as long as she can. The cat hooks a paw inside the screen, pulls it open, and pads across the floor to the bed. It jumps up and lands on Gert's chest, staring into her face and mewing.

When she still doesn't move, it bats her on the nose with its paw.

"You are a nuisance and an irritant," Gert says. She stands up and lets the cat fall to the floor. "What I was thinking when I fished you out of the creek, I'll never know."

But of course she does. She remembers exactly what she was thinking the day she walked by and saw a small, helpless form scrabbling along the sides of the creek bank. She pours the cat a saucer of milk. She takes a few deep breaths, letting the smell of the lavender from the open window revive her. And then she picks up the phone.

Her first call is to Fritz Kneeland. Until he retired from the position last April, Fritz served as the town's counsel, handling the rare legal issues that cropped up, as well as his own busy law practice. He's a handsome man, with a full glossy head of white hair. Gert suspects he has a soft spot for her. Just a few weeks ago during Sunday service she caught him casting a sidelong glance at her legs as he slid into the pew next to her. And while Gert's made it a point in life not to rely on her feminine assets, this is no time to be sanctimonious.

She explains the situation to him as best she can.

"Hmmm," he says. "I believe I might have caught a whiff of that down at town hall." They discuss options for a bit. Gert would like murder to be among them, but Kneeland talks her out of it. For now.

"What you want is to put the fear of God into your brother," he says. "I believe I have just the thing."

Kneeland's grandson, it turns out, is a professor at Yale

and something of a celebrity. In his spare time he consults for CNN on family law, and he's written several bestsellers on the subject.

"Here's his number," Kneeland tells her. "Tell him you're a friend of his granddad's, and he'll get right back to you."

To Kneeland's credit, he does. Gert's no sooner hung up the phone after leaving a message than the grandson's calling her back. He introduces himself, listens carefully as Gert talks, and doesn't interrupt once.

"Well," Leroy Kneeland says as she finishes. "That does sound like a problem. But the only way I can see it really working is if they declare you incompetent. Now, have you given them any reason to ... errr ... doubt your mental capabilities?"

There's a long pause as Gert reviews the events of the last few months, lingering longest on the goats inhabiting her back pasture.

"Possibly," she concedes. "But nothing I can't explain."

"And do you have other relatives or friends who might be willing to vouch for your mental acuity? Aside, of course, from my grandfather?"

Gert certainly hopes so, but today she's not sure of anything. They talk for a bit more, discussing strategy and plans, finally deciding on what Leroy terms "strategic escalation." She gives him her brother's phone number and thanks him. When she asks after his fee, he waves her off. "If this doesn't work and we have to go to the next level, then we'll talk. Right now though, it's a pleasure to help someone my grandfather thinks so highly of. The old guy has had a rough time of it since my grandma died," he says. As they hang up Gert makes a mental note to wear her blue dress, the one that best shows off her legs, and to sit beside Kneeland next Sunday.

Leroy promised to call her brother immediately, but Gert still waits a half an hour. She finds a Brillo Pad and gives the sink a good scrubbing, using a cotton swab and bleach to get into the cracks around the counter. When she puts so much pressure on the swab it bends into a vee, she realizes how furious she's become. She puts her cleaning tools away, turns on the faucet, and runs cool water over her wrists.

When enough time has passed, she dials her brother's number. The phone rings and rings, and finally Richard's voice comes on. It's a recording, asking her to leave a message. Gert does, the one she and Leroy had agreed upon, that essentially suggests Richard stop his infernal meddling or face his sister in a court of law.

But she's not satisfied. She paces the small living room, back and forth, like she's seen the cat do when she's confined it inside on cold winter nights. It strikes her that somewhere in the house she has Richard's cell phone number. He'd given it to her in case of emergency, sometime last year when Frank was dying, although it was clear he'd be of no use when the actual emergency came. She tears the house apart, looking for the scrap of paper he'd scribbled it on, and finally finds it pressed neatly inside her address book. She dials, gets a recording, hangs up, waits fifteen minutes, then dials again and gets the same message. She does this twice more before she remembers that on the newer phones you can see the number of the caller without answering. She calls

Richard's cell again and this time leaves a not-so-carefully-worded message suggesting her little brother check his voice mail at home and then call her. She hangs up emphatically.

It doesn't take long. Within twenty minutes her phone is ringing. She picks it up and waits.

"Gertie?" a voice says. "Are you there?"

"Don't you Gertie me," she snaps, and once she's started it's difficult to stop. Ever since this morning, when Walter called her into his office, she's been plagued with a self-doubt that's foreign to her. She wonders if this is how her niece lives, if the uncertainty she'd felt when she'd glimpsed her own face in the mirror is something Andie encounters every day. She lays into her brother with a fury.

"But you're forgetting, Gertie," he says, when she stops to draw breath. His voice is cool. "You've always forgotten, the lot of you. Andie's my daughter. By selling Evenfall, I'm doing what's best for her. What Frank would have wanted."

Spoken by her brother, the words are as much an untruth as anything else he's said, but still they give Gert pause. She stands by the kitchen door, twining the phone cord through her fingers, and wonders just exactly what it is that Frank wanted.

She knows about loss. She knows what it's like to stand close enough to touch your heart's desire, to stand there day after day, and not be able to reach it, to take what's yours. To search, every day, for the place you belong. Richard had that place, but he walked away. She can see clearly the part she played in making that happen, but the final decision was his.

For all those years she and Frank performed a careful

dance, with Andie at their center. To raise the dust on their past, to cross the line, could have cost everything. She'd not been willing to take that chance, and she'd assumed he hadn't either. Now she wonders if she's been wrong. Perhaps Frank hadn't seen Evenfall as a burden from which to shield Andie, but as a gift. A gift he'd left to her.

The cat rubs against her legs and she scoops it up, burying her nose in its fur. It smells of lavender. It occurs to her that she'd turned down Evenfall once before. To do so twice would be ungracious.

"Gert?" Richard says. "Are you still there?"

"Yes," she says. She takes a breath. "I am. I intend to be for quite some time." And then she tells her little brother what she should have said years ago, the one phrase she knows for certain of which Frank would approve. She tells him to go to hell.

A storm's coming, but still she chooses to walk the path through the woods instead of driving. The leaves rustle, showing their silvery undersides in the wind. When she reaches the big house the sun is setting, and the clouds rushing in are as black as the coming night. It's amazing, really, how seeing the house as a gift changes its appearance. The lights are on in the living room, and the house glows like a sentinel against the darkening sky. Still, walking up the front path, she shivers, though whether from the cooling air or what's to come, she can't tell.

The front door is ajar, and Gert knocks before pushing it

all the way open. "Hello?" she calls, but no one answers. She pauses, listening. Voices are coming from the living room, so she sets off down the hall.

When she looks in she sees Cort and Andie standing in front of the fireplace. If Gert had to guess, she'd say that until a few minutes ago they'd been doing more than talking. Andie's lips are swollen and her hair is half out of its ponytail, curling loose around her face. Cort's shirt is wrinkled and he's got a look in his eye Gert's never seen there before. Well, she thinks, it's about time.

Neal's standing in front of them, his back to Gert, and it's his voice that's the loudest. The dog twines between the three of them, whining, brown eyes glancing at Gert as if to ask for help. Aside from Nina, none of them have noticed her yet, so she stands in the doorway, waiting and listening.

"Look, I fucked up," Neal's saying. He paces in front of the two of them. "I made a mistake in Italy, I told you that. But this is how you try to get back at me?"

Andie raises her hand. "Stop it," she says. "This isn't about us. Just answer the question. Is it true?"

Neal stops his pacing and turns to face them. "You're going to believe your teenaged farm boy over me?"

"Just answer me, Neal."

"Fine. Yes, your father asked me to give him a hand, and I put him in touch with a couple of developers I know. That's one of the reasons I came down here, okay?" Neal pats his breast pocket, pulls out his cigarette case, and takes out a cigarette. The wind is picking up outside. Gert can feel the breeze through the open window. It lifts the hair on her neck, tickling like a caress. It takes Neal three tries to light his cigarette. He snaps the lighter shut, and Gert sees his hand is shaking.

"And yes, I took a couple of things to the antiques dealer, just to get some prices. Like you told me I could. And yes, I may have sold a few of them while I was there. So sue me. I've been doing it all for you. For us."

In a strange way, Gert can follow his logic, twisted as it. You cannot steal what you already own. As far as Neal seems to be concerned, Andie is his, as is all that comes with her.

He takes another pull on the cigarette. "You don't belong here. It's the ends of the earth. You've told me so yourself."

"That's not what I asked," Andie says, just as Gert clears her throat. The three see her for the first time. She steps into the room. There's an awkward silence, broken only by the roll of thunder. The storm is here.

"Perhaps I can help answer. I've spoken to my brother," Gert says, looking directly at Neal. "He admits he was a bit . . . misguided in his pursuit of Evenfall. My lawyer has convinced him to drop his efforts, and I strongly suggest you do the same."

Rain pounds against the house, hitting the windows like bullets. The house creaks like a ship, the wind swelling and breaking against it. The lights blink off for a second, then come back on with a buzz.

"Look," Neal says, turning to Andie. "Maybe I misspoke a little. I didn't mean to offend anyone. The house isn't the point, after all. The point is you and me."

The dog is growling, low, deep growls that Gert feels in

the pit of her stomach. Lightning hits somewhere outside and the whole house shakes.

"There is no you and me. Not anymore," Andie says.

"C'mon, babe," he says. He sounds incredulous. "You're going to throw away three years together for a one-night stand? For this?" He points to Cort, who looks to Gert as if he's more than willing to break the offending finger.

"You heard her," Cort says, but Andie speaks over him.

"No," she says, and a small sigh of relief escapes from Neal. Gert finds she can't bear to look at Cort. She watches his feet, instead. He's wearing yellow work boots. One lace is partially untied, but it doesn't matter. He's standing absolutely still.

"No," her niece says again. Neal crosses the room to her, but before he can reach her, Andie takes a step back. She gestures to the room and all that's in it, and Gert sees that the gesture includes herself and the boy. Possibly the dog as well. "For this. For all of it."

"What do you mean? I don't know what the hell you're talking about," Neal says. "C'mon, Andie. Don't do this."

"You don't have to know," Andie says. "It's enough that I do. But I want you to pack up. I'll spend tonight at the cottage, and I want you gone in the morning."

"Well, what if I'm not?" he asks. "What if I need more time?" A spoiled child, Gert thinks. Someone had a hard time saying no to this one, early, when it counted.

The dog cocks its head, as if listening, and then bares its teeth at Neal, backing him toward the door.

"Jesus Christ," he says. "Call it off."

Cort's making no move to restrain the beast, so Gert gives

him a look. The last thing they need is a lawsuit by this fool. Cort catches the look, gives her a can't-blame-me-for-trying shrug back and reaches for the dog.

"That'll do, girl," he says, but before his hand connects with the collar the dog lunges. Neal jerks back and there's the sound of fabric ripping. Neal's pants pocket tears open and a faded gray piece of cloth falls onto the floor. The dog releases its hold.

"Jesus Christ. Did you see that? The fucking mutt attacked me."

He bends to pick up the cloth, but the dog growls again, and he backs away. Cort muscles the dog out the door and down the hall. Andie scoops up the material, and as she does so something falls out of its folds. It hits the ground with a clink and rolls across the room to Gert.

It's a thin silver ring, and it spins in place a few times before falling to a stop in front of her. She can feel waves of energy pulsating off of it. She stares at it as if it's a snake, as if it's something dangerous and sharp instead of what it is, a man's declaration of love. She makes no move to pick it up. Her heart is beating too fast. The room is spinning a bit. She concentrates on Andie's face, on her cool blue eyes, and the world slowly comes back into focus.

Andie's still holding the piece of cloth, bunched in her hands. Gert takes it from her niece and unfolds it. It's an ancient handkerchief with a large, scripted W on the front.

"W," Gert murmurs. "For Wildermuth." She brings the cloth to her nose. It smells of dust, of age, and faintly, of lavender. There's an ancient streak of mud along one side.

Cort's come back to stand by Gert. He picks up the ring and holds it up to the light.

"There's initials here," he says. "Initials and some writing." He turns the ring, peering at the inscription. "A.W. to E.W. The rest is in a foreign language. French, maybe."

The wind hammers against the house and somewhere, an impossibly long ways off, a door bangs. To Gert, it sounds as if it's coming from the attic. If she breathes deeply, she thinks she can smell the sea.

"I want you out of here," Andie says to Neal. "Right now."

"What?" he says. "Over that piece of junk? I found it in the attic yesterday. I've been holding on to it to give to you, but the timing just hasn't been right. If I made a mistake, I'm sorry, okay?"

"Classy," Cort says. "Give the girl a ring she already owns."

Andie ignores him. "I'm the one who made the mistake," she says. "Out. Now."

Neal moves toward her, and Cort steps in between them. Neal eyes him for a moment, then shrugs. "Fine. Have it your way. But I'm telling you now, this is it. I'm not chasing after you again."

"Surprisingly enough, I'm okay with that," Andie says.

"Yeah, well, we'll see what you say when you've calmed down," he says. He tosses his cigarette into the fireplace, then crosses the room to the hall. Gert hears the front door open, a soft thud as it closes behind him. She turns to Andie.

"I think I'll sit down," she says, and then she makes her decision. "There's more, Andrea. Perhaps you should sit as well."

It happens quickly. Her niece takes her arm, and they are just settling on the sofa when the air crackles blue. The clap of thunder is immediate, so loud Gert's ears ring. She can't hear. Her hair is standing on end, she can feel it, and when she looks at Cort his hair is the same way.

There's an acrid smell, a metallic tang on her tongue. Lightning must have struck the house. Blue flames dance in the fireplace. They ought to leave, but when she tries to move she can't stand up.

"Aunt Gert? Aunt Gert? Wake up. We have to go. The house is on fire," Andie is saying. Gert opens her eyes.

"Frank," she says.

"She's stunned," Cort says. "I'll carry her." He bends, lifts her easily. But when he scoops her up and tries to walk, he stumbles, for just a second, over his unlaced boot. The ring slips from his hand, sails through the air and into Gert's lap. She clutches it. The metal is warm to the touch, and for just a moment the might-have-beens of her own life swirl in front of her, as real and hard as diamonds. She could reach out and touch them, pluck them from the flame—the child, the house, the warm presence at the end of every day. It's Frank's face in the fire, and she can hear every word he says, see the images as clear as photos. A good life, he says. It would have been a good life.

He shows her that day at the creek, but this time it is different, the way it should have been. He's taken the ring from his pocket. She's holding it in her hands. All she has to do is say yes, and everything will be different. She tries to fit the ring over her finger, but it won't go.

Somewhere in the distance an engine starts up. There's the rev of the motor, the whine of the accelerator. The ring slips from Gert's fingers. Andie bends to pick it up. There's a thunk and a screech of brakes. A dreadful silence, a howl that shakes the beams of the house, and then the flames lick higher, almost to the ceiling. They spread around the room.

"Yes," Gert says to the face in the flame. "Yes, yes, yes."

But the face can't hear her. Cort is carrying her away toward the door. Someone is calling to her, but she can't make out the words. She looks back at Andie. "My ring," she says.

"I have it." Andie holds up her hand. The ring slides easily over Andie's finger, sparkling in the firelight. "See?" And then they are outside. Someone else—her sister, perhaps—might have struggled to save the photographs, a quilt, Andie's baby blanket. But Gert, who is buttressed between Cort and Andie, knows that what matters can't be destroyed. Gert simply watches it all burn.

GERT, I call to her from the flames that lick the attic. *Gert.* I think she hears. But then that damn fool hits my dog, and the ring slides over my niece's finger. Andie will call the fire department. Cort will call the vet. But by the time they get here, we'll both be gone.

september

THE shipwrights who built Evenfall knew water. They built the house strong, the way they would a ship, with plenty of solid wood to withstand the waves. They caulked it well, to keep water out, using the pitch from local pine trees and filling the seams with cotton and oakum. They fitted the beams together as tight as they could, so close not even a piece of paper could slide between them. They understood water, respected and feared it. What they did not know was fire. They had no sense for it, for the snap and spark of it, the way it could climb a wall, faster than the fastest wave, consuming everything in its path.

The pitch and fiber acted as kindling, spurring on the flames. The dry aged wood, a shipwright's prize, served as the perfect fuel. Within moments the house was gone, or mostly so, even as the sirens wailed in the distance, tele-graphing the fire department's approach.

But if the men who had built the house, who had planed each board with care, had seen it after its wreck, when its ruins stood, still smoldering, they would have recognized that the power of fire and of water are closer than they appear. Like water, the fire stripped away the house's nonessentials, gut-ting it to its core. Gone were the trappings of the past two hundred years: the flowered wallpaper, the closets filled with clothing, the boxes of keepsakes. The house rose as it might have in the beginning, a simple dark shape against the early morning sky, bare to the elements. Picking through the shell days later, Andie could see the house's secrets revealed, the layers that hid them scoured away. In the master bedroom, where the wallpaper hung in strips, a tiny charcoal sketch of a boat at sea, drawn above the bed in a heavy hand. Mold-ing around the door of the kitchen was gone, and on the boards left behind two names, Abe and Frank, height marks showing how they hurtled toward adulthood neck and neck, Abe outstripping his younger brother by four inches the year they turned sixteen, the same year the marks charting their growth stopped. And in the corner of the attic, where Andie was not allowed to go, the fire inspector considering the flooring too unstable, came reports of tiny graffiti in the northern wall, the wall with the porthole window that over-looked the land, and beyond it, the glint of the sea.

He'd taken a picture of it, at Andie's insistence, and later, after he'd gone and the wreckage had cooled, she'd snuck up to see it, her heart pounding with every creak, afraid the stairs would fall down around her. Yet she was oddly exhilarated, too, the way she'd been as a teen sneaking out at night, doing something forbidden. She'd found her painting, the edges burned away but the center, her aunt Gert, still there, the canvas tangled in an enormous carpet too thick to burn at the far end of the room, most likely blown there by the wind from the broken window before the fire started. She'd found other salvageable items as well—the rocking chair, the sea captain's chest in the corner, a few old books and maps. And there in the corner, behind where a wooden box of old clothes once stood, was the writing the fire inspector had described. So tiny Andie had to kneel to read it, she could see the same words, written twice, by two different hands. The first was a delicate, feminine script, unfamiliar to Andie's eyes, but the second, the round, tidy letters of her aunt Clara's old-fashioned Palmer penmanship, was unmistakable. The words were simple: *Please Lord, bring him back to me.*

Andie knelt looking at them for a long time. By the time she stood up, the early morning haze had burned off and the porthole window filled the space with light. Since she was not supposed to be in the attic in the first place, she saw no reason to mention the writing to her aunt Gert. And over the following weeks, during meetings with insurance adjusters and the fire marshal and the cleaning and restoration companies, when her aunt's restiveness drove Andie from the cottage into an apartment in town, she found no reason to change her mind.

* * *

NOW it's early morning, and Andie has come one last time to say good-bye. It's foolish and sentimental, she knows, but still she rose before dawn this morning and drove in the chill morning air, the Nova's radio cranked as loud as it would go. The maples and oaks that line the road are licked with shades of crimson and orange. As she pulls into the driveway, she sees the house, blackened and gaping, pointing toward the sky.

She's been here several times since the fire, but still the smell of charred, wet wood catches her by surprise, an olfactory punch to the gut. It's happened every time she's come, and she takes a moment, letting her senses tell her what her heart insists can't be true. The wavy glass that once filled the windows along the side of Evenfall is shattered in a spray as fine as any wave. Pieces glint and shine from the grass. Black streaks mar the outside of the walls. The beams of the attic are visible through the roof; the fire inspector believes the lightning struck there, and the attic took the full brunt of the hit.

Andie gets out of the car and stands. In the weeks following the fire she's had little time just to look, to take in the image that's haunted her dreams for days. She notices the details now; the lace curtain, blackened but still recognizable, that hangs from the attic window; the scorch marks along the grass where embers from the house landed; the layer of ash that coats the leaves of the trees.

But it's not until she gets out of the car and walks around to the front of the house that she sees the table. It's covered with a blue cloth and the ends snap gaily in the breeze.

There's a small vase of asters in the center, place settings for two at either end. Champagne flutes. A pitcher of orange juice. And standing behind it all, Cort. He looks different, somehow, and it takes Andie a moment to realize that it's because Nina's not with him. Her throat tightens a little bit, and the space around her legs feels emptier than it should.

"Your table is ready," he says, and pulls out the chair closest to her.

It's an odd scene, the cheerful table in front of the ruins of Evenfall, and Andie hesitates, still thinking of the big shaggy dog. But then she shrugs, slides into the chair, lets Cort spread a napkin across her lap.

"How did you know I'd come?"

"I didn't, for sure. But I hoped," he says. "And maybe somebody might have mentioned your habit of saying good-bye."

At first she doesn't understand what he means, and then it comes to her. The mornings Richard came to take her back to school, Andie always rose early, just as the sun was coming up, to walk the acres around Evenfall. The air was cool then, like now, and she'd shiver as she wandered through the meadows, the grass damp with dew. She imagined the frost that would blanket the fields after she left, the ice that would form on the creek, and she'd wonder if the farm would miss her, if some part of it would sleep away the winter days under a covering of snow, dreaming of her return.

Gert must have seen her, all those years ago, and remembered.

"Andie?"

The painting of her aunt's own early-morning wanderings is packed in the trunk of Frank's old Nova. Andie has left it untouched, it's edges blackened and curled, although some day she may add the faintest hint of silver to it, like the ring, warm to the touch, her aunt wears around her neck on a slender silver chain. It's a reminder that traits can skip a generation, slide sideways, spring up where you least expect them. She knows now what she never saw on those childhood voyages of good-bye—that she was missed, that she was noticed, that she was loved by three people even in her absence. That the thaw at Evenfall came not from summer's return, but from her own.

"Andie?" Cort says again. She looks up at him. He smiles, a bit uncertainly, and opens a paper bag by his feet. He takes out miniature corn muffins, dotted with the season's last raspberries. There are tiny apple fritters scented with cinnamon basil, and brown hard-boiled eggs still warm in their shells. A container of goat's yogurt, thick and creamy, with a tang that makes her mouth pucker when she tastes it.

"The yogurt is from the girls," he says, reaching across to fill her flute with orange juice. "From Clarabelle, actually. But Clarissa sends her regards."

"It's really, really good," Andie tells him.

"The rest of the sendoff's from Chris," he says. "He's really going to miss you. He can't believe I'm letting you go."

"Are you?"

"I don't know, am I?" He's looking right at her.

It's true her bags are packed, loaded into the back seat of the Nova, which only has to get her as far as Pennsylvania.

It's the farthest the car has ever been driven, and she's a little nervous, if she's honest, that she'll wind up calling the dean from a roadside garage somewhere, asking for a lift.

"Have you ever been to Pennsylvania?" she asks instead. "It's only about four hours away. When I went for the interview, the farmland around the college went on for miles."

Driving there, she'd thought how much Frank would have loved it, the rolling green hills and valleys that made her feel instantly at home. It wasn't the urban setting she'd wanted, but maybe that was okay. She's willing to try it and see.

"Is that an invitation?" Cort asks.

"Maybe. Yes," she says. "If you want to."

He raises one eyebrow before turning in his seat to look at the house behind them. "You're not in a rush, are you? Because I have the feeling I'm going to have my hands full here for a while."

"You really think you can salvage it?"

"I do. Gert's giving me till spring, and if it works out, Chris and I can lease it. The front of the house by the living room and the bedrooms above it are shot, but the support beam in the attic is still sound. And the land's good. I can make something out of that."

When he looks at the house, Andie can tell he's seeing the future, an Evenfall built to his design, not the hulking wreck behind them.

"I don't know. Sounds like a lot of work," she says.

"You know me. I like a challenge."

"I have noticed that about you."

She picks at a bit of the muffin on her plate, cracks an egg and nibbles at the white, but she's too nervous to eat much. It's time to go. She pushes the plate away, looks at the house again.

"Will you keep an eye on Gert for me? Don't let her do anything too crazy, okay?" she asks.

"Define crazy," he says. "You have to remember she's a Murphy, and reason only goes so far."

That's more true than he knows. What happened the night of the fire depends upon who tells the tale, and who is listening. For Neal, the lightning caused a conflagration so large and sudden he swore to the fire marshal that the old house must have been soaked in gasoline. The blaze was so bright, he said, he never saw Nina behind his tires.

Cort has a different take. The fire, he told Andie, was a natural disaster, plain and simple. Put a big house up on a hill, factor in wood that's two hundred years old, and the surprise is that it hasn't happened before.

As for Andie, she's not sure what happened that night. If she believes her aunt, the same flames that drove Neal away from the house carried a message so enduring neither fire nor time could destroy it. Whatever Gert saw or did not see in the fire that night, she's found a measure of peace in the ashes. For Andie, who saw nothing, that is enough.

"Just promise me," she says.

He nods. "I will. If you'll tell me one thing." He stands, pulls her to her feet. He's so close she can see the individual lashes around his eyes, the way the tips catch the light when he cocks his head to look at her. She waits.

"If I kiss you right now, will you come back?" he says, and Andie gets the feeling those words aren't all he wants to say, that he's biding his time. He's so close now that she has to shut her eyes. When his lips touch hers, she feels dizzy. The kiss goes on for a long time, and when Cort finally lets her go, she doesn't move.

In the air above her, blue jays squawk in the tall pines. With her eyes closed, she can see the house untouched by fire: not the future, the way Cort sees it, but the past. The arbor to the right, plump Concord grapes ripened by the sun, the fieldstone steps, the porch where she spent so many hours. She listens carefully, and the noise of the jays fades. In its place she hears the rustling of the leaves, the faint murmuring sound of the creek rushing over rocks, the water dark and muddy. She listens more carefully still and thinks she hears, borne on the wind, the distant jingling of silvery dog tags, the whispered calling of her name. She stays, eyes closed, for a moment longer. When she's certain she'll remember, she opens them. She turns and walks down the drive. She can feel his eyes on her the whole way. She takes one last look, standing by the old car, and then she gets in and drives away.